...BY ANY OTHER NAME

Presently we [...] forest, where th[...] miniature totem poles with the *sasquatii* heads.

"Look!" cried Aaye, pointing toward the center of the clearing. "Monstrous footprints!"

"You know," Nikias said, "it would be nice to give this creature a proper name, rather than this barbarous *sasquatius*. How about *megapus*? Look at the size of that footprint. *Megapus*. Yes, Bigfoot. A good Greek word."

Just then, we heard a deafening roar. And a ponderous, pounding footfall. "Good heavens!" I cried. "The Sasquatii are approaching already!"

"Come, young Titus!" Aquila said. "When I first met you, you were ready to commit suicide at a moment's notice. Anyway, it is a good day to die."

"Lovely, Aquila, but—"

With a hideous, earsplitting laughter that seemed to rock the very forest, one of the *megapodes* lumbered forward and shoved the centurions aside.

"*Shalom*," it said distinctly.

THE AQUILIAD

Aquila in the New World

S. P. SOMTOW

A Del Rey Book

BALLANTINE BOOKS • NEW YORK

This book is dedicated to the Kenneys:
Ed, who likes alternate histories;
Ellen Jane, the Great Director;
and Angel and John

and also to the redoubtable "Dippy" Simpson,
whose efforts to teach me Latin
have resulted, alas, only
in this monstrosity

CONTENTS

PART ONE

AQUILA

CHAPTER
I

ONCE, WHEN I WAS VERY YOUNG, FATHER TOOK ME in the motor-car to the Via Appia, to see a man being crucified. It was some slave, some minor offense that I don't recall; but it was the first time I had ever seen such a thing. All the way there—and the way from our estate is olive-tree country, beautiful in the height of summer—Father was lecturing me about the good old-fashioned values. It was as much for the benefit of Nikias my tutor as for myself.

As we approached the Via Appia we would run across peasants or slaves; I remember that their awe at seeing my father's gilded motor-car, with its steam chamber stoked by uniformed slaves, with its miniature Ionian columns supporting a canopy of Indish silk, was sometimes comical, sometimes touching. Only someone of at least the rank of tribune might possess such a vehicle—although they are much slower than horses—for their secret parts are manufactured, somewhere deep in the heart of the Temple of Capitoline Jove, by tongueless

3

and footless slaves who can reveal little of the mysterious rites involved. Truly the Emperor Nero must favor my father, who had never plotted against him and always sent him curious and witty gifts, such as that funny glowing shroud from Asia Minor that had been used to wrap up the living corn-god, sacrificed each year only to be found reborn in some unfortunate young man.

It was stifling. My toga praextexta was drenched with sweat. When we got to the crucifixion, it was late in the day and hard to get a good view; and even my father was weary of lecturing me, and did so only intermittently as Briseis the pretty little cupbearer filled and refilled our goblets with snow-chilled Falernian. I was young then, as I have said, and remember little of the poor wretch's agonies; he put on a good show at first, shrieking hideously as the ropes were tightened and the cross raised, but presently he sank into lethargy, his eyes (which I only saw by virtue of being perched on the motor-car's driver's seat) glazed over, and flies stormed all over him. We gorged ourselves on melons and on a concoction of peacocks' brains and honey.

As we started home, my father, stimulated by the sight of bloodshed, harangued me all over again, standing proudly over the prow of the motor-car with his white mane and his senator's toga trailing in the evening breeze.

"Titus, old boy," he growled gruffly, dropping pointedly into Latin instead of using the Greek of casual conversations, "remember that you're a Roman. As a citizen you'll never be crucified, of course; but even so, a lesson well learnt and all that. The old ways are the best—I don't mean to espouse the Republic or anything foolish like that, Jove forbid, only to make sure you grow up straight and true and my son, eh, what! We should never have let those slimy Greeks come over and transform us into culture vultures... in the old days men were hard, fighting hard, playing hard, not like your mincing tutor over here." (Nikias and I were giggling in the back over some childish matter.)

"Listen, young man, when I talk to you! After all, the Divine Emperor Lucius Domitius (or Nero as he likes to be called) may do all this acting and singing, but he chose me, a sober and staunch man of courage and integrity, to receive the gift of this magical horseless chariot, of whose locomotive secrets only the gods Vulcan and Jove know."

"But Sire," said curly-haired, beardless Nikias of the gaudy tunic and scented hair, "it is said that this device was invented by a Greek scientist, Epaminondas of Alexandria, by enlarging on the theses of the ancients Aristotle and Archimedes; that this same Greek now holds an important, but secret, position in the Temple of Jove; that this mysterious engine, over which rites must be said and sacrificial blood spilt before it will run, is a simple mechanical device, the basis also of the equally mysterious ships which even now have returned from Terra Nova laden with curiosities—"

"Impudent scum! You can't buy a decent slave for a thousand gold pieces," my father said. "I suppose I'll have to beat you for impertinence." He pulled a little flail from a fold in his toga. "Damn these horseless monstrosities anyway! Nothing to whip, the thing just chugs along without any *feel* to it—" At that he began to lay into my poor tutor; but it was more of a gesture than anything, and he missed more often than not.

"Tell me about Terra Nova, Nikias!" I cried. It was the first interesting thing to happen that day. "Is it true they've found barbarians?"

"Yes, and giant chickens, too, that go *gobble-gobble-gobble*, and *vast* herds of aurochs, and the fiercest barbarians imaginable—thousands in number! Why, they decimated the Tenth Legion before General Gaius Pomponius Piso—"

"Insufferable!" my father said. "Everyone knows that

the Roman army, in its discipline, its order, and its bravery, has not been beaten in a thousand years."

"Tell that to the Parthians," said Nikias, deftly dodging a blow.

"They must be really fierce, these Terra Novans," I said. I know I had stars in my eyes, because even then I knew I was going to be a general and have a legion all to myself. Father could afford, after all, the kind of bribery that would get me some minor foothold in the establishment, and I'd go from there. "Are they as fierce as the Britons?"

"Fiercer. Wilder," said Nikias, and then added (keeping an eye out for my father) "but I'm not going to tell you a thing about them until *after* you've memorized all the aorist and second aorist forms of these contracted verbs. See, when alpha, epsilon or omicron stems come into conjunction with the conjugatory endings—"

"Bloody Greek grammar," my father grumbled as we pulled into the estate.

"He's just jealous," Nikias whispered in my ear, "and besides the Emperor only invites him to those parties so that wily Petronius can make fun of him when they have those poetry-improvising sessions, and your blessed father, who can't tell a hexameter from a hole in the ground, has to get up and warble to the lyre—I hear Petronius is writing him into his new novel, and the in-group at the palace is just in *stitches*—"

Perhaps I've painted too genial a picture of those days But alas, they were all too short. My father lost favor with the Emperor, got accused by the Empress Poppaea of some tom foolery, and was permitted to commit suicide. Despite the law, which is quite firm on the fact that descendants of traitors who honorably run on their swords may inherit as though the escutcheon had never been blighted, the Emperor somehow managed to confiscate the estate.

It was Nikias, that slimy Greek as Father used to call him, who saved my hide. He had a cousin, a eunuch, who was high up in the palace bureaucracy, who had become a millionaire simply by accepting one out of every three bribes that came his way, regardless of whether he followed up on the request to which the bribe was attached; and so our truncated family came to live at court.

Meanwhile I grew tall. Nero and a few other emperors expired in various unpleasant ways. Terra Nova was all the rage for a while, and several modern cities with all the amenities—baths, arenas, circuses—were built, mostly along the eastern shore of that huge land mass, and procurators sent to govern the thriving colonies of settlers and Romanized natives. The legions pushed westward into what is now the province of Lacotia. Some of our horses escaped and began to breed in the wild; the Terra Novans, in only a few years, became by all accounts the most adept of horsemen.

Frankly, I changed a great deal after Father's death, which taught me a salutary lesson about the human condition. I determined to become a fine Roman; to become, in fact, the very man my father had thought himself to be. I boned up on my Caesar and on all those battles; I studied Xenophon and all the Greek military historians; went off with the legion and got myself a few border commands; saw action in Britain, when the Picts came down on Eburacum, and again against some recalcitrant barbarians on the Dacian border. . . .

After a while I was noticed by the Divine Domitian; and it was on the very day that the Emperor granted Roman citizenship to all the barbarians of Terra Nova, and awarded himself the title of *Pater Maximus Candidusque*, or *White and Greatest Father*, that he also honored me with the command of the Thirty-fourth Legion.

CHAPTER
II

"TITUS, OLD CHAP," THE EMPEROR SAID TO ME, "have I conquered anything lately?"

We were ensconced in the Imperial Box at the Circus; Domitian was choking on a pickled lark's tongue with laughter over some lions who were making mincemeat of a bunch of recalcitrant Judaeans. His favorite, a peculiar-looking dwarf with an enormous head and staring eyes, sat at his feet.

"Well," I said, feeling very silly to be out of uniform and having long since lost interest in the sight of gore, "there's not much of the world left, Your Magnificence. West of Lacotia, perhaps, in Terra Nova—"

"Boring, boring, boring, you silly general. Those savages are fierce, and they certainly put on a spectacle in the arena, though I suppose you haven't seen any of the new shows, being out in the backwaters quelling Visigoths and Picts."

"True, my lord, but—"

"I want spectacle, Titus!" The crowd was roaring now

as the slaves with meathooks dragged the corpses out through the gates of death. A lone lion straggled. Domitian clapped his pudgy hands; a bow and arrow was handed him on a silver platter. He waved for silence, and it fell just like that, twenty thousand people gulping in mid-sentence. "I haven't had an interesting spectacle since...last year, when I had Amazons in motor-cars fighting pygmies on bicycles."

"Yes, where are the motor-cars these days, my Lord? I haven't seen a single one since I got back from the campaign."

"Shush, shush, old chap." He clambered up onto the seat of his throne and transfixed the lion in the neck with a single shot. The crowd burst out in carefully rehearsed spontaneous cheering. He sat down as they began to flood the arena for a mock sea-battle. "Ah yes, the motor-cars—I used them all up in the one circus show, Titus, and the priests of Jove haven't deigned to cough up another one."

"And how's Epaminondas of Alexandria?" I said pointedly.

"Oh, we tortured him. Didn't get anything, though; it seems that his 'visions from the future' have ceased. At least we got all the shipbuilding secrets from him before he passed on, or else we'd lose all contact with the New World. But you're changing the subject," he said warningly.

"Of course, my lord. The spectacle."

"Do you remember... Marcus Ulpius Trajanus?"

"How could I forget? Brilliant strategist. Taught me everything I know, Trajan did. Very clever of him to lead the Dacians up the wrong way on the Danube...."

"A little too brilliant," said Domitian. "Oh, he had plans—big plans. Subjugate the Parthians. Blah blah blah. Well, we got Cappadocia out of it, but after that he went a bit far—wanted to march on up the Tigris and push the Parthians into India or some other such grandiose notion. Fortunately, I was able to send him off to

subdue the Seminolii, an absolutely frightful tribe of
Terra Novan savages. Maybe I should recall him, but
you know how it is. These ships—even with Epaminondas's improvements—I mean the revelations of Jupiter Optimus Maximus—take a year to get here. And as
it happens, the Parthians are attacking now."

"Which Parthians, Sire? I thought they were all wrangling over the throne since old Vologesus died."

"God knows. Some petty king of theirs, fancies himself Vologesus's successor, busy reuniting the place. Just
a few thousand of them, Titus old chap, I'm sure they'll
easily be defeated by one of our matchless legions, eh,
what? I wouldn't even bother with it much, except that
...the point is, my precious aurochs herds are in
danger."

"Excuse me, Sire, but...I've been on campaign so
long..."

"The aurochs herds, you fool! You know, *bison*. I've
been breeding them in Cappadocia for the arena. Good
grazing, you know. You've no idea what trouble it is to
capture the damned creatures, to send good legionaries
up through Dacia and into the forests of Sarmatia north
of the Black Sea...and every one of the soldiers itching
to slaughter barbarians! And since the aurochs have
been rendered virtually extinct by the demands of the
games—you remember Vespasian and his hundred-day
opening celebration of the Coliseum, don't you?—these
Imperial aurochs are the only ones to be had on short
notice. I understand that gigantic ones roam the Great
Plains of Lacotia in Terra Nova, but shipping costs are
prohibitive. I'd have to impose some capricious tax, on
adultery or theatergoers or pumpkins."

"I see."

"You'll do more than see! You'll lead the expeditionary force, that's what you'll do!"

"Yes, my Lord," I said, my heart sinking. At lest I
would miss the reign of terror which, rumor had it, Domitian was about to instigate. I had no desire to end up

being devoured by lions—or crocodiles, I reflected
grimly as I saw them being released into the flooded
arena to mop up the survivors of the sea-battle.

"You'll take the Thirty-fourth," he said. "What a
spectacle! I may even come and watch the carnage."

"But your subjects need you here in Rome, Caesar," I
said.

"Beware, beware, I've a purge coming. Your best bet
is to be far from here; and fighting is, after all, the only
thing you do well."

That was true. I remembered the last major purge; for
a moment, after twenty-odd years, I saw my father as he
lay dying on a couch, back on the estate with the olive
groves. "Thank you, Caesar, for the signal honor," I
said, going down on one knee; but Domitian was busy
shooting the crocodiles, cackling with glee as the drain-
ing arena churned red.

We set sail shortly from Brundisium. We used traditional triremes because it wasn't too far; but to show our
status as purveyors of the Imperial Wrath, we were preceded and followed by a full escort of the new fast little
ships. They wove in and out among our old-fashioned
ones, making a thorough nuisance of themselves.

The Thirty-fourth was garrisoned in Thrace at the
time, fresh from its foray into the land of the Dacians.
My tutor Nikias was there, wizened but waggish as ever.
We marched eastward.

At first it was clear that we were in the land of the Pax
Romana. Town after town followed the prefabricated
Roman pattern: country estates of the rich, a temple to
the local god and another to Jove or Augustus or someone, a circus for family entertainments, an enormous
public baths, insular apartment complexes for the poor,
markets, and so forth. The terrain would change from
the hills of Bithynia to the plains of Galatia, but the
towns all looked alike; it was one of the less agreeable
aspects of the Empire.

Naturally I adhered to strict discipline throughout. I

didn't hesitate to have men flogged or executed, and all down the good straight Roman roads I never once heard a sour rhythm in the thump, thump, thump of infantry, nor did the legion's eagles once waver as the aquiliferi held them high. In spite of himself, Father had made a man of me.

When I got to Cappadocia I found that Domitian had been grossly misinformed.

The Parthian host had pushed right through the mountains and into the western plain of Cappadocia, where lies a great salt lake. We were outnumbered five to one, and they had already taken the border town of Domitianopolis, only a year old. The precious herds of aurochs and their grazing grounds were behind the enemy lines!

I did my dogged best. We set up castra about a mile from where they were, up the side of a hill, and engaged them in the traditional manner, to little avail. There were just too many of them. In the second battle I lost one of my eagles, the sacrificial ram had three livers and its heart on the wrong side, and I sat down to compose a letter to Caesar asking for help. I retired my legion to the next town, Trajanopolis (ah, human vanity) and prepared for reinforcements.

Some weeks later came the reply, as I was having my back rubbed in the local baths:

> To Titus Papinianus, Dux of the Thirty-fourth, greeting.
>
> Well, Titus old boy, got more than you bargained for, eh? Well, there's not too much I can do. Terra Nova's acting up—for some reason the Seminolii (who are a union of the southeastern savages, formed when we drove the Chrichii, the Chirochii, and the Choctavii southwards, and these barbarians interbred with certain of our runaway Nubian slaves) think there's something wrong with our teaching them to take baths and go to the circus

and so on. Trajan is busy quelling them—only the northern provinces, Iracuavia and Lacotia, are friendly.

So I'm afraid there's little I can do, unless I want to expose some other border elsewhere.

A curiosity, though, Titus. In his last shipment of entertainers for the arena, the impresario Lucretius Lupus, who is vacationing in Terra Nova, sent me a whole tribe of Lacotians. Their leader, Aquila (actually some barbaric tongue-twister, but it *means* eagle) was the very man who defeated Pomponius Piso thirty-five years ago. They were supposed to do battle against Numidian archers in the Coliseum, but... why not?

I'm sending them on the next ship. Who knows, perhaps these Lacotians may know something—and they're screamingly funny besides. Fight well —come back with your shield or on it, as the saying goes.

Ave atque vale,

Titus Flavius Domitianus, Caesar, Augustus, Imperator, Pater Patriae, Pater Maximus Candidusque, and various other titles, your Emperor and God.

Apparently I *was* a victim of the purge, after all. But at least I would fulfill my childhood dream of meeting one of those legendary Terra Novan savages face to face, before I died gloriously in battle.

CHAPTER
III

I T HAD BEEN AN EXHAUSTING DAY. WE HAD RETURNED to the old castra, and I was studying the war histories, trying to work out a viable stratagem, and, for fear of keeping the legion too idle, had detailed two maniples of infantry to dig more trenches and build more ramparts. Alone in the shade of my praetorium with a flagon of Chian wine, I tried different ways of deploying our meager artillery, our scorpiones, ballistae, and catapultae, by arranging pebbles around a clay model of the terrain. About two thousand men, a third of the legion, were dead or wounded. It was depressing.

I'd fallen asleep at the table. A lamp burned still, causing the shadows to flit along the flaps of my praetorium. I was in my bare tunic; outside, guards watched, their pila crossed over the entrance.

Suddenly I opened my eyes.

The shadow on the wall . . . was there someone in the room with me? I listened. Was it a breathing? Ah no, my own, but—

14

There. A shadow on the wall, dancing against the quivering lamplight...I reached for my dagger. It was jerked out of my hands. I whirled around. In the eerie flickering, an apparition leered at me.

"Jupiter defend me!" I cried, doing every avert-the-omen sign I could remember.

The ghost did not disappear. It didn't move either. I took a good cool look at it (I knew by now I must be dreaming, or else why would the guards not have noticed?) and Virgil's description of the hell-beings of Avernus, whom Aeneas saw on his descent into Hades, was nothing compared to this.

It was a weatherbeaten face with a hooked nose and hawklike brown eyes, and it was painted in garish reds and yellows and striped with black. Its hair was long and white; and, in a headband, a number of eagle feathers stuck out.

It was almost naked; it stooped with age, and its chest sagged like an old man's. A breechclout of some kind of leather hid its privates. It smelled of some strange oil; if it had bathed at all, it was no Roman bath it took.

It grinned at me.

"Who in Hades are you?" I gasped at last, when pinching myself several more times resulted only in an itchy arm. "And how did you get in here?"

It shrugged. "I've never yet met a Roman I couldn't creep up on," it said genially.

'You mean you're—"

"*Hechitu welo.* I am Aquila the Barbarian."

"Oh, but you *do* speak Latin, I see."

"What do you think? We've been taking your baths, reading your ghastly poets, and watching your indecently gory spectacles for the past thirty-five years."

So this was the famous tactician who had demolished the legions of Pomponius Piso! "I'm pleased," I said, "to have such a distinguished leader as yourself working under my command."

"Under *your* command!" The savage began to cackle.

I was somewhat disgruntled; he said, "The White and Greatest Father said nothing about working under anybody. We came of our own free will, in friendship, to make war with honor if we so choose. Do you have any wine?"

"Oh. Sorry." I picked up the flagon to pour some, but he relieved me of the whole thing and began to guzzle. "And your men? How many are there?"

"How should I know? Who can count the trees of the forest?"

"Show me then." I lifted the tent flaps; outside, the two guards lay bound and gagged. The moon was full, and a fire was roaring at the crossroads of the via principalis and the via praetoria. I saw them in the half-light, a comical procession such as you might see in one of Plautus's farces.

Some of the men were mounted; their horses were painted as bizarrely as they were themselves. Some wore their hair braided in the Gaulish manner, but unlike the Gauls' it was well-oiled and sleek. Feathers adorned their heads. They had little armor, although a few had borrowed cuirasses and one or two sported ill-fitting helmets. Some were bare-chested; others had bewildering neckpieces hung with beads, animal claws, seashells, and silver denarii. All the way down the via principalis they came. It was amazing that they had made no noise. Their women followed, carrying burdens, or leading dogs with packs tied behind them.

"Are these," I asked Aquila, "my reinforcements? Can they take orders?"

"I don't know," Aquila said. "Is there good fighting to be had here?"

"Well, there are twenty thousand Parthians back there," I said, jerking my thumb eastward.

"And who might the Parthians be?"

"Parthians," I said (slowly, in the legionaries' pidgin Latin, so they'd understand every word) "are a race of extremely wicked people from the east, who revile the name of Rome and seek, in their overweening hubris, to rob us of our territory and set up a rival Empire of their own. They have already taken Domitianopolis and are about to ravage all Cappadocia."

"And what about the Cappadocians? Perhaps they would prefer the Parthian masters to the Romans?" he said with a nasty chuckle.

What ignorant idiots! I cursed Domitian for playing this terrible trick on me. "Obviously," I said with painstaking clarity, "it is the destiny of Rome to rule the world; the Emperor, who is a god and bloody well ought to know, is divinely charged with the right to conquer all inferior nations! Everyone knows that. I mean, you Lacotians have been Roman citizens for some time now, haven't you? What a ridiculous thing to be arguing about, with those beastly Parthians beating at the very gates of the Empire...."

"You Romans never listen, do you? By what right, pray, are *you* in Cappadocia, as opposed to the Parthians or indeed, the Cappadocians?"

Casuistry has never been my strong point. Nikias could never get me to understand the simplest Platonic dialogue, so you can imagine my confusion as I faced this foul-stenched savage who was making me defend the obvious. I glared at these Terra Novans, getting very red in the face. "Damn it, we *own* this land here!" I said.

"What a strange philosophy! How can land be owned? You Romans came charging into Lacotia, you gave us horses and pushed us out of the forests into the plains. What we had we shared with you, but you wanted everything. And all you give us is those bloody spectacles. You don't have true wars, wars that hone a man's spirit and sharpen his senses; you have wasteful wars in which men are like the cogs of your motor-cars and ships. I do not come to fight in your war. The others, of course, may do exactly as they wish."

"You're not going to give them any orders?"

"Why should I? We are all equal; as their chief I shall

certainly advise them, but public opinion may gainsay me."

What a way to run an army. "Are you sure you're the great Aquila who vanquished Pomponius Piso?"

"Ah, that funny little Roman who watched from afar and never once got a spot of blood on his toga! That was a wonderful war indeed. Some mercenaries of yours, from Hispania I believe, taught us the art of taking scalps, which we have adopted into our culture." For the first time I noticed the grisly assortment that dangled from his waistband. "But you Romans didn't play by the rules. After you lost the war, you didn't return to your own land. Now that I have seen your land I can understand why, though."

What! This man dared to impugn the sacred name of Rome? I had a mind to have him flogged immediately, white-haired though he was. "How can you possibly say this?"

"Ugh! Your crowds, the noise of your thoroughfares, the ugly monstrosities you call palaces, the stone images that you dote on and pray to . . . I thought I was in hell itself, General. Where I live the land is green for a thousand miles, and the brooks are clear and men's hearts soar like hawks. Much like this Cappadocia which you are even now despoiling with aqueducts that change the flow of nature, with circuses that exterminate whole species of beasts—"

"That's enough," I said. "We'll fight this war without you! Go home!"

"How can we? We no longer have a home. Our sacred burial grounds were razed to make room for a public baths. An evil spirit has descended upon our tribe, don't you see, and there isn't much we can do about it. We went hungry; we ate even our own dogs, such was our shame. That is why we took Lucretius Lupus up on his offer to come to Rome. We look for an honorable war in which to redeem ourselves—we didn't know that Lucretius Lupus had signed us up to kill Numidian archers in the circus for the general amusement. But the Pater Maximus Candidusque heard our plea with compassion; that is why we're here. . . ."

"I see," I said without conviction. I was resigned to an ignominious defeat. I'd already lost one eagle after all, and in the days of the Republic I would probably already have committed suicide, but such was the decadence to which contemporary society had fallen that I did not even contemplate such a step. I decided to dismiss them for now and get back to serious work. "Go see the quaestor, Quintus Publius Cinna; he'll feed and pay you. You'll have to pitch castra outside, but in the morning I'll assign a detail to help you dig fossae and build vallae."

"Bah!" the old man snorted. "Are we women, that we must hide behind trenches and walls? We will put our tipis at the foot of this hill, in the very sight of the enemy—"

"But their catapultae—their ballistae—"

"What do a few machines matter? Since we have lost our burial grounds we do not care to live." So saying the old savage made a gesture of dismissal at me—*me*! and swept out; the weird parade followed him, silent as shadow. Even the dogs made no noise. When I returned to my tent it was as if the whole thing had been a dream.

CHAPTER
IV

AT DAWN, DRIVEN BY CURIOSITY, I RODE OUT OF the camp with Nikias and a couple of tribunes. I was hoping that the Terra Novans would miraculously have vanished, but far from it. An encampment lay at the foot of the hill, just as Aquila had promised. If the enemy wanted to storm our castra it would probably be over the Terra Novans' dead bodies.

What an undisciplined hodgepodge of a castra it was!

Their tents, scattered without any pattern or thoroughfare, were shaped like inverted funnels of the type alchemists use for straining their filtrates. Infants squalled; horses were tethered at random; and the tents, which seemed to be of the hides of cows or aurochs stretched over a frame of poles, were decorated with crude likenesses of animals and men. No doubt Domitian found these savages comical; lacking his sense of humor, I found them rather pitiable.

And were they engaged in drill exercises, or marching up and down the hill to keep in shape for the coming conflict? Not a bit? The men, all naked save for scant loincloths, beads, feathers, and soft leather caligae, were lazing about in clumps, muttering in their guttural tongue.

I saw Aquila among them.

"*Ave*, General," he said, looking up. "The Parthians have mobilized a wing of their army; I believe it's young Chosroes leading them. They're on their way."

"How in heaven could you know such a thing?"

Aquila got up and pointed to the east.

"Whatever do you mean?" At the limit of my vision, a hillock much like our own seemed to be emitting little puffs of smoke.

"Ah, some of our braves are restless, General, you see. They decided to go for a closer look. Those are smoke signals."

"Secret codes in smoke? Good heavens, how sophisticated," I said; in truth I could hardly make it out at all, in the dazzling sunlight, and I was certain that Aquila was having me on. "From behind enemy lines, no less! How large was the party you sent out?" I asked sarcastically.

"What party? You know how young men are. I could not restrain them from this display of bravery. . . ."

"Perhaps there is something in your savage tactics, Aquila," I said. "I shall look forward to your fighting by my side—"

"And whyever should I do that?" said the chieftain. His puzzlement seemed genuine.

I threw my hands up in despair. "Oh, Marcellus—"

The tribune by that name rode up to me. "Tell the signifer and the aquiliferi to ready their banners. Let the tubicines stand ready to sound my orders, and let the cornicines be not far behind, to relay the commands to the appropriate maniples."

"Yes, General. Any particular formation?"

I sighed. "Oh, acies triplex, I suppose." A doomed general might as well go out in good classical style.

"You haven't much time, General," Aquila said, chuckling. "They're due in about five minutes."

"How do you know?" I said, knowing that he would only come up with some outrageous boast of his men's prowess.

"Oh, I've been putting my ear to the ground—"

Suddenly an earsplitting din rent the air. My horse reared up. I waved vaguely to the tribune. Somewhere a bucina wailed, and then I heard the shouts of thousands of men as they fell into the three lines of Julius Caesar's favorite formation. I heard the deep-voiced tuba bray and be echoed by the shrill screech of cornua.

"Have fun," Aquila shouted after me as I spurred my horse down the hill.

CHAPTER
V

A T SUNSET WE STRAGGLED BACK TO THE CASTRA, roundly beaten. I didn't even want to reckon the casualties. I found my way to the praetorium and summoned Nikias to me. We had run out of the good Chian wine and were down to cheap Italian wines, but I was past caring. I downed a whole pitcher of it before Nikias arrived.

"Sit at the table, Nikias. There, opposite me, like you used to when you taught me all those contracted verbs. Did you bring your pen and parchment?" He opened his toolbox.

"Letters to write?" he said.

"Yes, I want to dictate a letter to Caesar. But first . . . write me up a document of manumission."

"You wish to free a slave, Master Titus?" An expression of alarm crossed his face.

"Yes. You." The oil lamp sputtered briefly; the wick was low. The tent dimmed; the shadows deepened.

"You're not planning to—"

23

"Yes, as a matter of fact I am. You can hold the sword while I run on it. But I want you to be a free man first."

"That's absurd! We Greeks have always considered the Roman predilection for suicide to be wasteful and unaesthetic, and—" He was in tears suddenly.

We were both sobbing our guts out, recalling the happy days of the estate with the olive orchard and the motor-car, wallowing in paroxysms of grief, when—

Behind me, in the tent, someone cleared his throat.

I nearly fell out of the chair.

"Am I interrupting something?"

"Aquila!" I was almost incoherent. "How dare you interrupt this most private moment, you impudent savage—"

"There now, there now. I have no wish to see you suffer so. I come to offer help."

"Help?"

As I looked around my tent, other savages resolved out of the shadows. Far from having an intimate tête-à-tête with my tutor and friend of thirty-five years, I might as well have been a clown in a Plautus comedy, waving my leather phallus at the hooting masses.

"These are," said Aquila, "some of the young braves of my tribe. Here is Ursus Erectus...Nimbus Rufus..." The names were, of course, in his savage speech; I have translated them into a humanly comprehensible tongue. "...Alces Nigra...Lupus Solitarius...."

"I am beyond your help," I said. "I'm weary. Domitian surely intends me to die here, and he shall be satisfied. I don't know what I've done to offend Caesar, but it appears to be the will of the gods—at least the will of one rather insistent one—"

"There now, don't kill yourself," Aquila said. "These four braves are bored. They've decided to invade the enemy camp, and they won't rest unless they penetrate to the tent of their very leader."

"What rubbish! Four people against ten, twenty thousand? Your boasts have been plentiful, but this one—"

"The Lacota do not boast," the chief said matter-of-factly. "You may have noticed that we sneaked up to your tent and were able to watch your entire little scene with Nikias unobserved. Rather maudlin, I may add."

I could not deny that. "Since you insist—"

"Oh, they certainly do. They haven't had a good raid since they crossed the Big Water."

"Very well then," I said, trying to gather up what shreds of dignity I yet possessed. "You shall each have a standard issue of weaponry: pilum, gladius, and scutum. Nikias, see to that. You will depart immediately."

"Thanks for the weapons, but our own will do very nicely," Aquila said. "As for leaving immediately, though—"

"Well?"

"They can't leave for at least two hours. A man's got to look his best for a sacred thing like war. It'll take them that long to get their warpaint on."

"What? What kind of fighting is this, where you stop to adjust your makeup and your hair? Is this a war or is it a Corinthian brothel?"

"Relax, General!" Aquila said jovially. "Honor and glory will soon be ours." I blinked and they were gone.

For the next five or six hours I sat twiddling my thumbs. Even if they didn't come back, I reflected, they might be able to slip into Chosroes's tent and assassinate him. A dirty trick, and hardly the Roman way to do business—my father would turn over in his grave!—but I could salvage my conscience by noting that savages could hardly be expected to know about the refinements of civilized warfare.

I pulled out my military texts and studied them. But I was too nervous to concentrate. I pulled out some light reading, a scroll of scientifictiones.

I was a little way into the epic poem *Fundatio: Fundatio et Imperium: Fundatio Secunda*—which predicts, amusingly, that Rome will collapse and we will enter an age of barbarity—when . . .

"What's that noise?" I shouted. Nikias was awake too, and hollering for the tribunes. "It's an ambush!"

I staggered outside.

Coming up the via principalis of the castra, the four Lacotians were dancing up a storm, screaming incantations in their language, and hitting their lances on shields. Alarums were sounding around the camp. Centurions rushed hither and thither, bumping into each other and tripping.

The Lacotians were cavorting around in a bacchanalian frenzy, and I saw that fresh scalps dangled from their spears and their face paint was streaked with blood.

When they saw me they calmed down a little. "What on earth—" I said. They began clamoring in their tongue all at once. I finally saw Aquila, shuffling up the via principalis.

"Victory!" he said. The braves began to throw assorted spoils at my feet. Chests of precious metals. An aurochs hide. Parchments written in the Parthian language. Aquila came forward and embraced me, beaming and smelling like a he-goat.

"They reached the tent of Chosroes?" I stared dumbly as one of the braves hurled what was unmistakably Chosroes's armor at my feet. I could hardly believe my luck. Surely the Parthians (whose military organization was far less disciplined than ours, and who would be thrown into utter chaos by the death of a leader) would be confused enough to return whence they came.

"You have evidence of Chosroes's death?" I said excitedly. "His head, perhaps, or some other such trinket I can send to Domitian?"

A pause. Aquila spoke to his four savages while I stood nervously.

Finally he said, "I have the honor to report that all

four of my braves have counted coup on the Parthian leader."

I smelled a rat. "Counted coup? What does that mean?"

"Among my people it is considered the mark of highest bravery to touch the enemy with one of these"—he held up a short, cudgel-like baton—"and return alive. *Killing* the man hardly seemed necessary."

"You took these spoils and you didn't...even... harm...."

"Oh, he was harmed all right. Nasty bruise on his forehead, given by Ursus Erectus, here. And Nimbus Rufus fetched him a smart one on the posterior—he won't be able to sit down for a week."

"I want him killed! I want him killed!"

There was a terse discussion amongst them; then Aquila turned gravely to me. "Alas, General, they've decided they don't want to kill him. Seems that he fought so gallantly that he's won their respect, or something."

"But I command it!"

"We've been through all this before."

I stalked into my tent. "Nikias! The sword!" I shouted. "It's now or never!" Nikias followed me, shaking all over; poor soul, I'd never dictated his certificate of manumission, and I was too distraught to think of it now.

Aquila—of all the impudence—followed me in. "Come now, General!" he said. "I'll never understand you palefaces. Here we come from over the Big Water to inspire you with noble deeds and courageous acts, and what do you do? You decide to kill yourself! It's cowardice pure and simple. All you Romans are cowards! When you fight you put up barriers of metal so you can jab safely at the enemy. You throw great balls of flame with your thunder-machines and watch from a distance. You are no true men, but a gaggle of women. Or if you are men then you are hawks whose wings Wakantanka, the

Great Mystery, has clipped. You are devils who have taken paradise from us. It grieves me to see such cowardice, for it declares your subhumanity to all men." He paused for breath.

"Are you calling me a coward? Me, Titus Papinianus, son of Caius Papinianus, nicknamed The Stalwart, equestrian by birth, dux by the Emperor's decree, scourge of the Dacians, a coward?"

"The same."

I leaped for the man's throat. Deftly he stepped aside and, I went crashing into the wall, ripping a hole in the fabric. "You see what I mean?" he said calmly. "Only a coward would attack a man old enough to be his father."

I lunged again; this time I knocked my head on a tent pole. "I'll prove it to you," I said. "Send me your strongest brave and I'll—"

"Brute force won't show anything," Aquila said. "However, if you wish to convince me of your bravery...."

I waited, glaring at him.

"Tomorrow," he said, "I have a mind to ride far to the east, behind the enemy lines; to see the limits of your Roman Empire. And while I have no enmity for your Parthians, yet I will ride into their very maw and taunt them, so you will see that Aquila is no woman. You see me here, a man past eighty; yet I will do this thing. Do you dare come with me?"

A general doesn't permit himself to indulge in personal challenges, I told myself brutally. My father had beaten good Roman ethics into me often enough. But when I looked at this old savage something in me cracked. Here they were, these people who had stolen straight into the enemy camp and yet had scorned the easy victory of dispatching the enemy leader. What was it about Aquila and the Lacotians? After all, they had defeated Pomponius Piso himself. Perhaps they were sorcerers; perhaps they had some cloak of invisibility or potion of invincibility. I had to know. I no longer cared about Domitian, or his purge, or his precious aurochs herds for which we had wasted the lives of thousands of good legionaries. All I wanted to do was teach this insolent, supercilious savage a lesson he would never forget.

CHAPTER
VI

THE SUN HAD NOT RISEN WHEN WE SET OFF DOWN the hill. There were four of us: Nikias and I came in simple tunicae, although it galled me to be so disguised; Ursus Erectus, the young brawny one I had met the previous evening; and Aquila himself, who came clothed in a painted aurochs hide and wearing a bundle around his neck which he called his *fascis medicinae*.

Exchanging not a word, we rode towards the east, the sky gray-purpled by impending dawn. At the horizon was a line of low hills, at the foot of which the Parthians lay encamped; beyond them, I knew, was Domitianopolis.

"To the north," said Aquila, bringing his roan abreast of me, "there is a way around the hill. My braves found it yesterday. The Parthians, being the invaders, are unfamiliar with the country, yet they have not the Lacotian knack for sizing up the terrain; this is to our advantage." His smugness was annoying me; and also the fact that he was easing himself into the position of leader. I thanked the gods that my cohorts were not here to see me made a fool of.

"Shall I believe this braggart?" I asked Nikias in Greek.

"Watch it!" Aquila said in the same tongue. "There are Greeks in every village in Lacotia, for we find the tales of their Homer far nobler than your superficial love poems and the boasts of your historians."

"Is there no way we can speak privately?" I said, frustrated. Nikias and I lashed our mounts on ahead; but I confess I did not know which way to go next, and had to allow the Lacotians to slip into the lead again.

Presently we tethered our horses in a copse at the foot of the hill and Aquila began picking his way through a rocky trail that led upwards. He moved swiftly, gracefully, like a wild animal. Ha! I thought, remembering one of the popular theories about the Terra Novans, which averred that they were indeed part animal, thus lacking souls and being oblivious to pain.

"I see you've snooped around here before," I said.

"No," said Aquila, "I'm just following the signs left by last night's raiding party."

"What signs?"

Quickly he pointed around us. Here an arrangement of leaves and twigs, there a few rocks heaped in a natural-seeming pattern. These he claimed to be sophisticated messages that warned of pitfalls, unsteady footholds, and the like. For a moment, I almost believed him. Then I realized that reading the signs of nature was a special ability of such primitive sorcerers, and that he was just having a little fun with me. I laughed at myself for being so gullible.

In a few hours we were overlooking the Parthian host from behind.

It took my breath away. Their tents were gaudy— brash reds, vibrant oranges, vivid against the green. They stretched far into the hill's shadow. There were chariots, points of fire in the carpet of grass. There were

alien standards. There were soldiers crawling like ants: I
couldn't begin to recognize all the types of costumes.
And in the center of it all, an oriental palace in fabric,
was the tent of their leader. How unlike my sparse, classical praetorium, or the rough hides of the Lacotians'
tipis!

"There are many," I whispered. It wasn't like the Dacians, who were, after all, barbarians not much more
advanced than the Lacotians.

"Bah! Old women, the lot of them. They are river
reeds that sway when a child blows on them. They are
even less courageous than the Romans, whom I once
subdued."

"Will you taunt them now?"

"No," Aquila said. "First I've a mind to see your precious Cappadocia. Let's go east."

"Very well," I said grimly, ready for anything. Now
that I had seen the extent of the Parthian host I knew
that death would not be far. I felt a reckless exhilaration,
as though I were a child again.

We scrambled down cautiously, fetched our horses,
and rounded the hill. A little forest hugged the eastern
slope of it; and then we were on a plain. Lush grass
thinned in the distance as the hills rose.

Suddenly there was a burst of gibberish from the lips
of Ursus Erectus, who had been silent all day. He was
pointing wildly at the far hills. I squinted.

At first it seemed like a scar, a brown patch on the
hillside; and then I saw it move.

"The *pta*! Our sacred *pta*!" Aquila cried. He sounded
younger. "At last our tribe may be freed of its curse, may
find new hunting grounds! Would that I were a young
brave, to find such *pta* and *pte*...."

Without waiting, reckless, the two Lacotians spurred
their horses into a gallop. Nikias and I caught up with
them, and soon I saw the brown patch resolve into little

brown patches; my vision blurred from the horseback riding—

"The Imperial aurochs herd!" Nikias shouted.

I knew that such creatures existed in the new world, but I had not known that they would exert such power over the savages.

The Lacotians were laughing now, whooping with glee, throwing their lances and catching them as they raced forward.

They were grazing. Thousands of them. Majestic creatures, bearded and sleek-furred.

And then, as we passed a rock mound, Aquila's steed stopped and whinnied.

I slowed to a trot behind him. A sickening sight greeted me.

They were lying in the grass, one or two of them, rotting. Carrion birds had settled on them, and when I looked up I saw more vultures wheeling.

The bison had been completely flayed.

"Why?" Aquila screamed at the sky, raging. I saw him weep copiously, without shame, like a woman. We rode on, but now their demeanor was grim.

As we neared the herd we found more carcasses. Always the skin would be stripped from them and their flesh remain moldering in the heat. Aquila's weeping did not cease.

And then, peering from behind a boulder, we saw mounds of piled pelts. And armed guards watching over them.

"Poaching," I said, "on a grand scale. At this rate they'll have killed and skinned the entire herd by year's end."

Aquila said, "Can this be true? Can they really take the skins and leave the flesh to rot, disrupt man's balance with nature?"

"Probably they plan to trade them further east. To the people of India, or those folk with skins of gold who inhabit the lands beyond, these pelts may be worth more than silks and spices."

"We have rediscovered paradise," said Aquila, "only to lose it a second time."

The Lacotians exchanged words rapidly in their tongue. I caught the words *pta* and *pte*, which seemed to be the male and female aurochs. Then Aquila turned to me and said, his voice quavering with emotion, "My heart is like a stone, General. I can no longer even weep. When your people drove us into the great plains and gave us horses, we hunted the aurochs and our bellies were full. We took no more than what would fill us, and the hide and the bones we made good use of. When we were full we made war: holy war, not a war of senseless killing, but war to strengthen a man's heart and give him honor. Now when I look upon this land I see what could be another paradise. We could be happy here, for when we hunt we are part of nature's harmony. But these Parthians hunt wantonly, they take only the skins and discard the meat. They must truly be cursed. I cannot bear to look upon this—" He faltered. "I have seen too much. I am too old. It is a good day to die. I shall lie here on the grass until death comes for me."

I was moved by his words. The savage spoke of strange ways and customs; but when I thought more deeply I saw that we were kin. For my father had had much the same thought, the day he learned of the Emperor's disfavor and took it upon himself to execute sentence. But I didn't want Aquila to die. I said, "Old man, last night you forced me to live. You called me a coward. Must I remind you?"

Aquila seemed puzzled for a moment. Then he chuckled and said, "Of course, you're right. That isn't the answer at all, is it? Obviously we shouldn't take this lying down. Instead, we'll take on the whole bloody pack of them."

"You'll fight beside us?"

"What do you think?"

"So finally I'll get to see the fabled Lacotian art of warfare . . . the unorthodox tactics so elliptically alluded to by Pomponius Piso in his *Memoir of the Lacotian Wars*?"

"*Huka hey! Alea jacta est!*"

CHAPTER
VII

LATER I SQUATTED UNCOMFORTABLY IN AQUILA'S tent. There were four or five of them, the quaestor, one or two of my tribunes, sweating in their full regalia, Nikias taking notes, and me. Aquila pulled out a pipe, filled it with herbs from his fascis medicinae, and lit it, whereupon a foul stench filled the tent and I could hardly see for the smoke; this he puffed on, and then insisted I do the same. On complying I seemed to fall into a shadow world; everything felt hazy, unreal. So this was one of their secrets...a magic drug that no doubt rendered them invulnerable.

"Does the nearby town have a public baths?" said Aquila.

"Of course," I said hazily. "How could a Roman town not have any?"

"I want exclusive use of them for my braves for a day."

"Righty-ho." Perhaps they *were* getting civilized.

"I want some trees, felled in a ritual way which I shall prescribe, set up at the foot of this hill—"

"Aha! A Lacotian war machine!" I knew they'd have something up their sleeve; for magic, in itself, is rarely effective unless blended with careful planning, as I had myself learned in my dealings with the Dacians and Picts.

"You might call it that," Aquila said, and he started to giggle ferociously.

A few more puffs, and it was as if I was seeing the world from underwater. The Lacotians rippled. In the distance, Father drove up in his motorcar, scolding me, and off in a corner Domitian was shooting some chimera full of arrows, and I was laughing helplessly...

There was a great deal of grumbling from the townspeople when I requisitioned the public baths. But eventually we barricaded them off and the Lacotians— perhaps two hundred strong—trooped inside. A maniple was dispatched to a nearby forest to fell the trees Aquila had requested, accompanied by one of their priests or *homines medicinae* who would perform the appropriate ritual.

After a while I wearied of pacing the colonade outside the baths; I decided that I might as well join them. It's good to get the kinks out of your body before a major battle, even one you've little chance of surviving.

I went inside. Signs led to the tepidarium, caldarium and frigidarium. The place was unusually quiet. Normally the buzz of social banter never ceases at a bath. I disrobed in the vestiarium, which was piled high with the animal skins and feathers the savages wore, and then tried the caldarium.

I rubbed my eyes. At first you couldn't see for the steam and then—

The pool proper had been drained. Lacotians squatted in ranks inside. Steam poured out from the heating vents; the slaves must be working overtime underneath. Steam tendrilled out then as they sat, unspeaking, each of them apparently lost in some private vision. Fetishes, the skulls of aurochs, ritual pipes littered the tile floor, which was a mosaic depicting the rape of the Sabine women. I made out Aquila, a shrunken man with age-blotched skin, kneeling in the center of the throng.

I descended into the empty pool, my feet smarting against the hot tiles.

"Ah, there you are, Aquila old chap!" I said. "Thought we ought to discuss a little strategy, eh, before tomorrow?"

Silence. The man's eyes stared ahead far away. He didn't move.

"Hello? Hello?" I said.

He snapped to. "Oh, General Titus. Sshhh"—his voice dropped—"wouldn't want to disturb these fellows, would you?"

"What's going on?"

"Lacotian custom. Sweat bath, you know. Some of the men are, oh, far away, on spirit journeys. Usually we have special tents for this purpose, but it seemed a good idea to take advantage of your modern Roman technology. . . ." He fell into a trance again, and I couldn't rouse him.

I bathed alone in the tepidarium for a while and returned to the castra, where an even more incredible sight awaited me.

At the foot of the hill, some distance eastward from the camp, several circles had been marked off with stones, aurochs skulls, pipes, and fetishes. At their centers stood the tree trunks that my soldiers had felled, and from them radiated hundreds of strings.

"Ho, there!" I called out, dismounting. "What's the meaning of this?"

A tribune came puffing up. "General, these savages have gone out of their minds!"

"Is this some kind of war engine?"

Distant hoofbeats. The Lacotians were returning from

the city. In a moment they had all split into groups and were lined up naked in the circles.

"I don't rightly know, General, just *what* the blighters are up to. It could be some kind of rapid-firing slingshot, I suppose."

"No," I said, "those strings are strips of hide; anything for firing ammunition would require tormenta, twisted ropes with a spring action as in the catapultae. I can't see any possible use for them."

"Perhaps they mean to swing down on the strings, as apes with vines in Africa."

"Then surely they would camouflage the engines so that their swoopings might contain some element of surprise."

"Good heavens, sir, what are they doing now?"

One of the homines medicinae was solemnly mutilating the young men one after another, cutting slits under the skin of their chests, sliding in little sticks, and then attaching them to the poles by means of the strings. Another homo medicinae distributed rattles to them and placed little wooden flutes in their mouths. The braves gave no show of pain at all, but walked out to the edge of the circle, facing the center, stretching the strings to their limits.

"It seems awfully gruesome," Nikias said, approaching from the castra with welcome bowls of Lesbian wine, just purchased in the town.

All at once came the pounding of drums and a most monstrous caterwauling from a group of old men, chanting a wavering, out-of-tune melody whose long notes were punctuated by peculiar rhythmic gurgling sounds. At this the braves began to dance and blow on their flutes, staring steadfastly at the sun, which was shining fiercely. As the men danced they tugged at the strings, trying it seemed to yank themselves free; blood spurted from their chests. The din was astonishing. Presently a crowd of legionaries had gathered, and were staring at this display, cheering and jeering with the typical

Romans' love of spectacle; one might as well have been at the bloody circus. Even I, professional butcher as I am, felt queasy at this eerie exhibition.

I finally caught sight of Aquila, moving unconcernedly through the crowd.

"What the hell is going on?" I yelled above the cacophony.

"Oh, nothing," he said. "They are merely offering up their pain. It is the sundance, you know. You do want to win the battle, don't you?"

"Yes, but—"

"They must dance," he said, "until the skin tears and they break free. After that they will dress in all their finery and go to war."

Children were running amok, poking at the men with grass blades. Women sang, their voices blending with the grunting hey-hey-hey of the old men.

"Do you mean to say," I began indignantly, "that you have made me go to all this trouble, just so you could have some horrid rite?" Never had these people seemed more alien to me. I had been wrong even to attempt to gain their co-operation. We were doomed, and I had only been stalling for time. The best thing would be to fling ourselves on the Parthians and die with a good grace.

Well, as if in answer to my sentiments, bucinae and cornua began to bray above the din. I looked to the east. A line of glitter was rolling slowly across the plain, like a monstrous worm of gold.

"The Parthians!" I cried. Instantly the tribunes were by my side. "Aquila, enough of this rubbish!" I said. "We're in real trouble now, and we need all the men we've got! Let everyone grab a weapon!"

Aquila just laughed at me. "What?" he said. "This is a sacred thing the men do. We cannot interrupt it. When they are ready, they will come."

It was useless. I should have known better than to attempt to deal rationally with savages. Superstitious primitives. It was our job to civilize these people—with fire and sword if necessary—not reason with them. With a final shrug of exasperation, I mounted, barked some orders to the tribune, which were presently relayed by tubae all over the castra above. Legionaries rushed for their shields and weapons, and the audience for the Lacotians' curious ritual of self-mutilation wilted away in an instant.

CHAPTER
VIII

I HAD BARELY TWO SQUADRONS OF CAVALRY, AND ALL save one of my praefecti equitum had perished. These I held in reserve, placing them on the hillside under my own command. I had five cohorts of infantry and a scattering of auxiliaries: a few slingers, perhaps a hundred of the Cretan sagitarii, and so on. These, under the command of the quaestor Quintus Publius Cinna, I deployed, again in Julius Caesar's favorite acies triplex formation, in three lines directly facing the onslaught, the troops in front forming an iron barrier with their shields. The artillery I scattered at intervals throughout the lines.

As I shouted my commands and the tribunes hastened to obey, the Lacotians continued their frenzied dancing, jerking at the rawhide strings and wildly piping on their flutes, so that it was almost impossible to make myself heard. The tramp-tramp of the distant enemy was something you felt more than heard, like a heartbeat, an impalpable dread. It had oozed halfway across the plain now, that multicolored worm of an army, and there was no time to lose. I chose a little cliff from which to watch the fray, as far as possible from the distracting noise of the Lacotians' rite. Nikias was there; this time I remembered the certificate of manumission, and he was at my side a freeman and my hired scribe. Behind me I concealed the cavalry as best I could.

I gazed over the plain.

It seemed infinitely slow, the crawling forward of the enemy, froom my lofty vantage point. But I knew there was little time. I saw Cinna ride back and forth behind the lines, haranguing the pedites.

The enemy stopped.

I looked them over. They were neat squares of color, each square perhaps a thousand men. We were strung out a long way, but not very deeply; it was only a matter of time before they broke through. I saw, in the distance, the range of foothills in which their camp nestled; behind them were the cursed aurochs herds which Domitian was about to make me die for.

I heard their trumpets sound. They charged in one chaotic melee: chariots, infantry, cavalry all jumbled together. It was their numbers that had been our bane, not their brilliant organization. The first wave crashed into our shield wall; the shields clanged open at a single command and a volley of fire-arrows burst forth. Horses whinnied and perished. Chariots overturned and upset other chariots. But they kept coming.

And lo! Our wall of scuta was breached by a suicidal charioteer, and hundreds of the Parthians were streaming through the gap, swords waving! Even from on high I smelled the blood, and the dust clouds were dyed scarlet, obscuring the view. I averted my eyes; the sight of hacking and bloodletting was not new to me, and held no interest. It was now up to me to decide whether to condemn the cavalry too, or to sound the retreat and commit suicide. It had been hardly an hour, and the outcome was already clear.

"Nikias," I said, adopting a brusque tone to hide my sorrow, "bring the sword at once."

"Yes . . . master." His eyes were red. I did not weep—we had been through all that before, in the tent, when Aquila and his braves had so callously spied on us.

Suddenly—

An earsplitting screeching assailed my ears! Down below the fighting froze for a moment, the dust started to settle, everyone turned and stared to the east.

Demons on horseback were charging from behind the enemy lines, firing streams of fire-arrows into the dumbfounded Parthian ranks. The figures were painted in dazzling colors, the horses' legs were decorated with bright lightning streaks, and they wore bonnets of feathers that trailed behind, and they were uttering such piercing screams as would make the very mummies burst forth from their pyramids. In the hills, I saw pillars of flame and smoke, and my spirits lifted. I knew the enemy camp was on fire. The Lacotians must have ridden as fast as the wind, and as silently, to have been able to accomplish all this.

Now the Parthians were scattering randomly, and my infantry were having an easy time of it as they rushed, crazed with fear, into their arms. I gave the order to give chase. The Lacotians had formed a circle of horsemen that surrounded the enemy host, and were riding around and around and firing.

"Quite a spectacle, eh, general?" I started. It was Aquila. He was mounted on a white horse, decorated with crimson lightning-stripes; his face was painted in red and white, and on his wrinkled brow sat a crown of feathers; behind him more feathers streamed. In his right hand he held high a feathered lance. He was magnificent. Although he wore no golden cuirass, his horse carried no gilt caparison, no cloak of purple flapped behind him . . . yet he looked like a god, his demeanor stern and implacable. The Parthians, who had never seen a Lacotian decked in his war regalia, must surely have thought them devils, for they are a superstitious folk, without the benefit of the Empire's enlightenment.

"Aquila!" I said. "You've saved us! I've a mind to make all the legionaries perform your sundance from now on—"

"You are far from saved," he said. "Quickly. Bring your cavalry. Your men on the plain will pursue them; my men there will lure them. Meanwhile your cavalry and what remains of mine will round the hills, swifter than thought itself. If we become one with the wind, and soar like eagles, we may be able to head them off at yonder pass." He pointed to a crack, far off behind the enemy camp, which I could barely distinguish. But I wasn't going to argue now. I sent the herald with the summons and we were off.

The war-fever was in me now. We hurtled over the other side of the hill, Lacotians and Romans together, following Aquila's white steed. When we reached the pass I saw that Aquila's men had been busy indeed. For, as the Parthians fought their way through the bottleneck, pushed by our men and terrified out of their wits by the screeching of the Lacotians, other Lacotians had been at work rousing the herds of aurochs. Hither and thither they galloped, in and out of the herd, prodding, poking, luring.

A few at a time, the Parthians broke through the pass —to run head-on into a stampeding herd of aurochs.

"*Huka hey!*" the Lacotians shouted in thunderous unison. Then they broke into a babble of war cries and shrill ululations, and charged frantically into the fray. Aquila turned to me and winked; then he too charged.

"*Huka hey!*" I yelled madly, wondering what it meant, as it finally dawned on me that a handful of eccentric savages had rescued the honor of Rome.

CHAPTER
IX

IN THE EVENING THE WOMEN DANCED THE SCALPS OF the slain around a roaring fire, and the Lacotians feasted on fresh meat from the humps of aurochs. We Romans were all invited. In the midst of the festivities we had a surprise visitor—Domitian himself.

He came up the hill in a palanquin borne by eight burly slaves. Couches had been set up for the Romans, a little way off from the dancing; Aquila and I were quaffing Samian wine from the same goblet as though we'd known each other for ages. When Domitian stepped off the litter I gaped and dropped my goblet.

"No ceremony, Titus old boy," the emperor said. "I told you, didn't I, that I'd half a mind to come along and observe the spectacle? And you didn't disappoint me. Ah, if only I could recreate this battle on the Campus Martius outside Rome ... set up bleachers for the populace, with vending stands for cold drinks and sausages ... how the people would love me! I imagine I could stave off assassination for quite a while with a show like that."

"Caesar—"

"Imagine it! This sundance they've described to me—could it be done in the arena, do you think?"

"Certainly not," Aquila said. "It is a sacred thing."

"Oh, don't worry, old chap, I'm only joking. That's what I like about savages though—you dare to contradict me, unlike these spineless Romans." I started to say something, but checked myself. "What's this you're eating, barbarian victuals? Let's try some." He stuffed a piece of roast aurochs haunch into his mouth. "You shall have a triumph, Titus! And a new title. And I shall make you a procurator."

"I'm deeply flattered, Caesar," I said, hoping I would not be packed off to some rebellious wasteland like Judaea.

"Though, frankly, things haven't gone according to plan. I was rather hoping you'd be out of my hair by now."

"Caesar is merciful."

"And as for you, Aquila—"

"O Pater Maximus Candidusque," Aquila said softly, "I have seen the land of my dreams. When I was a young brave I came to this land in a spirit journey. I knew that the old ways were dying in Lacotia, but still I hoped. . . ."

"Very well, old man," said Domitian. "You and your people shall stay here in Cappadocia. I only ask that you defend my herds. Take what you need for sustenance, and cull the best each year for my games, but protect them and see that they multiply."

When Aquila had translated these words to the Lacotians, they cheered the Emperor loud and long. Domitian beamed. He was like a child, really, and liked to do the right thing, when it didn't involve too much work.

"As for you, Titus, what do you want?"

What did I want? I turned it over in my mind. I

wanted to retire from fighting. I wanted a comfortable house in the country. Simple things. I didn't think the Emperor would understand, so I said, "I want whatever you want, my lord."

"Yes, yes, old chap. You're rather lucky in a way, you know, being an incompetent idiot and all that. No one of any competence has been permitted to rise in power ever since my father Vespasian became Emperor. Your well-meaning stupidity has served you well . . . and you're damned lucky besides! After your victories in Dacia you were on the short list for purging, you know . . . so what do you think of these barbarians, eh? Do you think you could whip them into shape, lead them down the golden path to Roman citizenship, and all that?"

"Well—er—" Frankly, I don't think I ever wanted to set eyes on another Lacotian again.

"How succinct of you. Well, you're leaving for Lacotia right after the triumph—as my new governor."

I looked wildly about me. Was I seeing things, or had Aquila and Domitian just exchanged a sly wink? Mustering all my confidence, I said, my face getting redder by the second, "You can rely on me, Caesar. By next year, these barbarians will bloody well enjoy taking baths and going to spectacles. They'll read Virgil every morning before breakfast, and they'll all wear togas and speak Latin and they'll worship Venus and Mars and Jupiter and Minerva instead of their heathen idols, even if it kills me!"

I turned and saw Aquila guffawing uproariously. Then I took another swig of wine and laughed myself into a stupor.

CHAPTER
X

O F THE TRIUMPH, THE CEREMONIES, AND THE
orgies I shall say little; there was all the usual sort
of thing. Marching through Rome, you know, with the
throng cheering and old Nikias whispering in my ear the
traditional words, "Remember, thou art mortal. . . ."

Eventually I found it irritating beyond all measure.
"Look here, you old fart," I said fondly, "just because
I've given you your freedom—"

The crowd roared. My white stallions reared up and
whinnied in tune with the braying of bucinae.

"It happens to be traditional, my Lord," Nikias
said. "Remember, thou art mortal. . . ."

"I know, Nikias, I know. And I'm just dying to find
out how Domitian means to test my mortality next."

"You soon will, I'm sure. Fact of the matter is, Master Titus, you're better off in Terra Nova; if he should
decide to execute you or something of the sort, it'll take
months for the command even to reach you, and the

49

Empire is far less under His Magnitude's control than he'd like to think."

"Look, Nikias! They're throwing flowers." Blooms of every color and scent were flooding into the chariot now, and the steps of the Temple of Capitoline Jove, at the summit of which I would accept a laurel wreath from Caesar, loomed ahead. Of course, I kept my demeanor stern as befitted a general of my importance—wouldn't want the peasants to laugh at one, you know—but secretly I was actually somewhat elated. By the time I reached the top of the steps, though, my legs were aching terribly, and my expression of languid composure, which I had been practicing all day in front of a polished shield, had petrified into a grimace of anguish.

"Ah, there you are, Titus, old chap!" the Emperor said. I noted that he had no trouble at all with the decadent facial expression that had given me so much grief. But then, he'd been carried up the steps on a litter. "Pleasant view here, eh? Look at the throng...they're here to see *you*, my goodness, you bumbling bulbosity! They're not even paying any attention to *me*. Despite the fact that I happen to be their god, eh, what? I've half a mind to have you executed for casting your perfidious little shadow on my limelight."

"But Caesar...wasn't this little spectacle your idea?"

"And I'm already bored silly with it!" He summoned his dome-headed favorite, who had the laurel wreath all ready on a little platter. "Here, I suppose I shall have to give you this now." As I knelt humbly, the Emperor plonked the thing hard on my head, shoving it down my brow askew so that I could not see out of one eye...my eye watered horribly. My head itched. I had to scratch it, but protocol demanded that—

Meanwhile, the Emperor had begun his little speech, each little phrase of which was punctuated by a pompous sennet of brasses, thus:

"I, Titus Flavius Domitianus—"

Tat-ta-rat-tat-tat-tat-ta-ra-ta-rah!

"Caesar—"

Tan-ta-ran-tan-tan-tan-ta-rah!

"Augustus—"

Tara-tara-tarah!

"Imperator—"

I was itching all over now. The trumpets shrilled in my ears, making me even redder. What was I to do? I took off the wreath and began scratching furiously—

The music died down to a gurgle.

"Good heavens, man, what's the matter?"

"Caesar, I appear to—" I looked at the wreath. "This laurel wreath appears to be laced with poison ivy, my Lord—"

His Imperial Majesty began to giggle wildly. I realized that once again I was the butt of an Imperial prank. "Ha! Don't you realize, old chap, that if a *single* thing goes wrong with any official ceremony, it must be repeated all the way through from the beginning? Hee! You didn't think I'd let you get out of my clutches lightly, did you, you naughty general? That I'd give you the procuratorship of my newest and vastest province without at least a teeny-weeny little joke? Put the wreath back on at once!"

I obeyed.

"I, Titus Flavius Domitianus—"

"The itching began again, relentless. I gritted my teeth and forced my face back into the expression of elegant composure.

By all the gods! I have seen the walls of cities crumble under the onslaught of our Roman testudos. I have seen battlements battered. I have suffered savage defeats. I have flown for my life over the harsh terrains of Thrace and Caledonia. But never in my life had I known such indignity as on the day of my investiture as Caesar's representative in his most distant realm. It was bad enough that I would lose the comforts of civilization—the baths, the afternoon spectacles in the arena, and so on—to rule over a collection of savages all as eccentric as this

Aquila I had encountered. But to begin my reign with an itchy head! I think it can safely be said that no procurator of the Roman Empire ever took office in so ignominious a manner.

Just you wait! I thought bitterly. I'll be revenged on you! I'll outlast the pack of you Flavian Emperors! Then burning pain consumed my scalp. I closed my eyes and thought of wine: snow-chilled Chian wine, a nice capacious wooden vat of it! How I longed to dunk my head in it, to drown my sorrows and my soreness in the oblivion of inebriate excess! Already my pain seemed to take flight.

PART TWO

AQUILA THE GOD

CHAPTER
XI

O F THE JOURNEY ACROSS THE OCEAN ATLANTICUS I
shall relate but little. The time to visit the vomi-
torium is when one has had a surfeit of rich food; parties
and orgies are fine places to display one's regurgitory
prowess. But when one has had nothing to eat but a few
hunks of dried meat and stale bread, and there is no
music to listen to but the slap of the oars on the water
and the sound of the lash and the hortator's drumbeat,
the enforced vomiting of sea voyages has nothing to rec-
ommend it at all.

Nevertheless, there were certain advantages to leaving Rome. I was relatively free from Domitian's ca-
prices; I was, after all, going to be almost an emperor in
my own right; and I no longer had to cope with Aquila,
whose rise to fame filled me with the utmost oppro-
brium. Each time I had to make a report to the senate, he
seemed to have acquired a higher status. He was first a
senator, then a tribune, then a consul, and always Domi-
tan's favorite. He wore the senatorial robes particularly

well, combining them with the eaglefeather warbonnet; this style became much affected even by those not of Terra Novan ancestry. Indeed, there was such an up-surge in the popularity of Terra Novan fashions that it was rare to see a senator whose head was not adorned with a feather or two, or, at the very least, shorn, as is the custom with the citizens of Iracuavia, into the style of a mohawk.

I travelled to Terra Nova with my tutor Nikias. As soon as I arrived there as the Emperor's newly appointed procurator of the provice of Lacotia, I made all the usual decrees: renovating the procurator's palace at Caesarea-on-Miserabilis, engaging the impresario Lucretius Lupus to provide sufficiently astounding beasts and gladiators for the weeklong games in my own honor, and sending parties of surveyors to check up on the aqueducts, temples, and other public works that my predecessors had created.

In my time I had traveled most of the Roman world— I had been as a tourist to Egypt and Hispania, and as Dux of the Thirty-fourth Legion to Dacia and as far east as Cappadocia. But I was unprepared for Terra Nova. They had warned me that the place was at least as huge as the rest of the Empire, that the two provinces under our control, Iracuavia and Lacotia, were as vast as Europe, wild and impenetrable, and swarming with savages of a thousand kinds and languages. I had heard of the mighty Miserabilis, a river longer than the Nile; of the Montes Saxosi, mountains at the Empire's limits that dwarfed the Alps and the Caucasus. But none of the stories was as astonishing as the reality. It was the little details that were most alien: the strutting, giant chickens; the skin-tent villages; the feathered counte-nances of my new subjects. And the distances, for it took me almost a year, even with the advanced new ships, to reach the port of Eburacum Novum, and then many months of overland and upriver travel to reach the realm I was to rule.

I have told of my official acts on reaching Caesarea, a jewel of a little city, nice Roman temples and insulae and fora and agorae and a little amphitheater and racecourse, nestled in a fork of the River Miserabilis, a comforting chunk of Rome in the midst of unending plains dotted here and there with clusters of tipis and vast herds of aurochs. My first private act was to have a marble statue of Aquila made, and to install it in an atrium of my palace.

For I knew that Aquila was responsible for my being in this forsaken wilderness. Oh, he didn't mean anything by it, I'm sure. And a great deal of it was simply Domitian's annual purge of the up-and-coming. But here I was, and he was in Rome, no doubt enjoying all the things I couldn't have: peacocks' brains! raw unborn dormice dipped in honey! and the wine, the good Greek wine that cost a whole aureus here for a single jug.

Each day, as I sat in the procurator's seat and signed documents or pronounced judgments, I would be looking straight at the statue's face. I'd made sure the sculptor made it quite unflattering; the beak of a nose, the coronet of scraggly eagle feathers, the unkempt, stringy hair, the stooped shoulders, and the smirky expression, had been very accurately displayed. When particularly frustrated I would pelt it with rotten fruits.

Indeed, I was doing just that one fateful morning, when I found out just how devious, relentless, and unmitigated Domitian's dislike for me really was.

I was on a couch by the fountain, having my morning Lacotian lesson. In every other land of the Empire we had established Latin or Greek as the lingua franca, but not here; we had been beaten to it by a system of peculiar hand-signals and gestures with which all the savages, no matter which barbarous tongue they used, could communicate. My boyhood tutor Nikias, a sexagenarian by now, who had preceded me into Lacotia, had made it his life's task to study the dialects of Lacotia and to compile a monstrous Lacotian-Greek lexicon. It was easier to learn from him than from some savage; and so, though it was almost forty years since I'd sat on his knee and recited my *alpha beta gamma*, it was as though nothing had changed.

"No, Master Titus," he was saying, pointing at the scroll on which I had been laboriously trying to translate Virgil from Latin into Lacotian using the Greek-letter transcription system Nikias had devised (for the Lacotian savages wrote only in pictures before our coming). "Not at all. You see, here you've written *mit'awichu* for 'my wife' and *mit'achink'shi* for 'my son.' But you see, 'son' takes the *intrinsic* possessive, so that should just be *michink'shi*. The extrinsic possessive is used for alienable or distant possessions, such as a wife who might after all be divorced, whereas a son—"

"Jove blast these Lacotians!" I said. "Why can't they have simple declensions and conjugations, like civilized languages? Maybe we *do* have six hundred different endings in Latin, but at least we bloody well know what the word's doing in the sentence! None of this extrinsic and intrinsic possession...oh, I'd give anything for a good old irregular Greek contracted verb. Well, I suppose you might as well finish correcting the paragraph."

"Well, actually the rest of the sentence is wrong too. You see, when 'thou' is the subject and 'them' the object, the two pronouns are replaced by the prefix *wichaya-* and for the plural you must add *-pi* to form *wichayak'tepi*, 'you (plural) kill them,' but then—"

"Curse it! How did *you* ever learn all this nonsense?"

"I was a slave once, Master Titus. Slaves learn very quickly, or else end up as spectacle-fodder for the circus."

I sighed. The sun was rising over the Temple of Augustus. I cursed at the statue of Aquila, smug and smarmy in his warbonnet and toga. Damn them all! "Just *one* goblet of Chian wine, that's all I want. Half a goblet."

"First you have to hold court awhile, my Lord; then I'll go down to the steward's and see whether there is any."

"There isn't. I drank the dregs yesterday." I stood up and shook my toga straight. "Any good court cases?"

"Nothing; just a run-of-the-mill crucifixion or two, and oh, a raid on the southern town of Cansapolis by the wild Apaxian tribes beyond the border. A delegation of the Cansae are here to ask for help."

"Oh good, I'll be able to practice my Lacotian on them."

"Wrong dialect, I'm afraid. Related, I think, but not mutually comprehensible."

"Damn these Lacotians and their squabbling tribes and their countless languages."

"If you say so, my Lord."

I hefted half a pumpkin at Aquila's face.

Just at that moment all hell broke loose outside the palace. Hoofbeats thudded. Shields and weapons clanked. "Oh no," I said, "Not another coup-counting expedition!"

Tubae blared. Slaves scurried in and started swabbing at Aquila with mops. "Visitors," said Nikias. Gathering my dignity as my body slave handed me my vestments of office, I ascended the steps to my procurator's seat. The riders were near now. Suddenly slaves and officials were scuttling in at the main entry to the atrium, scattering in the wake of the mounted messengers, while the trumpets barked raggedly and out of tune. "Those savages!" I cried. "They ride into one's very house. Nikias, have them executed or flogged or something on their way out."

They dismounted.

I recognized four Praetorians in spanking new uniforms. A pretty, overdressed page was bearing a scroll

on a silver platter. And behind them—in the toga praetexta of a senator yet—an ancient man with a beak for a
nose, wearing a ridiculous headpiece that was a tasteless
mismatch of golden laurel wreath and eagle-feather warbonnet.

"Aquila!" I shouted.

"I see you've been getting good use out of my statue,
my dear General Titus," he said, approaching my throne,
and curiously eyeing the slaves as they scrubbed at the
still pumpkinified nose of the marble image.

"What's it to you?" I snapped. Then emotion overcame me. "Oh, Aquila . . . I've been so miserable here!" I
had missed him terribly, but had never had the guts to
admit it to myself. I got off my throne and went down to
embrace him. "My friend! Has the Emperor recalled me?
Perhaps he's dead and one of my friends is on the
throne?"

"Come, come, stiff upper lip and all that, you know,"
he said.

"A year in Rome and you talk just like my father," I
said, and he shrugged.

"To business, Titus, and I think you'd better get back
on that official chair of yours—"

"You dare to command—" I stopped. He picked up a
purple-bordered fold of his senatorial toga and whisked it
in my face.

"I'm not a savage, you know. In fact, the Emperor
has made me next in line to the procuratorship—although I've frankly declined the honor. Sooner or later
one gets purged, I found."

I climbed back on my throne. I am now the voice of
the Senate and People of Rome; that is to say, Caesar's
mouthpiece. I put on a good menacing mien as befitted
my role.

"There's a good lad." I pretended to ignore his pa-
tronizing tone. In spite of my five minutes' of enthusiasm, I was already wishing the uppity savage into a nice
hot niche in Hades. Then Aquila came forward and

placed an object in my hand, cool and smooth, I looked at it.

"Strange," I said. It was a statuette, carved in jade, only a few fingers tall, but worked in lavish detail. It was a baby—no sex could be distinguished—caught in the middle of some supernatural transformation, for parts of its face and body were shifting into those of some feral cat-creature, leopard or tiger perhaps. It was not exactly beautiful; any Greek craftsman would have inveighed at length about its lack of proportion, its complete disregard of natural human posture. But the expression was what held me; for it was both anguished and joyful, unhuman. I knew it as the face of some god.

"What is it?" I said.

Aquila said, "It came to Rome with Trajan's triumph, one of the many spoils of the campaign against the Seminolii and the Chirochian Confederation. Caesar was so captivated with it that for weeks he stared all day at it, neglecting the government, not even participating in the customary banquets and orgies."

Looking at the statuette, I understood. "But what culture has fashioned this thing? The only jade-works I have ever seen have come from the distant east, down the silk route from the empire of the yellow folk which no one has ever seen; but this workmanship is different from theirs. And this is no god I've ever heard of."

"General Titus, the Word of Caesar!" Aquila said. Tubae brayed resoundingly, and the silver platter with the scroll on it was presented to me.

This is what I read:

To Titus Papinianus, Procurator of Lacotia, from the Divine Domitian, greeting.

Titus old boy!

Thought you'd got out of my hair, did you? Thought I'd never bother you again, eh, out there in the middle of the wilderness with nothing but barbarians for company? Well, you thought wrong,

I'm afraid. My famous sense of humor prompts me to issue new commands.

I have a new favorite at court, Leukippos son of the philosopher Epaminondas whose visions created the motor-car and the quick-sailing-ship. He is one of those scientists, you know. He's recalculated the old figures of that ancient Eratosthenes, and has decided that Eratosthenes's estimate of the circumference of the earth is wrong by some vast factor. The upshot of it all is this: that the fabled Middle Empire, called by the Hindish traders *Chin* or *China*, ought to lie somewhere within the great continent of Terra Nova. This statuette—which I can hardly bear to part with—is further proof, since everyone knows that only the Chinish peoples have the art of carving jade.

Well, can you guess yet, my dear Titus, how I plan to bring about your downfall? Yes indeed! I want more of these things. I want that kingdom discovered at once. In time we'll send a *real* general, someone competent like Trajan, to do the actual conquering, but in the meantime I want you to explore beyond the Empire's borders until you find this Chinish Empire. A small party will do very nicely, nothing fancy, since I have no intention of paying for this out of the royal coffers when the mob outside is howling for more bread and more spectacles!

I'll expect some kind of report, Titus Papinianus. And beware—I've my eye on you. I still haven't forgotten what your father did to poor old Nero.

Good luck,

Titus Flavius Domitianus, Caesar, Augustus, God-Emperor of the Universe, Pater Patriae, Pater Maximus Candidusque, *et cetera, et cetera.*

"Good heavens, Aquila," I said, passing the letter on to Nikias.

"This is absurd!" Nikias said. "Eratosthenes's figures are clearly impeccable, measuring as he did the parallax of the sun's shadow in two different locations in Egypt. And besides, the extra space is necessary. After all, where does the sun go when its chariot comes to rest at the day's end? Where do all the deities of the world live, and where are the thousands of heavens and hells, if not in the 'lost' spaces?"

"And," I added, "this simply is *not* a Chinish piece of artwork. I'd wager twenty talents on it. Domitian's gone mad!"

"Alas, Titus, I wish I could agree with you," said Aquila. "But I happen to know that this whole thing is simply a rather imaginative, roundabout way of getting you on the purge list. You see, simple executions and things have gone out of style in Rome. Indeed, I was there at the very banquet when Domitian and Leukippos (who, I'm afraid, shares the Emperor's bed as well as his confidences) concocted this elaborate scientific hokum while downing endless bucketfulls of Chian wine."

I was furious. "It rankles," I said, "especially the Chian wine. *Onze mayahu kte lo!*" I added (it was the one obscenity I knew), hoping to impress Aquila with my new grasp of the Lacotian tongue.

Instead, he and Nikias laughed uproariously. "I suppose I shouldn't make fun of you, General," said Aquila, "but you just told me that I am about to perform an unspeakable act upon your inviolate person."

"Oh, sorry. Wrong pronoun again, eh?" I said. "I intended to say that *I* would perform this act on the Emperor."

"Yes, you should have used the nominative *wa-* prefix. But seriously, it was then that I knew Domitian planned to do away with you and play a fiendish joke besides. That's why I insisted on bringing you the message myself, all the while pretending to laugh myself silly over Caesar's brilliant wit. You see, I'm the only person who can possibly help you solve the riddle of the jade statuette. Besides, Rome was beginning to bore me. The decadence! You've seen one orgy, you've seen them all. And the Lacotian tribesmen who settled in Cappadocia —dissipated, every one of them. Gone to boozing and orgifying. Some of them have taken up in the arena, where they even perform the sundance nowadays, although it goes against all I believe in. I'm bitter, Titus. I'll come with you on your quest for Caesar's golden fleece."

"But you said you knew—"

"Perhaps so. It's a legend, nothing more. Of a race far, far to the south, who worship the were-jaguar and carve mysterious heads. For all I know they may have died out."

"And their name?"

"I don't know what they call themselves. But the Apaxians of the desert talk sometimes of an ancient empire-building race they call the Olmechii."

CHAPTER
XII

IN A FEW DAYS WE SET OFF DOWN THE GREAT MISERA-bilis River by paddleboat. I was proud of this new acquisition: Epaminondas of Alexandria, who had perfected the steam engine and had since been executed for refusing to give up its secrets, originally created such a barge for Nero's state visit to Egypt, so that Caesar could journey down the Nile in style. It was occasionally powered by steam; more often, the huge paddle was kept in constant motion by an assemblage of treadmill-jogging slaves. They were lazy, shiftless good-for-nothings, captured from the Algonquian and Athapascan tribes of the icy north, less civilized even than our somewhat Romanized Lacotians.

It was an idle month. I and Nikias and Aquila would sit in our couches of state; an elegant little temple to Minerva graced one end of the boat, while the prow was carved to resemble a naiad in a somewhat pornographic pose, and inlaid with several talents of solid gold. The trappings were as luxurious as in Rome; the food and drink were not, and for some weeks we ate nothing but aurochs: stewed, boiled, roasted, fried, but never once metamorphosing into some more palatable creature. Aquila disgusted me by frequently eating the liver raw; even as a senator he had not given up all his filthy barbarian ways.

Aside from the paddle slaves, of which a certain number expired daily and had to be replaced from stock, we had brought a few attendants. There were about a dozen guards, mostly of the tribe of Tetonii, in their half-Roman, half-barbarous garb; and the usual consortium of body slaves, cooks, scullery maids, bed wenches, foot washers, masseurs, singers, lyre players, dancers, Nubian palanquin bearers, toga stitchers, pot washers, and so on: only a few score of these, hardly enough to call a decent household, but then Lacotia was still something of a hardship post. An escort of charioteers rode alongside, and we had horses below deck.

Lacotia went by slowly—for it is a vast terrain—and we soon grew weary of endless plains. Here and there stood a little shrine to Caesar, whom the natives had graciously been permitted to worship under the aspects of their own rather nebulous god Vacantanca, a god whose vagueness is equaled only by the formless thing the Judaeans worship. Or we would pass a little tipi cluster from which smoke curled into the brilliant blue sky. Or a Roman town, an islet of marble in the great green grassy ocean. It was a beautiful land; but I wished we could get on with it. I had the slaves lashed harder, but nothing came of it.

Soon we went by the last frontier fort. We encountered rough waters where the River Ochaio runs into the Miserabilis. Now we were in the enemy lands. We had catapultae and ballistae aplenty on board, and I set the Lacotian centurions to constant watching. On the right bank was Caddonia, on the left Muschogea; so the first explorers had named these lands, after the principal languages the savages spoke. But we knew little about them, and their names were meaningless to me.

For a week or so we continued downriver. We ate dried aurochs now, salty and tough to chew, and a little river-fish. We watched the dancing girls and talked of old times, and at night I stared at the Olmechian figurine, trying to divine its secrets.

One day we were eating breakfast on deck. I was just stuffing my mouth with a chunk of aurochs when I heard a zinging, whistling sound. I stared incredulously as an arrow pierced the meat, flew into the temple of Minerva, and nailed my breakfast to the goddess's nipple.

"Whaa—" I said.

"Hostile riding alongside boat, General, sir!" said a centurion. "They've killed half the chariot escort—"

"Dispatch them, for heaven's sake! I can't have my breakfast ruined, you know."

"Duck, Titus!" I heard Nikias shout. As I did so arrows began to rain on us from both sides.

"Get the catapultae out!" I screamed. "Lash the paddle-slaves, maybe we can outmaneuver them!" As I looked up I saw the slave-whipper clutch at the arrow in his throat and tumble from the treadmill. The slaves, who were chained and couldn't escape, were screeching with terror.

"China, my arse!" I cried. "We're not even going to get out of Lacotia alive!" Then I ran into the temple of Minerva and bolted the door. I found Nikias there already, hugging the altar in supplication, whilst Aquila was waving his arms and doing some hoppity-skippity dance while singing in a wheezy monotone. "Aquila, do something! You're the bloody expert on the savages."

"I *am* doing something," he said, and continued his dance. "This war-dance happens to be excellent medicine, and will render the three of us quite invisible to the Apaxae."

"Apaxae?"

"Yes," he said, not missing a beat of his dance. "They

are the hardiest of all the tribes; I am not surprised to see them come raiding this far, for they often venture even into Roman-occupied territory. Now, if you'll excuse me . . . *hey-a-a-a hey-a-a! Eya-heya-ey-ey-ey-a-a!* . . . let me see . . . *eya-hey-hey-heya—*"

I gave up on him. Behind the goddess there was a window; I looked out and saw them.

There were several dozen. They were riding up and down the riverbank, whooping and taunting us. Their flowing black hair, held in place by headbands of old rags, streamed behind them. They were the scruffiest savages I'd yet seen, and the fiercest-looking.

Aquila stopped dancing. "*Huka hey!*" he shouted. "Let's attack them!"

"But the war-machines—"

He threw open the door of the temple. The Lacotian guards were letting the horses out from below decks; they were whinnying and rearing. Above the gleaming cuirasses and bloodred cloaks, their faces gleamed with war-paint and their heads were crowned with feathers.

"*Huka hey!*" they screamed in unison. The Apaxians were charging straight into the water at our paddleboat, pelting us with arrows.

"Catapultae!" I shouted, grabbing a bucina from an astonished slave and blowing on it myself. The engines were wheeled into position. Great rocks soared and brained one or two of the Apaxian horses. They were diving into the water now, one after another, knives in mouths. I ordered the boarding ramps lowered. The Lacotians' horses leapt overboard and the men were fighting hand-to-hand, half in, half out of the water. Meanwhile Aquila had mounted himself and was rushing straight at the Apaxians, who never seemed to notice him.

"If an eighty-year-old man can do that—" I said to myself. Soon I too was calling for my horse. The temple of Minerva was on fire and so was the paddle-treadmill, and lines of slaves with buckets were busy quenching the flames. I jumped the side of the boat and rode down the ramp, cursing Domitian with a will.

"Quick!" I shouted at the last of the on-shore escort. "Put all the chariots in a circle!" One of them heard and relayed the order. In a while we were driving the Apaxae back over the river and right into the circle of chariots. The carnage was incredible, for these savages fought as if insensible to pain.

After some hard fighting we drove them off. The Lacotians scattered to strip and scalp the corpses. In the distance, a shout went up. Two Lacotians on horseback were returning, pursuing a man on a bicycle.

"Good heavens!" I said. "I haven't seen one of *those* since Rome—and Domitian wrecked almost all the bicycles in the world in an epic spectacle in the arena ten years ago!"

They had knocked off the bicyclist, pinned him to the ground, and were about to scalp him when I rode up to investigate.

"Let go!" a voice was squealing in Greekn "You can't do this to me, I'm a Roman citizen! You don't speak Greek? What about Latin? Sum civis Romanus! *Romanus*, d'ye hear, sum . . . civis . . . *Romanus*!"

"Release him," I said.

The man got to his feet. He was middle-aged, clad in a torn, dirt-streaked tunic of fairly decent Greek wool; but he had a decidedly dusky complexion, and his Greek was strangely accented. Once before, in my African peregrinations, had I heard such an accent. "Jove help us!" I said. "You're an Egyptian! Whatever are you doing here among these barbarians?"

He brushed himself with his hand. Then he said squeakily, "I was captured. They were going to torture me to death! Please help me, help me, I'm on a mission from the Library of Alexandria, and—"

"That seems unlikely," I said, "considering that library was burnt down a century ago."

"No, no," he said, like a tutor addressing a stupid child, "not that Alexandria. Alexandria in Iracuavia! You know, Terra Nova's center of learning, dedicated to humanizing the savages! What are *you* doing here, anyway?" he added sulkily.

"How dare you use that tone to me? I am Titus Papinianus, procurator of Lacotia."

"Well, how was I to know? Procurators come and go; the turnover is amazing; what with purgings, recallings, treason trials, and compulsory suicides. Never even heard of *you*. Wouldn't know you from Amenemhet!"

Just then Aquila and Nikias came riding up. They were jabbering away to each other in Lacotian, much to my chagrin. Then Nikias saw the Egyptian and exclaimed, "Well, if it isn't grumpy old Aaye!"

"Nikias! Why this is—this is—" He was overcome. Nikias got off his horse and they hugged each other, weeping.

"My Lord," Nikias said to me, "this is the most bad-tempered scholar the world has ever known, the astrologer whose full name we could never pronounce at the Academy; but he answers to *Aaye*. We studied together before my unfortunate enslavement."

"What a coincidence! But what's a scholar like you doing far from civilization, a slave to savages?"

"You Roman pseudo-intellectuals are all alike," he grunted. "Always afraid you'll soil your delicate fingers, never leaving your slave-ridden palaces to quest for those hidden meanings to be found in the backwaters and cloacae of existence! But *I* am a true philosopher. I search for truth. At the moment, thought, I'm searching for the pyramids."

I laughed. "The pyramids? In Terra Nova? I've heard of people losing their way, but this is ridiculous! You're out of your mind!"

"Perhaps so, though it's impertinent of you to point it out," he said. "But there is a scrap of parchment in the Library—dating, it seems, from the first explorations of this continent—that mentions pyramids. Somewhere to the south. At least, I took it to mean that. Literally. They all laughed at me. How they laughed! Those rationalizing scholars with their theories of hallucination, symbolism or some explorer's bout with a jug of bad Falernian wine. If it doesn't warp to fit their theory they'll ignore it or ridicule it . . . not me! I am a proponent of the scientific method. If it was good enough for Aristotle, it's good enough for me."

"But how did you come to be among the Apaxae?"

"Patience, Roman! We Egyptians have been civilized for four thousand years. We were building the pyramids when you were coming down from the trees. That's why you're all so damned impatient. Well . . . I journeyed here after learning a little of the Apaxian speech from one of my slaves, hoping to get corroboration for the parchment at the Library. I lived among them for some months—no luxury at all, let me tell you!—when the village was raided by a rival tribe. They intended to trade my bicycle for some horses, and to kill me by some fiendish means; but as they journeyed towards their trading rendezvous they chanced upon your paddleboat, and, thinking of the booty on board—"

"Enough of this longwindedness! We are traveling south at the emperor's behest, on a wild-goose chase as preposterous as your own. You can come with us if you choose; if not, there's not much I can do for you."

"How dare you call it a wild-goose chase! I had already found evidence, before wicked fate cast me into this predicament—"

"Evidence?" I snorted.

"Yes! For when I inquired among the Apaxae about pyramids, when I drew them in the dirt to illustrate my meaning precisely, I would often elicit a certain response. It was a single word, foreign to their tongue, that appears to be the name of a race of pyramid builders."

"And that name?" Aquila said. I noticed that he had leaned forward suddenly, and seemed to be taking this fool seriously.

"Olmec."

CHAPTER
XIII

WE REACHED THE DELTA OF THE MISERABILIS without much more incident; for the local natives, who were by no means Apaxian and lived in as much fear of their ravaging hordes as we did, were friendly, and we were often able to get food from them in exchange for a few of those valueless, heavy old copper coins that are still in vogue in Egypt and carry the images of the long-deceased Ptolemaic dynasty. It was lush country, rich in fruits and meats.

When we reached the sea, we had no idea what to do next.

Aaye to the rescue, then. Faded old maps hastily copied from the Alexandria Library documents were pulled out and pored over. They showed the seashore curving to the west; the words *terra incognita* were everywhere evident. I ordered a fort built on the left bank of the Miserabilis, stocked it with catapultae and other artillery from the ship, and left most of the slaves there under guard, while Nikias, Aquila, Aaye, and I rode southwards with only a handful of cavalry, Lacotian and Roman, and two weeks' supply of that hideous buffalo jerky.

Two weeks! We were very optimistic then; no one dreamed that the world could be quite as large as we came to discover. In any case, we followed the coastline at first, coming to the mouths of many rivers. After a fortnight we began to go through harsh terrain. The heat was stifling, and we had little water. To my surprise, Aaye proved the most stalwart among us in the desert. I supposed it was because the Nile is a mere ribbon of greenery in the midst of a vast ocean of hot sand, so that the Egyptians have, perforce, learnt some of the ways of deserts. Aaye had apparently learnt one or two things from the Apaxae, too. How to trap and kill those alarming serpents with rattling tails, and how to suck the juices from the prickly, clublike vegetation.

The worst was yet to come, though. I thought I had seen forests, but I was not prepared for what came next. You could have sworn this forest was alive. It was dark, wet, swarming with vermin; snakes masqueraded as vines, alligators as logs, and mosquitoes bit our skin raw.

"Wherever we are," I sighed, "this certainly isn't China!"

"Clearly not," Aaye agreed. Then, settling into his pedagogic tone, he said, "For it is a well-established fact that the Chinish lands are full of golden towers and ziggurats, and that silken tapestries hang in every home. Indeed, I have heard it mentioned by Apollodorus the Bithynian, that the Chinish silk is manufactured by a giant worm, seven leagues long, that continually runs in a circle, eating its own tail, and that the effluvience of saliva that drools from its maws, hardening in the path of its circumperambulatory meanderings, forms the thread used in the warp of the silk; for the woof, however, the Chinish sages entrap moonbeams by midnight and—"

"Rubbish!" Nikias said. "Aaye old chap, you were always the most gullible boy in the academy. If some two-obol authority had told you that the oceans on the moon's surface were deserts you would have believed it."

"You bastard! You stole Master Harpocrates's apple and *I* got the strap for it! How dare you—"

"Enough, you fools!" I said. "Look at Aquila; he never argues with anyone, and he's borne all these hardships better than any of us."

We had found a little clearing. Bones and the remains of fires littered the forest floor; it was our first evidence of humans. They were likely as not to kill us, but at that point I would rather have died at the hands of recognizable people than be torn to death by beasts like a criminal in the arena.

"And to think," Aquila said, as he tethered our horses (some had succumbed to horrid diseases, and these we had eaten, much to the discomfiture of our bowels), "that I did this all for you! Those deadly boring orgies at the palace are beginning to seem more and more attractive by the hour!"

The Lacotians were pitching a tipi and spreading aurochs hides on the ground to sleep on. If we fumigated it thoroughly with incense, and sealed the thing completely shut, the mosquitoes only bit one an average of once a minute instead of continuously.

Drinking the vile water had given me a flux; so I spent the day groaning in the tipi while Nikias read to me from a stack of the latest scientifictiones, which Aquila had had copied in Rome and had been kind enough to bring me: in particular a collection of pieces in the avant-garde style that characterizes all the decadent literary efforts of Domitian's reign, entitled *Visūs Periculosi*. While I found none of the visions particularly dangerous, especially in view of the actual horrors that surrounded me, I was amused by the frantic blandishments of Alienus Elysianus, the scribe who had anthologized and annotated the various scrolls.

"Reading that rubbish again!" said Aquila. "You should be working on your Lacotian grammar."

"And what of it?" I spluttered, gripping my bowels. "Why don't *you* do something useful?"

"I intend to! I am going hunting."

"What?"

"A brave can't laze around all day. Lack of action ages a man. I shall go stalk some creature for our supper." So saying, he took his quiver and a dagger and a sackful of skinning tools, and he strode out. Knowing the mosquito problem, I didn't care to follow.

Presently, though, a bloodcurdling scream cut across the jungle's cacophony of buzzings, croakings, and screechings.

"Jove help us!" I cried. "If it's Aquila, what'll we do?" I rousted some of the others and we crept out, hacking at the undergrowth with our short swords.

"Aquila!" we called, our voices fading into the gloom. It suddenly occurred to me that we were lost, hopelessly lost, and even if we weren't lost we weren't going to get home anyway—

When I heard a familiar hooting sound, such as the Lacotians used as a secret signal in warfare.

"Come out of there, by Hades!" I said. "I'm in no mood for another trick; this flux is killing me, and—"

The hooting again.

"It's coming from the left," Nikias whispered.

"The right," hissed Aaye.

I listened. "The left." We tiptoed farther into the darkness.

Now from the right. We passed huge trees, greater than the columns of the temples at Karnak, twined with vines. No light fell at all in the depths of this alien forest.

Then—

"I see light," I said.

"Ahead," said one of the Lacotians.

I took another step.

Something tightened around my foot! I was jerked up

into the air. I saw my companions dangling head downwards from trees on either side, and so was I, and my helmet clanked onto the ground and the jade figurine that I had kept on my person all these months fell down beside it.

And then there were torches, blazing, blinding. Brown-skinned, lithe-looking natives had rushed to pick up the jade statuette, and were fingering it reverently.

"What the hell is going on?" I yelled. For in the center of the clearing ahead stood Aquila, large as life, his head thrown back in laughter; and all around him on the forest floor, prostrated in obeisance, were dozens of natives in elaborate costumes. And right at his feet was the corpse of a huge and frightening creature, the leopardlike demon that I had heard Aquila call *jaguar*.

"Tell them to let us down!"

Aquila said, "How can I? I've no idea what's going on, although it's about time a high chieftain of the Lacotians got treated with the proper respect. Why shouldn't I let you Romans hang for a few days, like pheasants ripening for the oven?"

We started yelling imprecations in every conceivable tongue. Finally one of the savages came and cut us down, after which we were led, with out hands tied behind our backs, to Aquila's feet, and forced to make the prostration also.

"This is shameful!" I said. "That a Roman and an equestrian by rank, and a procurator at that, should be compelled to kneel down before some . . . some. . . ."

"Now you know how we lowly savages feel, O noble procurator! But to be frank, I'm as much in the dark as you are. I just went out and happened to kill this jaguar."

"With your bare hands?" I gasped.

He chuckled. "We Lakotah have always been excellent hunters—although I did cheat a bit. I made friends with him first, by pulling a thorn out of his foot. Now, if someone would care to translate—"

One of the natives—whose earrings, I saw now, were

enormous sun disks of solid gold—came up and began
barking, bellowing, and braying in various languages.

"Ah!" Aaye said at last. "One I know. This one
speaks Apaxian!"

So our interchanges began. Their leader spoke in
whatever language it was (and I had a feeling it wasn't
Chinish); their interpreter translated into Apaxian; Aaye
relayed in Greek with a sprinkle of Latin and an occa-
sional Egyptian curse; and finally Aquila repeated the
exchange in the Tetonian dialect of Lacotian for the benefit of the native centurions who were still swinging by
their feet. In this laborious way we spent the better part
of a night; mercifully the need to discharge my flux did
not yet visit me.

Yes indeed, these people knew of the Olmechii, although they themselves were only a subject race.
Aquila, who had killed the jaguar, had unwittingly become the victor in their regular competition for the rank
of God-of-the-Month, and would soon be going in
triumph to his coronation.

We were mortals, on the other hand, would be sacrificed to the glory of Aquila and the entity He repre-
sented, the Great and All-powerful Flying Disk of the
Sun.

Indeed, I, whom the Great Were-Jaguar in the Sky
himself had chosen by causing his image to appear beneath me as I dangled, was to have the honor of being
the first to be sacrificed to Aquila the God—and all this
by the charming expedient of ripping my still-beating
heart from my chest with a crude obsidian knife.

"Delighted, I'm sure," I said. "At least it's a nice,
simple death; none of Domitian's labyrinthine jokes."

"It's good to look on the bright side," Aquila agreed,
as the flayed skin of the newly killed beast was placed
over his shoulders and a palanquin brought in to receive
him, and as two of the natives stooped down for him to
step up on their backs. "At last my dream has come
true," he went on, as eight burly, oiled natives hoisted

his throne up on their shoulders. "A nice, quiet retirement far from civilization; all the comforts of Rome without any of the bustle."

"But what about us?" I said. And then I saw the cages. They were double-decker ones with wooden bars. We were herded into them, and they too were carried by natives: mangy ones, gap-toothed and cross-eyed, clearly litter-bearers of lower quality than those of Aquila the God.

The forests thinned. In a few days we were in open plains, sunny and verdant. We passed villages where we were eyed with disinterest; Aquila got all the attention.

Eventually we came to a broad paved road. As good as a Roman road it was. And in a few days we could see the walls of a vast city in the distance.

"Curse you all!" Aaye said for the thousandth time. He was in the same cage as I, in the lower compartment, so I was forced to listen to him. "You should have left me to die with the Apaxians. Oh, I know they'd have tied me to a rock in the desert and cut off my eyelids, but at least with them you knew where you were. You've certainly led me off the trail, you idiot general. No wonder Domitian made you procurator; it's a well-known fact that only the utterly unintelligent can ever rise in office, and—"

My fever had worsened. I was in no mood for any of this talk. As far as I was concerned, Domitian's ruse had proved all too successful; I was anxious to get it all over with.

We were coming into the gateway.

"They're—they're—it's true!" said the Egyptian, losing his ill humor at once. "They *do* have pyramids!"

I opened my bleary eyes and saw them. At the end of the avenue there was a huge one of gleaming stone; it must have had more than a thousand steps. The street was lined with sculptures of heads as huge as buildings, their features a curious hybrid of Asian and African. Golden disks—sun-signs, clearly—hung from the wall like giant saucers. People thronged the squares and marketplaces. I could have sworn this city was as big as Rome, if I hadn't know it was impossible.

"Maybe this *is* China after all," I said.

"Oh, no," said Aaye, falling automatically into his lecturing mode. "It's not China at all; for one thing, I haven't seen a single silkworm, and it is an established fact that the Chinish citizenry ride these silkworms, after disengaging their tails from their mouths, by driving great hooks into their segments and urging them forward by the irritations they cause—"

"I think I read that," I said, "in one of the recent scientifictiones."

"Oh no," he said, "it's the truth! You can't have opinions about truth! No, this is the land of the Olmechii for certain; the pyramids prove it. I'll show those doubters back at the Academy! They'll have to believe me now! I'll make them grind up every papyrus they've written against my theories and eat every word of their unscientific rantings!"

"We," I said, "are about to get sacrificed . . . or had you forgotten that, eh, old chap?"

"Minor matter, General; they're pyramid-builders, I'm an Egyptian, give me a couple of days and we'll be tighter than brothers . . . why, I'll bet they *are* Egyptians, stranded here in antediluvian times. We'll get along famously. It's an incontrovertible fact that we Egyptians, deep, inscrutable and mystifying as we are, can talk our way out of anything."

"Shut the idiot up!" Nikias moaned from a neighboring cage.

"Call me an idiot, will you? Me, the greatest theorist of all time, now that my theories have been vindicated?"

It was then, finally, that the flux hit me, and all at once at that. I hit upon an elegant solution to the problem of the ranting Egyptian. Using what little dexterity was still left to me in my condition, I managed to claw my way painfully along the railings of my cage until I was positioned directly above Aaye; and I proceeded to void copiously at him, drenching him thoroughly with the liquidescent contents of my bowels. I had hopes that, like one of Jove's mighty thunderbolts from on high, this downpour might shut the man up; but it merely gave him another thing to complain about, and complain he did, incommoded though his speech had become by its issuing perforce through the muddy gurgle of my ordure. By then, though, I was too sick to notice.

CHAPTER
XIV

WE WERE DUMPED INTO A SPACIOUS PRISON, OPPO-
site the gargantuan pyramid-temple and overlooking the city square, and they gave me a potion that
did wonders for my flux. Aquila had been installed in the
temple across from us. Every day we would see him
holding court from a throne of solid gold; I could tell he
had been watching Caesar carefully, for many of his imperial gestures were an amusing parody of Domitian's.
He mimicked to perfection, for instance, that wave of
the hand that signaled a concealed guard to execute the
suppliant; but he seemed to do so merely in sport, for I
saw no executions. He would never have made a good
Roman emperor; our rulers know well the efficacy of the
well-timed, spectacular execution of some important figure. It is thus that they are able to appease the mob, and
thus that the Empire will last for ever, even though any
individual emperor is lucky to survive a year or two. In
short, Aquila seemed constantly to be showing such
unkingly clemency that I was afraid the crowd would

soon be bored to death and assassinate him. And that we could not have; for Aquila, savage that he was, was our only hope of rescue.

Day by day we watched. Far and away the most mysterious sight was that of golden disks that flitted about in the sky, resembling nothing so much as levitating dishes or saucers. Sometimes three or four of them would hover over the large pyramid for some minutes, and then vanish into the sky. We could not decide what they were, although Aaye, who naturally had a theory handy, said that they were sun sculptures and that the flying effect was brought about by constant rubbing of the pyramid's summit with huge house-sized cloths, just as a piece of electrum, or amber, can when briskly rubbed be observed to attract small particles of papyrus, engendering that ineffable and mystic force to which amber has lent its name.

The argument over this consumed several days. Food came at a slot in the prison door, a slab of solid rock that would not budge. Our clothes had been taken from us and we were forced to wear ridiculous loincloths; the material was soft and comfortable, and therefore effeminate and unworthy of a staunch and stalwart Roman.

The sights from the window were remarkable—

For these Olmechii (Aaye had convinced us they were not Chinese by the sheer weight and intricacy of the learning at his disposal) were by any lights the most technologically advanced nation in the world. It galled me to see them travel about in gilded motor-cars when Rome's motor-cars had almost all been destroyed in the Coliseum and the secret of their manufacture lost. It rankled to see they had a hovering device, floating from pyramid-top to pyramid-top by means of enormous leather balloons containing heated air from which dangled baskets of people. I will not say that such sorcery is beyond the Romans, because we are, by the grace of the gods, the dominant nation of the world after all, and are by nature superior to all peoples, whether as-yet-subjugated or not; but *I* had not seen it before. I longed to send a few such devices to Caesar.

"Imagine the spectacle!" I said, gnawing on an ear of maize. "We could stash gladiators in the baskets, and they could have at each other with catapultae and ballistae, flinging fireballs at one another as they soar over the sands of the Circus Maximus!"

"How can you think of such things," said Nikias, "when our death is imminent?"

I was brought down to earth. "If only there was some way of contacting Aquila—"

"He'll do nothing!" Aaye said gloomily. "Savage blood will always show, that's what I say. Gullible, unreliable, and a dullard, there's your standard savage."

"Are you out of your mind?" said Nikias. "This is the man who singlehandedly won the Battle of Domitianopolis in Cappadocia by driving the Parthians into—"

"And made an utter fool out of *me!*" I grunted. "No, look at him out there. He's happy now; not many people get to be a god in their own lifetime, you know. Even the old Caesars had to wait until the Senate declared it after their death, although *these* days—"

"A plan!" Aaye cried. "I have a plan!"

"Ha! You, a plan!" Nikias said. "I remember well your scheme to make a few obols when we were children, selling lemonade in the streets of Alexandria in the middle of December."

The Lacotians among us were sitting apart, grunting or singing softly to themselves, with a great deal of *hunh-hunh-hunh*ing and *hechitu welo*ing. The three of huddled together.

"What you don't realize, Nikias old chap," said Aaye, "is that I am by profession a trained astrologer, and as such am in the position of knowing a great deal about the proper motions of the sun and moon and stars. I happen to know a few things that will scare the living daylights out of these Olmechii."

"I doubt it," I said. "These Olmechii seem rather sophisticated to me."

"Appearance only, my dear General! For it is a well-known fact, a truism, indeed, that those not blessed with the . . . ahem . . . *Roman* citizenship are by their very natures superstitious, credulous, and incapable of rising above the status of simple peasants."

"If this city is but an appearance of civilization disguising utter savagery, it's bloody convincing, I say."

"Stuff and nonsense! Are these savages not making a big song and dance about sacrificing us to their gods? Back in the *real* Empire, people may be killed for amusement, as in our great epic spectacles of the arena, but it is hardly something to be taken *seriously*, as they are doing. The lack of a cynical attitude to life and death is a telltale sign of barbarianism. We'll never talk sense into them! No, I shall perform my patent razzle-dazzle, just as I once so impressed the King of Parthia, who held me captive, with my lightning wit and arcane knowledge of trivia that he awarded me safe conduct to the country of my choice!"

"Poor Aaye. Never knows when he's being tactfully gotten rid of," Nikias said.

The two were at each other's throats; soon their beards had become entangled, and I had to extricate them from each other.

Just then one of the Lacotians, staring out of the window, began yammering. We all rushed over; an awesome sight greeted us.

Huge heads, of the kind we had seen lining the city streets, were hanging in the sky. Each was taller than three or four men; each dangled from a convoy of the heated-air-balloons, which soared high above thick as birds. Sun-disks hovered or darted above them; it could now be seen, from the scale of the flying balloons, that these dishlike floaters were actually the size of palaces or temples.

"Extraordinary!" said Aaye. "A remarkable method of transporting heavy objects. . . ."

"Which would leave no trace on the ground, no evidence of where the rock was quarried," Nikias said.

"Goodness," I said, "I'm going to *have* to wrest away the secret of these levitating baskets; I can just see them being used against the Parthians! Imagine a squadron of these things pelting the enemy with rocks...we could easily cross Parthia and maybe have a stab at conquering India."

Now who's daydreaming?" Aaye said. "First you pooh-pooh my plan without even listening to it, despite the fact that I am (admittedly by default) the most capable astrologer in this land. Then you talk as if we've already freed ourselves—"

The door opened at that moment. Olmechii, dressed in jaguar skins and armed with lances, came in and bound us fast.

"Well, fellows, this looks like it," I said, deciding that an eve-of-the-battle speech was called for. "Remember—"

"My plan! Don't you want to know my plan?"

"Oh, all right," I said, "let's have it. And it had better be something with a little more substance than your airy speculations."

"Ha! You have the gall to come to me now, after deriding my learning and abusing my person? I've half a mind to let you all perish—"

"Come, Aaye," Nikias said, "we're all in this together."

"Oh, very well, very well."

CHAPTER
XV

THE LIGHT WAS BLINDING IN THE SQUARE. THE AVE-
nues, the rooftops, the balconies were crammed
with spectators in all their finery: spangled loincloths,
headdresses of feathers, furs, even the actual decapi-
tated heads of various forest beasts; while overhead the
traffic of golden disks and floating heads never ceased.
But, in contrast to the festive atmosphere of a Roman
spectacle, the rivers of wine, the carousing and the
whoring and the catcalls, this was a very sober throng
indeed. It was just as the Egyptian had said: these people
were simply far too serious about the whole thing; they
lacked the good Roman sense of sport and fair play.

"Which is precisely what I shall rely on," said Aaye.
"They'll swallow anything I tell them."

As we progressed down the avenue we were joined by
other prisoners; most of them were of unfamiliar tribes,
but there were a certain number of Apaxae, Caddones,
and Comanxae. Whether these had simply ventured too
far south, or whether the Olmechii had raiding expedi-

tions that traversed the very desert and crossed into the land of the River Miserabilis, I could not tell.

Soon were sounded tremendous cornua of stone from the tops of distant temples, a bleating noise with a tinge of croak to it. We reached the foot of the pyramid, and I assumed that we would now be forced to ascend the summit; instead we were ushered into a little chamber within the base, which—wonder of wonders—began to rise, by pulleys or by some hydraulic mechanism as is used for the raising and lowering of scenery in the arena in Rome. Thus, without any expenditure of effort, we reached the top. There was a huge chamber there; from its windows I could see a panorama of the city, stretching limitlessly in every direction. It was clear now that these Olmechii were masters of super-science, so powerful as to be beyond the imaginings even of the writers of scientifictiones.

We were pushed to the ground in prostration. When I looked up I saw Aquila seated upon a throne, every inch the ruler; and at his feet, voluptuous and elegantly dressed in jaguar-skins and jade, was a woman. When she spoke, the walls reverberated; and to my astonishment I found that as the words re-echoed they reformed into translations, into Lacotian and Apaxian among other languages. This was sorcery indeed! I no longer doubted that we had penetrated into one of the supernatural realms, for it was impossible that any race could be this much more advanced than Rome without divine intervention.

"I am," she said, "the High-Priestess and Chief Consort of the Were-Jaguar-Golden-Sun-Disk-Almighty."

"Glad to know with whom I am dealing," I said in my halting Lacotian, which words immediately rebounded from the walls in a foreign tongue. (So the old man had been very well served indeed, I thought enviously, with such a woman as his official bride!) "Aquila!" I said in Greek. As I hoped, there was no wall-translation. "You've got to get us out of this!"

"Whatever for?" he said, waving a hand languidly. "There seems to be nothing I can do, so I've decided to be philosophical about the whole thing."

The priestess said: "Here, then, is the order of the sacrifice. First the man who calls himself general, he with the bulbous nose—" I fought the guards who held me at this physical insult, but I was bound too tightly. She went on down the list of names. "And finally, at the last rays of sunset, the great Personification Himself, the Living God"—Aquila beamed at this—"will condescend to resume his place in the sky among the High Ones from whom he has come—"

"Wait a minute," Aquila said. "Does this mean—"

Guards ran up and dragged the god down from his seat. "Oh, yes," the high priestess said. "Your sacrifice comes last. I thought you already knew."

Aquila shrugged. "Ah well. I am an old man, and I have seen much evil come to the world. I have seen the *washichun* take my children's land from them; I have seen them made subjects to a distant self-named god whom I have myself met—a man who daily eats and drinks and indulges himself into a stupor. I am old, old, old. I have fought against the Romans, and I have fought for them; and I know that they will never leave our land. It is best that I die here in a foreign country. Today is a good day to die! And though the manner of it *might* be a little unorthodox, there is, I think, some honor in it; for when I reach the Land of Many Tipis, I shall say to all of them: *Here comes the Flapper of Wings, the man called Eagle, who has counted coup a thousand times and ended his life a god.*"

"But Aquila, old chap . . . can't you simply *command* that we be released?"

"I already tried. Oh, I tried. I know what cowards you Romans are."

I bristled.

"Wait!" Aaye said. My heart leapt. I knew he was

going to try his ruse, which depended on a somewhat shaky astrological calculation.

"We are," Aaye said in the Apaxian tongue, which the walls translated, "terrible sorcerers from the north. I tell you that we have power to control your god! For lo, in precisely . . . ten minutes, I shall summon a great dragon from heaven who will swallow up the sun, and your days will be dark forever unless you release us!" The guards were so surprised he was able to shake them off; he hobbled up to the high priestess and looked her in the eye. "For behold!" he said. "The dragon has even now begun to swallow the sun!"

For this was indeed what he had told us: that, based on the calculations of Apollodorus of Bithynia, a solar eclipse happened to be due that very day.

As we stood there the light began to dim very slowly. I heard the crowd murmuring outside.

The high priestess stared at Aaye curiously; then she began to laugh. At this all the guards laughed too, pointing at him and hooting hysterically.

"But it is happening at this very minute!" Aaye said. "Do you not believe me? Do you deny that I, as a full-blooded Egyptian, am born with the power to perform this feat?"

"Poor, silly man," said the priestess. "I suppose you must have been listening to the guards. Why, you superstitious little foreigner, you! Everyone in the whole empire knows there's an eclipse of the sun today. We Olmechii have never, in our thousand years of history, found anyone to equal us in the accuracy of our astronomical calculations. Not to mention the fact that the Great Were-Jaguar-Sun-Disk Himself frequently comes down and tells us things. Why do you think all those thousands are gathered out there? Surely you could not be so egocentric as to believe they are here to witness a mere sacrifice of the kind they can see any day of the year?"

At this Nikias too began to laugh. "First time in your

whole life," he spluttered, "you actually make a correct prediction—and everyone in the whole town knows it before you do!"

Then I had to laugh too. There was no hope now. It was over. *Vale, Roma mea!* Darkness was falling rapidly now; the Olmechian guards had kindled torches and were holding them up. They pushed us out onto the top of the steps, where there was an altar and other priests, dressed in jaguar-skins, waited. It was then that I saw the knives.

Madness overcame me then. I laughed and laughed until my eyes were blurry with tears. As they bound me to the altar I saw the sun's corona, dancing, shimmering, and the stars in their millions, and I thought how insignificant my death really must be in comparison to this awesome sight. The crowd wasn't watching *me* at all. Their eyes were trained on the sun, stunned by the beauty of it. Then the blackness began to ease a little, and a corner of the sun glistened like a diamond on a ring of ebony.

I saw the high priestess nod.

Just then, the sun disks that had been flying to and fro changed formation and started to swoop down in my direction! The priestess was shrieking something in her language. The crowd's attention was diverted for a moment.

They were coming straight for the top of the pyramid!

Suddenly all the terror I should have felt before burst loose from its cage within me. I started to scream. The golden disks, a dozen or more of them, grew enormous as they neared me. I knew they would crash into the pyramid and kill us all, that whatever mystic force was holding them in the air must have dissipated—

I was blacking out fast. "Zeus help us!" I heard Nikias yelling as I lost consciousness. "The flying saucers are attacking!"

CHAPTER
XVI

W HEN I CAME TO...
A chamber with walls of solid gold, it seemed; the walls curved inward, into a flattened dome. A huge window, glassed in with some transparent substance, looked out over terrain: forests, rivers, plains, cities. We were very high up indeed. This must, I decided, be the actual interior of one of the golden disks that had descended upon us sacrificial victims and seemed to have snatched us up.

"The gods have intervened!" I said.

I looked around. The others were stirring beside me.

"Why, this is heaven itself!" Aaye said. "Walls of solid gold ... death isn't so bad after all. I hope the ambrosia is everything they say it is."

Nikias just smiled.

"I don't think we're dead at all." It was Aquila speaking. "*I* don't remember dying."

"Stuff and nonsense!" The Egyptian said. "You can see for yourself that we have been elevated far above the condition of men. Why, the view from this very window proves it. It is a fact, proven and incontrovertible."

"Bah," said Aquila.

"I want to go home," I said.

Suddenly a presence materialized in the middle of the room. With a shock, I recognized it.

Large as life! It was the very figurine that Domitian had sent to me, the very statuette that had precipitated this whole madness! A little green creature, perhaps an arm-span in height, resembling an enormous human baby in the throes of turning into a jaguar.

So we *were* in the domain of the gods! What else could it be?

The thing began to address us in a high whiny voice. The walls mumbled a little, then shifted into Lacotian.

"We have saved you," said the were-jaguar, "because you just don't seem to be the regular run of sacrificial victim. I would be most interested in knowing how you got here; you are Lakotah, aren't you? From the north? My name is V'Denni-Kenni, and I am an officer of the Dimensional Patrol. We protect the continuity, consistency, and integrity of the millions of alternate universes within this continuum." I understood very little of what he was saying, but he went on to explain that they were from the far future and that they had come in search of certain criminals who had to be brought to trial, who were guilty of attempting to tamper with the past.

"I see," I said in my halting Lacotian.

"Now," the little green man said, "which of you is the leader?"

All of them looked at me.

I looked at Aquila. He shrugged.

"I suppose I am," I said.

"Well, perhaps you can help us in our search. We have carefully avoided appearing in other hemispheres, in order not to change your continuum too much; but we suspect our criminals may have gone elsewhere—"

"I don't know what you're talking about."

"Oh?" the god seemed puzzled for a moment. "Ah, you mean . . . you don't know what I'm . . . I see. Well, with verbs beginning with *y-*, in Lacota, the *wa-* prefix for the first person usually mutates to *b'l-*, so the translating device was a bit puzzled by your dialectical variant—"

"Damn this intractable language!" I burst out in Latin. "I've had enough of barbarian languages. Mutating prefixes. Pronouns that get stuck into the middle of verbs. Extrinsic possessives. Male and female particles—I'm a Roman, and I'm fed up!" I knew that I wasn't in heaven. Not if the gods were going to correct my Lacotian grammar. And since this probably wasn't China either, I was almost certainly in hell.

The were-jaguar fiddled with some device he wore on a bracelet. The translating wall buzzed and squeaked for a moment. Then it said, "Good heavens, old chap! A Roman, eh?" in perfectly good Latin. I could have cried with relief.

"Yes, indeed. I am Titus Papinianus, Your Divinity, Procurator of Lacotia, sometime Dux of the Thirty-fourth Legion."

"Wait a minute. What do you mean, Lacotia? *You* people aren't even supposed to be on this continent! By Jove! Are you sure?"

"Why, certainly. Crossed over on a sailing ship, you know."

"And you rule over these Indians?"

"Indians? These are not Indians. These are Terra Novans; India is another country altogether, and remains unconquered."

The god muttered a few things which the wall did not translate. Then there were several dozen of them in the room at once, jabbering away like a cageful of cats and dogs. I caught the odd phrase on the wall, but the more I heard, the more mystified I became.

". . . must have made a wrong turning at the third tachyon nexus. . . ."

"... nothing for it now, we'll have to tell head-quarters, we'll have to abort the mission...."

"... can you get a fix on the right universe? Perhaps a wrinkle within the Riemannian time-construct...."

"... Romans in America, indeed! It's all K'Tooni-Mooni's fault, I'm afraid; he brought this frightfully *intelligent* specimen from outside the official surveillance territory on board... Epaminondas, I think his name was, must have run off with a few newfangled notions and made a whole new universe split off at timesector 101.24...."

"... anyhow, I resent having to abandon these Olmecs to their fate and take away their source of power. You remember what happened in the last universe, when we had to pull out four hundred years earlier?"

"... yes, their civilization vanished practically over-night! Mighty strange parallel world that was. Y're-member those Americans coming into power, with their cult of hamburgers and shopping malls?"

Well, we were standing around, getting more and more confused by the minute; you can tell from the scraps of conversation I overheard, which I have set down literally, even the bits which can't possibly make sense, that madness reigned supreme among these peo-ple.

"Am I going insane?" I said. "Is this some hallucina-tion I am having to cover up my terror as the knife slices into my chest?"

"Don't worry," Aquila said. "Back in Lacotia, we make a kind of tobacco mixed with a certain dried mush-room, and it induces dreams very similar to these. It'll wear off."

"But what's to become of us?" I shouted. The walls reverberated with the translation.

They stopped their chatter for a moment, and the one who had first addressed us did so again. "Oh, don't worry, chaps. You'll be released at the spot of your choice. Sorry to be such a nuisance to your dimension, and everything will be back to normal just as soon as we can arrange it. Oh, and we'll have gifts for all of you. Here." The ceiling opened and we were rained on by several hundred of the little jade were-jaguars. "Some small mementos of our visit in your universe. Oh, and don't noise it about too much that you've seen us, eh? We're in enough trouble as it is with the Central Dimensional Patrol Authority."

"The delta of the Miserabilis will do very nicely," I said stiffly.

CHAPTER
XVII

WHEN WE GOT HOME I SENT A SHIPLOAD OF JADE were-jaguars to Domitian together with a note explaining as little of our adventure as I could get away with—for I knew we would not be believed. Aaye and Nikias opened an academy together in Caesarea-on-Miserabilis, and I went back to ruling my unruly savages.

It was a whole year before a reply arrived. As it chanced, our whole gang was together, for it was high summer and I had decided on a grand aurochs hunt to celebrate some festival or other. We had followed the herd for some days, making Lacotian camps by night.

It was towards evening; we were exercising our horses in the plains, when a messenger arrived from Caesarea with a message from the Emperor. When I unsealed the scroll I beamed with pleasure at first.

"Why, it's from General Trajan! Domitian, it seems, has been assassinated. Well, I'm awfully glad a decent military man has become Emperor; we won't have any of these elaborate madcap jokes for a while at least."

But as I read through the letter my face fell. For Caesar had new orders for me.

Dear General Titus [it ran],

We have received your report on the Olmechii with interest, and your jade statuettes make welcome additions to the Imperial Treasury. Nevertheless, We are somewhat distressed that you have not yet found China. It is Our conviction that the fabled Empire of Chin must be conquered, for Rome cannot tolerate a force greater than herself, even in hearsay.

We charge you, therefore, and authorize you, with due dispatch to seek out this land of Chin, wheresoever it may be upon the continent of Terra Nova; to furnish maps and charts of this empire, or at least to establish once and for all its mythical nature so that We do not have to fret constantly about the possible military challenge.

Ave atque vale,

Marcus Ulpius Trajanus, Imp. Caes. August. and so on so forth.

"What shall I do?" I cried in despair. A wind blew from the west, making the tall grass sigh. In the distance the aurochs herd moved, dots of brown in the twilit hills. "Trajan has no idea of the vastness of this land! From here to the Montes Saxosi lies an endless wilderness of nature and savages. And beyond them?"

Aaye said, riding up to me, "You must go about this logically, procurator. You have tried the south, without any success. To the north are Athapasca and Algonquia, and frozen lands where surely the giant silkworms may not survive, for they are well known to be of a delicate disposition, and must continually be suckled with the milk of young Chinish maidens."

"If you know so much about the Chinish peoples, tell me where they are!"

"I was just getting to that! You impatient Romans . . . is it not true that gold deposits have been found in the Montes Saxosi?"

"Yes, but—"

"Let me finish. The Chinish folk are reputed to have yellow skins. Indeed, Apollodorus of Bithynia claims that their visages are normal in hue, but that their country is so rich that even the poorest among them paints his face with a paste of water and gold dust. . . ."

"And who *is* this Apollodorus who knows so much?"

"It is the pseudonym of a very great scholar, P. Josephus Agricola—"

"Another writer of those blasted scientifictiones! A dreamer. A weaver of escapist tales."

"When will you ever learn to trust me, General? Did I not cause the solar eclipse that enabled us to elude the altar of the Olmechian sun-god?"

I could see that he had convinced himself that he had indeed saved our lives; but I did not bother to contradict him, because I was feeling too sorry for myself.

"What I'm telling you, General, is that this Chinish land may well be very near—just on the other side of the Montes Saxosi. If you would but follow the line of the setting sun—"

"Aquila," I said, looking to the old man for support. "What does he mean?"

"I think, young Titus," he said, "that he's telling you to go west."

I looked towards the sunset. Truly this was a beautiful land; and now it was no longer an alien one. Shafts of red light broke through the clustered clouds. "West, lad, west," Nikias whispered. They were treating me like a child or younger brother, even though I was nominally their leader; but I was too confused to rebuke them. I had grown too fond of them all.

Far over the horizon, I knew, were the Montes Saxosi, the most imposing mountains Romans had ever looked upon. Behind them was the land of the setting sun. Could it be that east met west there? "China," I said softly.

We sighted a wild creature in the distance—an elk, perhaps—silhouetted in the sunset. With whoops and cries—and mine were as hearty and savage as the Lacotians'—we galloped towards it and the last of the daylight.

PART THREE

AQUILA MEETS BIGFOOT

CHAPTER
XVIII

C HINA INDEED!
    It was easier said than done. Indeed, it was to be a whole year before our merry company was able to venture westward once more. For the governance of Lacotia, under the auspices of our newest Pater Patriae, was even more difficult than it had been under Domitian. To put it mildly, His Magnitude was the worst skinflint ever to sit astride the throne of the Augusti, and I was forced to tax and tax—though Rome seldom allowed me the leeway to spend and spend.

    Of the rebellion amongst the Cansae I shall say but little; suffice it that Cansapolis is no longer the thriving city that it was, and its magnificent baths have now been permanently converted into a Mandan sweat-lodge for the performance of savage rituals. Nor shall I remark about my visit to Eburacum Novum, where, upon using the wrong secret entrance at the arena, I found myself face to face with an extremely emicturated lion. I have always suspected that this was a secret plot on the part of some faction or other in Rome to have me disposed of; but since I was conveniently rescued by an arrow loosed by Aquila from the governor's box, there was no point in my making a fuss.

The days passed quickly enough. I sat in judgment; I held the usual floggings and crucifixions; there were few orgies in the palace, since our Emperor's parsimoniousness allowed us few luxuries—indeed, I had to sell off half the kitchen help one month just to pay for a banquet —only to discover that there was no one to cook it! If Nikias hadn't had a cousin visiting from Byzantium, who had once managed a chain of sausage shops in Paestum . . .

At last, however, our Emperor's command, which had been hanging over our heads the entire time, could no longer be ignored—especially since he was coming to Terra Nova in person, and I was summoned to meet him in Alexandria.

I arranged to have the entire company from the last adventure travel to see the emperor with me: Aaye, who had grown even more pedantic and cantakerous over the past year; Aquila, in ludicrous garb of war-chief and senator; Nikias, who was stooped now, but still aging gracefully. Our plan was to journey down the mighty Miserabilis to the Ochaio River, whence we intended to journey to the city of Chirochiae and onward to the Iracuavian Capital of Alexandria by way of a pass in the Montes Apalatii.

"Never!" I said to Nikias over a loathsome breakfast of sour wine and buffalo paté, "Never will I travel by paddleboat again! Never! *Never!*"

For right now we were stalled on a sandbar; and the slaves, chained to the treadmill that worked the boat's one enormous paddle, stood idle, jabbering away in the barbarous tongue of Northern Algonquia. A brace of Lacotian legionaries poled frantically and fruitlessly on one side of the boat.

"Are we free yet?" I shouted. To Nikias, who was wolfing down his boiled buffalo with gusto, I said, "Damn the Emperor Trajan! Why can't he leave us alone? You'd think there was nothing to do in Rome, the way he traipses around the Empire overseeing us like a vulture, constantly inspecting the troops, making sure *we* don't pocket the taxes."

"Counts every brass *as* of it himself, too." Aaye said, looking up from an Egyptian newspapyrus. "Ill befits an Emperor, if you ask me."

"Slave overboard, General, *sir!*" came a shout from somewhere above. I cursed; the supply was limited. After all we were—in theory at least—within the confines of the Imperium, and it really wouldn't have done to go off on a slave-catching expedition; might snare a citizen, you know. Nasty repercussions.

"Worthless good-for-nothings!" I railed. "What we need are some decent Numidians. Proper lash-fearing stock, been under the Romans for centuries, know their place and so on. Not these lazy savages."

"They feel, General," said Nikias, "that it's woman's work. It shames them to be jogging the treadmill when they could be doing a man's work, raping, scalping and what have you."

"Ah, yes, the savage mentality," Aaye said, munching fastidiously.

"Fool!" said Nikias. "Mustn't assume they don't speak Greek and Latin, you know."

Just then the boat pulled free. I ordered the drummer to set a faster tempo, and the slaves were off and running. Their chains clanked merrily in counterpoint to our conversation. I would have used the steam device invented by the late Epaminondas of Alexandria if I could; but the boat's engineer, a brawny barbarian slave imported from far Caledonia, had caught an arrow in the throat from a surprise Apaxian raid, and I dared not send our centurion escort out woodcutting so near the border. I ought to have been better prepared; but now it was too late. "Well," I said. "I still say blast the bloody Emperor. Domitian would never have crossed the Atlanticus to meddle in his procurators' affairs!"

"Trajan *is* paranoid," Aaye agreed, using a newfangled term introduced recently by a new school of Gothic faith-healers. "Always worries about the Imperium being threatened from within and without...by whom, in heaven's name? Always seeing a menace to national security in every mud-eating savage tribe we encounter."

"Doesn't even give good orgies," said Aquila, wiping his mouth on his toga. I glared at him. *I'd* never been invited to one of the Emperor's orgies. I hadn't so much as set foot in Rome in four years, whereas Aquila had jaunted over twice, being a senator and much in demand besides at high-society receptions, orgies, banquets, and private spectacles as a token barbarian.

"Skimps on the games, too," Aaye said. "It says in this newspapyrus that Trajan tried to stage a venation at the Circus Maximus with hardly any animals at all—a mere fifty ostriches, twelve hippos, a single unkempt herd of aurochs that should have seen the butcher, not the arena, and not one single crocodile or exotic big cat! What's more, instead of dispatching the remaining victims after each act, he saved them and brought them on later to be devoured a second time...it's scandalous! What kind of Emperor economizes on spectacle, in Isis's name?"

"Egyptian broadsheets," Nikias said. "Bah. Stale hearsay embroidered with staler invention."

"But this news is a mere six months old!"

The paddleboat shuddered to a stop again.

"Sandbar ahead ho!"

All hands turned in the direction of the shouting. More legionaries emerged from below deck, brandishing poles and staves. In a moment the Greek and the Egyptian had resumed their bickering; so I turned my attention to Aquila.

"So, Aquila old chap. Been to Rome again, eh? Why

has the Emperor summoned me to Alexandria? Surely not to attend one of his less-than-lavish spectacles?"

"You will see, General. *Hechitu welo!*" He chuckled softly.

"Don't give me any of this Lacotian vagueness. You have acquired—as you seem to have with every previous Emperor of your acquaintance—the confidence of the Pater Patriae, whether through trickery or through some native hocus-pocus I don't know. In Jove's name, you've just come from Rome! Now *Domitian* would have had some fiendishly humorous trick planned for me, but that doesn't seem to be Trajan's bag—not quite his brand of lunacy, eh, what?"

"Then you've nothing to worry about."

"But am I to be recalled? Or executed, perhaps? You know how the Caesars are with their purges, and Trajan's long overdue for one of those, I suspect."

"You forget, O procurator, that while I have the Emperor's ear, I retain it only so long as I don't use it for political purposes." Then he began to cackle uproariously. I shall never understand the Lacotian sense of humor.

"I know what it is," I said. "He's going to send me off to look for that fabled land of Chin again, isn't he? He's lusting desperately after new worlds to conquer?"

"It is perhaps fortunate that you didn't tell Trajan about the teeming thousands, the levitating stone heads, the hot-air balloons, the gilded motor-cars, and the flying saucers of the southern Olmechii," Aquila said, reminding me rather uncomfortingly of our last little attempt to find the western route to China.

"Trajan wouldn't ever have believed any of it."

"*Hanh, hanh, hanh!* Caesar is most credulous when it comes to tales about territories he hasn't conquered yet."

"Who does he think he is, Alexander the Great?"

A hissing sound came, startling me. I looked up. A

flash of light scudded across the threshold of our portable Temple of Minerva. My mouth fell open.

"Of all the—"

There it was! Skimming the clouds, a spinning sundisk of gold that glittered high in the sky, catching the summer sunlight.

"It can't be!" I said. "Of all the rotten luck!"

"It seems, indeed," said Aquila, "that the flying saucers have come back."

"Leave us alone!" I shouted, shaking my fist at the sky. "I've had enough adventures! Nikias, turn the paddleboat back."

"Too late, my Lord; besides the Emperor's summons—"

"Damn the Emperor; and damn this huge savage monstrosity of a continent where you can't buy a glass of decent wine; and damn the lot of you; and damn those flying saucers with their were-jaguars from the future Dimensional Patrol or whatever it's called—"

"Perhaps I should remind you," said Nikias, "that they *did* save your life."

"So they did, so they did." I glared ruefully at the sky, at the zenith of which more sundisks had appeared. They were darting to and fro like a school of fish, a beautiful sight. "And yet . . . I think it's an ill omen, Nikias. Why wouldn't they just stay down south, in the land of the pyramid worshippers, exercising their godlike superscience and ruling the natives? Perhaps this *Time* the *Criminal* they claim to be searching for—"

"Rubbish!" said Aaye. "Rubbish and bull's pizzle! Let me give you my expert opinion as an Egyptian on that! It is clear that the utterances of the were-jaguars, cloaked as they are in astounding, polysyllabic jargon, are not to be taken literally, but merely to suggest the ineffability and inscrutable grandeur of godhead. I wouldn't worry, if I were you, about it having to *mean* anything."

"You mean it was all mumbo-jumbo, just to impress us?"

"Of course! What else could it be? 'Dimensional Patrol' indeed! 'Policing the time-lines,' 'Hot on the trail of a Time Criminal who is going around altering your continuum'—what else is one to make of such nonsense, if not that its purpose is more sibylline obfuscation? I've heard more convincing double-talk from the least of the priests of Osiris. Heavens, *I* wasn't taken in for a moment. After all, we are a very ancient people, very close to the gods, and we learn from birth to separate the wheat of truth from the chaff of verbosity—"

"So you're telling me," I said, "to disregard those *things* up there. To ignore these blasted sandbars. These cheap, low-quality slaves who are dropping like flies. Not to mention Caesar, who probably has some ludicrous new adventure lined up for me. Don't tell me things could possibly get any worse!"

I happened to glance down at my breakfast. "And where did this arrow come from?" I said querulously, pulling a feathered shaft out of my aurochs-liver pâté. I looked around wildly. The others were nowhere to be seen, except Aquila, who had doffed his toga, was reaching for his quiver, and humming some incantation.

On shore, smoke billowed. Horses neighed. Dead ahead, a pack of angry Comanxae were charging into the river, lances waving, shrieking such war cries as would make the very catacombs spit forth their corpses.

"Couldn't get any worse, eh, General?" said Aquila, grinning as he nocked his bow and picked a Comanxa clean off his horse.

"Catapultae! Ballistae!" I screamed.

"Huka hey!" said Aquila.

CHAPTER
XIX

I WAS STARING INTO THE FACE OF MARCUS ULPIUS
Trajanus, Caesar Augustus, Pater Patriae, Pater
Maximus Candidusque, *etcetera etcetera.* He was sitting
in a grand palanquin borne by burly Nubians; his
demeanor, far from the languid decadence affected by
previous Caesars, showed an earnestness that boded ill
for me. The day before, so I'd heard, he'd already reduced G. Pomponius Piso the Younger, procurator of Iracuavia, to a quivering jelly in the course of a tirade on
the necessity for parsimoniousness in the governance of
our remote provinces here on the western shore of the
Oceanus Atlanticus; would he do less for me, procurator
of Lacotia?

I was tired after my long journey by paddleboat. Here
I was in Alexandria, capital of Iracuavia, an eastern-
shore city egregiously sultry in summer and unpleasantly
chilly in winter, its glistening-new marble edifices loom-
ing from clusters of Iracuavian huts in a bend of the
River of Pluto Maximus.

"Found the place all right, eh, Papinian?" said Caesar. "Not too many brigands, I trust?"

I started to approach, but a eunuch stepped out and stopped me. "Ten paces forward," he warbled, "genuflect three times, then kneel until he tells you to stand up."

"Oh, we can dispense with all that," said Trajan. "Oh, bother! The things We've had to do, General, to make sure these nasty plebeians realize that We are their god! Ceremonies, protocols . . . and these frightfully expensive eunuchs from Asia Minor! Come, tell me about your journey." His use of the newfangled royal We was intermittent, as if he couldn't quite make up his mind. "Roads all right, eh?"

"Yes, Caesar. Perfectly safe."

Well, what was I to do, tell him all about how we'd been beset by Comanxians and Apaxians all the way down the Miserabilis? It hadn't been too hard to polish off our assailants, who had in any case been roaming a little far from home; it *had* been a good opportunity to get hold of some able-bodied slaves to use on the treadmill of the paddleboat.

Once east, in the Iracuavian territory, we had found the Pax Romana in full force in Pomponius Piso's province. We had left the River shortly into Iracuavia and then taken this magnificent new road, the Via Augusta, to Iracuavia through a pass in the Montes . . . the Montes Allegenii or Apalatii or some such barbarous name. Here and there were huge cities of ten and twenty thousand souls. There were public baths everwhere, and even the natives seemed to enjoy them, a sure sign that the process of Romanization was well in hand.

Ahead loomed our destination: the Circus Neronis of Alexandria, a towering edifice of gilt and white marble that paid tribute both to Roman ingenuity and to the monumental vulgarity of the Julian Caesars, long since dead and defied. Trajan had planned games there to celebrate his state visit to the transatlantic provinces that comprise Terra Nova. I had heard that His Magnitude's miserliness was such, however, that one might as well have stayed at home as gone to the spectacle; nevertheless, an Imperial Summons *was* an Imperial Summons.

"Very well, procurator. Come, we'll travel to the Circus together." I took this to be an invitation to join Him in His palanquin, but when I attempted to do so a second flabby eunuch came out and began to search me thoroughly, not neglecting my most personal of orifices; only then was I permitted to climb up.

"Can't stand these beastly things meself," Trajan was saying. "Spectacles . . . pfagh! Depleting my treasury for nothing. Saw enough killing in the war, you know, what. Come, you'll share the Imperial Box, Titus, and you'll tell Us all about how your search for China is progressing, won't you now?"

I should have known. My heart sank as I joined the procession into the Circus proper. As we reached the box I saw that a venation was in progress: female hunters, their left breasts amputated in the manner of the mythical Amazons, were pursuing a herd of scrawny-looking moose and elk, with only a few dozen ostrichs and crocodiles crawling around for exotic effects. The women were going at it with abandon; but the crowd seemed hardly interested at all, and the Emperor sat facing the other way, sucking delicately on an orange.

"China!" he said. "Tell Us about China!"

"Your Magnificence," I stammered. "I've been unable to make any progress since our little southern venture—"

"I might have guessed," said Caesar, still not looking at me. "Look here . . . the people are discontented! I give them lavish games . . . in Rome my grain coffers are almost empty from the constant handouts . . . but they must have something new and wonderful to dream about, some new enemy to frighten them in their beds at night . . . what complacency! They think they own the world!"

"But Caesar, they do own the world. At least, *you* do." If he would only put a little more gold into the spectacles, he'd have had all Rome eating out of his hand, of course. But it wouldn't do to tell him so. "It seems, in any case, that there is a natural border to our westward expansion—the Montes Saxosi. I have scouted out a few passes—" I hadn't, but it was time to start improvising—"but so far our explorations have borne little fruit. . . ."

"Hannibal crossed the Alps," said Trajan testily.

"True, O Caesar, but *he* knew where he was going."

"Indeed, General. Do you mean to say that you do *not* know where you're going? Is the land of Chin not an actual place? You dare assume I'm feebleminded?"

"Your Magnitude—" So this was *paranoia*.

"Watch the spectacle. I paid good money for those ostriches."

I looked down. The Amazons had carefully avoided killing any of the ostriches, and after the corpses had been cleared slaves entered and began yoking the ostriches to little chariots. The people—a mere thousand at the most, scarcely filling one-fifth of the arena—seemed listless. "A clever idea, Caesar," I said. "I mean, using the ostriches twice."

"Oh, We'll use them more than twice before the day's over," the Emperor mumbled, poring over a map of Terra Nova. I turned my attention to the entertainment. The band sounded a lugubrious sennet; at least a cheer went up from the throng, and I saw several elephants being led in through the gates of life. At last, I thought, some genuine expense! "Your Majesty had these elephants brought over with you by ship, I suppose?" I said, hoping to lighten the tone of our conversation.

"Good heavens! Who do you take me for, Nero? These elephants have been here since the founding of Alexandria; Nero sent them over, you know, frighten the natives and all that sort of thing; Vespasian sent a few dozen more to liven up the games . . . got a whole herd of them now. The Chirochii have proved excellent elephant trainers. Watch this now—elephants mounted by Numidians racing against pygmies in ostrich chariots. Just like the days of Vespasian, eh?"

"Didn't the late God Vespasian use five hundred of each?"

"Ah well, hard times, hard times. And he didn't have this blasted Chinish question to contend with." Trajan staggered off his seat and offhandedly threw a handkerchief into the arena. The race began; soon the ostriches had lost their direction and the pygmies were being trampled by elephants, much to the amusement of the populace. Trajan watched, slitty-eyed with rage for a moment, then shouted, "Don't kill 'em! Wasting good pygmies like that...cost me five hundred sestertii apiece, you nincompoop! There, there—"

Without question it was one of the most uninteresting spectacles I had ever watched; not that I love gore for its own sake, as the plebeians do, but one does require new twists, imaginative killings, and so on. I sat back on my couch and turned to look at the others in the Emperor's Box. One, in particular, overdressed and overripe, whose breasts heaved like watermelons, kept making cow-eyes at me, much to my dismay.

"You like the Lady Oenothea, daughter of the King of Cilicia?" Trajan said. He nudged my elbow and leered.

"Well—"

"Very good. It's settled then. She is to be your wife, and will journey with you to the land of Chin."

"I—"

"Yes, my word." Caesar fussed with a fold of his frayed tunic (not, I noticed, the latest in color or fashion) and continued, "You see, Papinian, I'm instigating a new image for the White and Greatest Father. You know, soften up the old harsh paternalistic bit, have a little more of Old Mother Rome and what have you. That's what the Lady Oenothea will provide. The other face of

Janus, you know. Satisfies one of my client kings, too, in the bargain."

"Your Majesty has a wondrous eye for . . . a good bargain," I said, almost choking. The stampeding of the beasts below was now evoking the odd belly-laugh from the audience.

"And one more thing: you are now to be surnamed *Lacoticus*, conqueror of the Lacotii."

"But I did no such thing."

"Of course not, but propaganda goes far, and I'm not giving you very many men, so you'll have to make do with a reputation, fabricated by me, of fearlessness and ruthlessness."

"Yes, Caesar." What more could he do to me? The Lady Oenothea began sidling in my direction. I coughed and stared at the spectacle beneath.

"It only remains," Trajan said pompously, "to determine now the exact *means* of your glorious journey into the Montes Saxosi. Did you say something about Hannibal, old fellow?"

I looked at the elephants.

"You don't mean—"

They were standing on their hind legs now, trumpeting as they trampled giant and dwarf alike, now and then swatting ostriches with their trunks.

"But Caesar—"

"Why not? This herd of miscreant pachyderms is a great drain on the privy purse, you know. They eat too much hay . . . and I'm not planning to stage anything this lavish in the provinces again, not for a long time. Why not give them to you, have them forage on the way to China rather than siphoning gold from Our pockets with their trunks? Besides which, Hannibal . . . ah, Hannibal. . . ." I noticed him counting off the points one by one on his fingers, with relentless logic. "I need something to strike the fear of God, that is to say of Yours Truly, into whatever lower beings you may encounter. Part of the new image, you might say."

"My Lord, we don't even know whether the Montes Saxosi are indeed the only barrier to a westerly route to the silklands. Besides that, Hannibal...didn't exactly win the Punic Wars, you know, Sire."

"My dear General Titus Papinianus!" he said, oozing charm. "Hannibal, you recall, was going against the Might and Majesty of Rome Itself, while you are simply to swat down a few miserable peasants."

"You can't have it both ways, Caesar: they can't be both miserable peasants *and* a vast threat to national security." He glared at me. I had said too much. Now I knew for sure that Trajan had been touched by the madness that affects all Emperors, no matter how benign their original intentions.

He continued to glare, his beady eyes glittering, as my heart sank slowly down my toga, down to my very caligae. What was he waiting for? Ah yes, of course. I hadn't thanked him for the elephants..."I say, your Omnipotence, awfully decent of you, what...."

He relaxed his gaze a little, then raised his hand and said, almost inaudibly, "All hail, Titus Papinianus Lacoticus, scourge of the Lacotii!"

The others echoed in a straggly sort of unison, and one by one came up to congratulate me.

Congratulate!

There were Praetorian guardsmen. There were the Imperial household eunuchs. There were senators. Finally, from the throng, came G. Pomponius Piso the Younger himself, a ratlike man, quite different from his grandfather, the magnificent general who had conquered most of the new world for the Emperor Nero. He was such an insignificant sort of person that I hadn't even noticed him squatting in the back of the Imperial Box. He pressed a sweaty hand into mine and whispered: "Thank you, oh, thank you, those elephants were the ruin of me, I'm awfully relieved to have you take them off my hands, old chap, you know, what...."

The Lady Oenothea enveloped me in a rancid embrace.

I was speechless for a long while. Then a stream of inconsequential platitudes came bubbling forth: "Er... *sic transit*... um, *morituri te salutant*, eh, what?... *alea jacta est*, if I say so myself...."

"Fine sentiments," said the Emperor, beaming expansively, "and worthy of a true Roman."

CHAPTER
XX

O F THE PREPARATIONS FOR THIS EPIC JOURNEY I
shall say but little. Suffice it that Trajan, having
overwhelmed me with lofty and comprehensive commands, was rather more reluctant to back up his words
with gold. He had an accountant figure out the market
value of one dozen elephants in fine condition (a somewhat inflated figure, since one or two of the beasts he
gave us were hardly in the pink of health) and then proceeded to deduct this amount from the already ungen-
erous ten thousand aurei allocated for this enterprise.
The result being a negative figure of some few sesterces,
he actually had his chief eunuch bring me a bill for the
difference! Naturally, fearful as always for my head, I
sent the Emperor a note praising his magnanimity, fore-
sight, and frugality in flowery terms; and upon reaching

Lacotia and my own capital city of Caesarea-on-Miserabilis, I immediately set about raising money.

I was forced to levy a most unpopular tax on the exchange of scalps among the Lacotii. This was a rather
frequent event, and, since the Lacotians consider the
obtaining and trading of scalps to be a matter of religious
significance and personal pride, there were few who
would purposely shirk the obligation of declaring a scalp
exchange. But the paperwork was excruciating. I appointed a whole army of quaestors whose sole function
was the notarization of scalp trades and the marking of
fresh scalps; for this we used a serial numbering system,
affixing the number to the scalp by means of a little tag
of buffalo bone. Of course, a new industry sprang up:
polishing and marking the little bones, which, for a
number like MMMMM, might be a mere splinter, but for
a serial number such as MMMMMDCCCCLXXXXVIIII
might be a considerable chunk of humerus or tibia, add-
ing considerable weight to the scalp itself. Luckily there
was no lack of petty criminals in my Caesarian dun-
geons, and these same were only too glad to do something that not only let them out in the open air now and
then, but also required relatively little flogging. One
could not exercise too much clemency, of course, since
this among my subjects was viewed as womanly weak-
ness; indeed, those criminals who were Lacotian often
complained bitterly that our excruciations were less ago-
nizing than their regular initiation rites.

But surely these dull details of a governor's day-to-
day duties are an uninteresting digression; so I will continue with the tale of our Great Quest.

A strange procession it was indeed that began lumbering up the River Miserabilis that Kalends of May.
With some difficulty I had persuaded the two cantanker-
ous pedants to come along; it was with greater ease that
I persuaded Aquila to leave this (as he termed it) life of
decadence.

First, then, came half a dozen elephants, with their

Chirochian mahouts, each bearing upon its back one of the little battle-towers we had seen used by the Indish race. Our infantry numbered a mere century, our equites a single squadron; and we had a mere two or three hundred of the usual camp followers: slaves, merchants, smiths, prostitutes, cooks, and what have you. I, my... ah... wife, and the triumvirate of old men followed last, in a sort of mobile palatium drawn by four yoked elephants; two mangier ones lagged behind, performing no duties more onerous than eating and eliminating. We were forced to live in an atmosphere befouled by the constant exercise of the latter, and it was not long before I yearned for the relative comfort of the old paddleboat.

A fortnight after we left Caesarea we reached the Lacotian border, having left the river and headed due west. There was a little garrison there, a minuscule tidbit of Rome in the midst of a vast expanse of great plain sprinkled with impenetrable forests; for the last time we were able to bathe like civilized people, and were even entertained by the modest spectacle of a few military executions and a fairly workmanlike crucifixion of a runaway slave.

And then... the wilderness of Siannia! An untamed territory as vast as Lacotia, perhaps, but more inhospitable and riddled with hostile Siannii, a race much like the Lacotii before we civilized them, but whose language was incomprehensible. Here too lurked other tribes: Apsarochii, Arapahovii, and others whose names cannot be rendered at all in an unbarbarous tongue. I sent out scouts regularly now to look for passes: for soon the Montes Saxosi would be upon us, and already we were skirting a minor range that we had named the Montes Negri.

While not a day passed without some minor skirmish with the natives, they were annoyances, nothing more. Soon the Lacotians among our centurions were all sporting a scalp or two (with serial number attached, of course—for where *I* was, Rome's long arm had perforce to be felt) on their cuirasses, or perhaps hanging gaily on a corner of their scuta or from the sharp tips of their pila.

For a time nature was bountiful; we hunted and feasted on aurochs and venison, and there was plenty of elephant fodder.

As we approached the Montes Negri, the terrain deteriorated into badlands, and life became considerably less idyllic. The elephants ranged far in search of the dry, husklike shrubbery that dotted the stony waste; the landscape was barren, interrupted only by fantastical spires and monoliths of rock, unnatural shapes no doubt left long ago by the battles of the Titans at the dawn of time. The nights were bleakly orchestrated by the baying of *quoiotuli,* exotic feral dogs whose meat even the Lacotii found unpalatable.

In all that time I bedded the Lady Oenothea but once; then I left her to her own devices, finding better pickings among the camp followers. It was a few days after that lardy tussle that we found ourselves encamped beneath a certain hanging rock, sitting around the fire imbibing the dregs of the sorriest Falernian, which I had been forced to dilute with muddy river water.

"We will never reach China," I said. "There is no hope. We must turn back. Perhaps there'll be a different Emperor by then—"

"You will find China," said Oenothea, making it sound like an order. "Trajan says so."

Nikias and Aaye began to nod excitedly to one another. "Ah ha!" said the latter. "I think it's time to bring out the book."

"What book?" I said. "More Egyptian hocus-pocus? More slapdash scholarship and overhasty conclusions?"

"Fetch the book," Nikias said. Grinning, the Egyptian went into his tent and returned with a scroll.

"Here!" he triumphantly hefted it into my arms, knocking me backwards into an elephant's outstretched trunk. It wrapped itself around my neck, half-choking me, and raised me high into the air, dangling me over the campfire.

"Let me down at once, you miscreant!" I shouted, letting go of the book. The two scholars dashed after it, giving no thought to their general as he swung over the flames.

"General, how can you possibly think of your own safety now, in view of one of the most exciting discoveries of the century?" said Aaye. "Proof that your legendary land actually exists, in exactly the place we calculated, to wit, just beyond the Montes Saxosi—"

"Down! Down, you perfidious pachyderm!"

The creature dashed me on the hard rock, giving my tender buttocks quite a turn. I found the opened manuscript brushing the end of my nose, with the Greek and the Egyptian on either side of me jabbering furiously.

I looked at the title, which stated in large red letters:

"My hieroglyphics," I said testily, "aren't quite what they used to be." For, of course, I couldn't read a word.

"Come, come," said Nikias. "Surely you recall something of what I taught you as a child. You know: determinatives, triliterals, what have you? And those signs that are used for suggesting vowels when transcribing Greek and Latin."

"Indeed," I said, "I see a snake, two reeds, a wiggly line, a quail, a triangle, and a man stuffing something into his mouth. The last glyph being a determinative, this suggests to me . . . a cookbook?"

"You fool!" said Aaye. "How dare you mock the sacred wisdom of the ancients? Listen, barbarian of a Roman, and I'll construe the thing to you. The determinative is of speech. The other characters, from left to right, spell the name of a language:

TCH-Y-N-W-K!

In short, *Chinook!* It is a dictionary of the *Chinook* speech! Now what else could that mean, but that we have here a transcription into Egyptian letters of the *Chinish* tongue? Incontrovertibly and indisputably the two words are cognate. And—as to the location of the Chinish land—an inscription ensues in Greek, which I trust the General is literate enough to follow."

I read:

Copy of a scroll of the Alexandria Library, Iracuavia; original scroll dated the Seventh Year of Lucius Domitius who is known as Nero, Emperor of Rome (a whole slew of concatenary titles followed here).

I, Rennut-Keb, philologist of the Terra Novan exploratory party (licensed by the Emperor) of Anaxagoras of Athens, do hereby set down these words in the hieroglyphic tongue, that the learning I have gleaned may pass only to those worthy of receiving it. On the Kalends of May last, a certain prisoner, of unusual facial aspect and speaking both Lacotian, Athapascan, and a smattering of Greek, was charged with treason and sentenced to a routine slow torture and death. I visited the prisoner during the process of excruciation, and he informed me (between groans, which I have not bothered to insert into the body of the text proper) that he had been captured by Lacotii, but that in reality he was the son of a rich chief from a distant land beyond the Montes Saxosi, eaters of the fiery-colored fish; that his father's kingdom was vast beyond our imaginings (I set his words down *ver-*

batim, poor wretch that has not seen Rome, Athens, or Alexandria): and that if released he would "potlatch" us many gifts. While it was not possible for me to ameliorate his fate, I was nonetheless able to obtain much instruction in this *lingua franca* Chinook, which, he claimed, was spoken throughout a territory a thousand miles in breadth. The dictionary (many of whose words I must render only approximately, given the condition of the informant) follows forthwith.

There followed a series of words, all transliterated into hieroglyphics, with translations into the Egyptian tongue alongside them. Aaye read out such strange-sounding words as *muckamuck* for *food,* *ticky* for *desire, want, lust,* and so on.

"I have looked over the manuscript myself," said Nikias, "and am reasonably convinced."

"Good heavens," I said in utter amazement. "Bloody brilliant bit of reasoning, eh, what?" I was impressed despite my determination to believe nothing the Egyptian said.

Then Aquila, who had been sitting with his eyes closed, smoking some foul-smelling weed from his *fascis medicinae,* suddenly opened his eyes and began to laugh uncontrollably.

"What's the matter with *you?*" I said.

"My dear General . . . oh, ho, ho, ho . . . it so happens that you have merely uncovered the trade jargon of the western lands, used to communicate between tribes, and not dissimilar to the sign language of the great plains. I myself have seen such western Terra Novans captured, and head the language spoken. . . ."

"My dear Aquila," I said, mustering my patience. "You are a senator and a Roman citizen, but a certain savagery clings to you even now. Don't you realize that books are sacred? Do you dare distrust that Roman scholarship which has made her might secure throughout the known world?"

Aquila closed his eyes and returned to his reverie.

"Ah yes," I said, "it must remain our divinely appointed duty, onerous but necessary, to open the eyes of and lift the veils of darkness from the savage mind. . . ." Realizing that my metaphors were now hopelessly mixed, and that Nikias would be squirming, I stopped. "Where's Oenothea?"

"Slipped back to her tent," said Nikias. "Had a grim look about her."

It was, as I adjudged, now time for my husbandly duty again; so I decided to go towards her tent.

As I approached it (its entrance was hidden behind the legs of an elephant, making my egress most unpleasant) I saw a man slip away.

"Cuckolding me, eh?" I wrestled him to the ground beneath the belly of the elephant, who promptly annointed us both. A scroll slipped from his hand. I seized it and stalked into the tent, where Oenothea was lolling about on the bed.

"What is this, pray?" I waved the letter. It rolled open; in the dim torchlight I made out a few words:

To   the . . . Trajan . . . greeting . . . have   uncovered Egyptian manuscript . . . Titus is . . . a fool. . . .

"My dear woman," I said, astonished. "You're—a spy!"

"Of course," she said, "and the more fool you, not to have guessed by now."

"Of course. Wife—new image for the Empire—spy, all rolled into one. Three for a single price. And I don't suppose you were that expensive, eh? The Emperor's killed too many birds with one stone this time, if you ask me!"

Tears began streaming down her flabby, kohl-stained cheeks. "My dear Titus," she said, "please don't send me away! I'll let you do anything you want, but don't do that . . . Trajan has blackmailed my father and—"

"*More* birds with this single stone!" I said. "Must be a veritable megalith."

"If you send me back he'll have my father killed—"

"Good heavens!" I said. "Well, I'm no great lover of His Niggardly Majesty myself, so I suppose compassion is in order, eh, what? But don't let me catch you again, or you'll have the nearest lions eating out of your hand, if you get my drift."

"You're very kind, my Lord," she said, gulping. "Perhaps you'd care for a few . . . rites of the bedchamber?"

"Not at the moment."

Suddenly a dozen war-painted savages leapt out of the shadows. Oenothea screeched. I heard a shout outside: "Siannian raid! To arms!" and bucinae began braying. I threw a torch at the nearest Siannius; it missed and set the tent wall on fire. Oenothea threw herself on a nearby savage and sat on him, gouging at his eyes. Just then the elephant parked outside our tent flap, roused by the commotion, came charging into the tent, scattering the natives. I unsheathed my gladius and found myself hacking away at the empty air.

As I left the tent I found Aquila, fully awakened, unleashing arrow after arrow into the distance.

"They've stolen all our horses!" he shouted. Legionaries were bustling about, dragging heavy ballistae; but there was nary a savage to be seen except for our own.

There was an ominous silence save for the howling of a distant quoiotulus.

"That's no quoiotulus," said Aquila, "but one of *them*, signaling. I think I'd better do one of my dances."

So saying he doffed his tunic and stood in a breechclout in the chilly air.

"You'll catch your death," I said.

"Oh, I'll be warmed up in no time," he said, and began to prance energetically about, wailing, and wheezing his mystic formulae. As he began I heard the cornua hooting, and I saw the hostiles, mounted, massed in the moonlight, coming for us in a cloud of dust.

"Torches!" I shouted. "Fireballs! Burn a few tents so we can see!" As I spoke, tents blazed behind me. Elephants trumpeted; I ordered them placed in a straggly line facing the Siannii, and the few men we had to form a wall of scuta. I knew the shields would not hold for long, and that we were a mere hundred men; but we were Romans, by Jove, and we'd fight them to the finish.

The dust came nearer, hoofbeats pounded like a distant earthquake. "For heaven's sake, Aquila, will you stop dancing? We're doomed, old chap!"

"*Heya*...can't stop now, it's working!"

Presently came the ululations of the savages, and the first rain of arrows stuck the shields at once with a resounding clang. The braves were bearing down now, and our Lacotian legionaries were answering them with whoops of their own. Horseless as they were, they broke ranks and began to rush toward the hostiles.

"What the...come back, come back, you fools!" I screamed.

"They're Lacotii first, Romans second," huffed Aquila, never missing a beat of his maenad dance. "Can't expect them to listen to discipline, you know. Glory's what they're after—"

"But they'll get killed!"

A Siannian warrior landed at our feet. Aquila paused to count coup, then continued, dancing the while, "Precisely! It's a good day to die, as we Lacotii always say." I watched him, bug-eyed, as he nonchalantly continued with his wheezing song. "Ah...ah...I feel it working now...yes, indeed...." As suddenly as he had begun, he stopped.

"Come to your senses at last?"

"Oh no, O procurator. Now I'd like a good steam bath. Have one of your orderlies prepare one, please."

"But—but—"

"My dear General, relax! It has worked. Look, there, up at the sky."

I looked.

I screamed.

Flying saucers were streaming from the sky! It was just like that day in the land of the Olmechii. The night exploded with a thousand brilliant colors. Thunder crashed. Streaks of light rained everywhere. I saw the Siannian braves look up in horror, their horses rearing, whinnying wildly. They were fleeing every which way. Behind me, our elephants had fallen asleep, tired out from carrying the war towers on their backs, the poor dears.

"Good heavens, Aquila!" I said. "I thought we were done for for sure!"

"That we are not, my dear General, is a tribute to the excellent discipline of the Roman Army, and can hardly be attributed to *your* bumbling leadership," said Aquila, snorting.

"But the Olmechian flying saucers... to have them appear so far from their super-scientific abode... I must instruct everyone to wear their were-jaguar amulets at once!" For it will be recalled that these little jade trinkets, each a representation of one of the godlike green were-jaguars who ruled over the Olmechii, had been given us as a remembrance by our old friend V'Denni-Kenni, the leader of—what was the mystical title of their sect? Ah yes. The Dimensional Patrol. "This Lacotian magic is astounding!"

"Indeed! Not to mention amazing!"

"But seriously! I mean, to be able to summon the godlike Olmechian flying saucers from their homes in the south... however did you do this?"

"You Romans never notice anything, do you? These saucers have been following us ever since we left Alexandria. I have sighted them somewhere almost every day: peering through the branches of a tree, peeping from a cloud, popping up between the rifts of mountain peaks."

"But the dance to summon them—surely a very powerful Lacotian magic! Tomorrow you shall teach it to all the troops. How did you ever learn to do such a dance?"

"Frankly, General, I just made it up as I went along. I couldn't do it again if I tried."

"But—"

"Clears the mind, dancing, you know, when you're desperately trying to figure out what to do in what is clearly a hopeless situation. Keeps you lot mystified, too, this prancing around. You Romans are so superstitious."

"I am too much a Roman to be riled by the ravings of a barbarian," I said stiffly, automatically. "But this leaves us with one more question." I looked up at the sky. No trace remained of the recent pyrotechnics. It was a cold, clear, beautiful night. "Why, in the name of Hades, are these flying saucers following us, and why have they bothered to save our lives . . . twice?"

"Beats me."

CHAPTER
XXI

Although our skins had been saved by the fortuitous appearance of the flying saucers, not many of our horses remained, and our casualties numbered fifty wounded.

I resolved to command that a garrison be built in a suitable spot; that the standard of Rome be set up within this garrison, thus creating in the name of the Emperor a sort of province of Siannia, though how long we could continue to hold it was a matter of some conjecture.

Nikias, Aaye, and I argued a little about what to call the fort. I argued in vain for Papiniana, but it was not to be. Speed, naturally, was of the essence; and so I chose a simple name, expressive of our purpose: I elected to call it the Castra Celeritatis, or Camp of Rapidity.

Upon reflection, though, I decided that a more grandiose name was necessary, if we hoped thereby to make Trajan think this construction of logs a city worthy to be capital of a new province.

We therefore aggrandized the fort's name to Tachyopolis, or Rapid City. I dispatched an epistle to His Magnitude at once, informing Him of the latest annexation and of the founding of another urbs, making somewhat inflated claims about our prowess and about the number and mightiness of the enemy's powers.

Clearly, though, the search for China could not continue.

But it was sensible old Nikias who said: "My Lord, it is now almost June. Surely this continent can't be much wider. The Montes Saxosi lie but a short way westward; beyond them, the Land of Chin, if it exists at all, is sure to lie. It can't take more than a couple of weeks at the most."

He was right, I supposed. It couldn't hurt to move on a bit, just for a little peek. Surely not! And so I left most of my little army behind under the command of one Cornelius. Nikias had been my tutor so long ago, and I didn't want him dying of snakebite, but he insisted on going. Aaye could have survived anything, he was so thick-skinned; and Aquila, oldest of all of us, would clearly not be persuaded to remain, since he was by far the ablest warrior among us. Yes! Even I, a stalwart Roman, was forced at times to admit that this barbarian possessed an innate cunning despite, or perhaps even because of, his savage origins, for a civilized man might not have stooped so low as to acquire that oneness with the elements that enabled Aquila to sniff out his way through danger with the adroitness of a forest animal. It was with such circuitous reasoning that I justified to myself my need to have the old bastard by me.

We had the small band of friends, thirty legionaries, a handful of horsemen, and the full complement of elephants. My wife Oenothea came too, for I couldn't very well trust her to run loose at the fort without my supervision.

Scouts ahead found a fairly wide pass in the Montes Saxosi, towards which we made our way. I had hoped that we would now be rid of the Olmechian flying saucers; but now that I knew of their existence I too sighted them almost daily, and it looked as if they were trying to show us the way. So I gave up on the scouts and followed the saucers; always they showed us the least impenetrable route.

The Saxosi are the most extraordinary range of mountains I have ever encountered. Even from a distance they seem like the very walls of the universe: an endless blue expanse, the highest peaks capped forever in white. It was hard to believe that an advanced civilization might lie beyond them, but at the same time it was difficult to question the validity of a document from a source as august and impeccable as the great Library of Alexandria-in-Iracuavia.

While the attacks of Siannii and others had become less frequent, owing no doubt to the rapidly spreading news that we controlled vast supernatural powers and were able to bring down spirit armies from the transetheral plane (rumors I neither deserved nor discouraged) and the presence of the Roman garrison beside the Montes Negri, we soon found nature even more of an enemy than any hostile natives. For, as Aaye pointed out, mountains, being by their very nature tall and therefore a little closer to the cold and chaste purity of the quintessence whereof the superlunary bodies are made, are not particularly suitable environments for humans, bound as they are by faulty admixtures of the four elements. "Do humans live on Olympos?" he said as we shivered in the towering shadows of one promontory. "Of course not. Perhaps we are guilty of hubris . . . of meddling in that which man was not meant to know!"

"Yet Trajan is a god," I replied, throwing a fourth blanket over my cloak, "and it is by his command that we are here."

"A god by decree of the Senate," said Aquila, who seemed not to feel the cold at all, and occasionally even performed a rousing dance wearing little but his breech-cloth. "Besides, it could be a lot worse. We could be scaling that peak yonder, where even an eagle—an *aquila*—would have trouble roosting." He laughed at his own pun.

"I only hope your crackpot theory is right, Aaye," I said "about being able to find another river, twin to the Miserabilis, to lead us downward from the mountains."

"There is absolutely no doubt, General."

"That is precisely what I fear the most."

"But General Titus. . . ." Aaye said. "The Platonic theory of ideals decrees specifically that the world must strive towards symmetry."

"To strive is not to succeed."

A hideous groan, like the water organ at the Flavian Amphitheater in Rome, drowned our conversation for a moment.

"Good heavens!" I said. "Another elephant collapse, eh, what?" Running against the bitter wind, I made my way towards the sound. The elephant was unsalvageable; I directed that its trunk be removed, this being the only edible portion, and the creature buried in a seemly fashion, for we had come far together. As I was seeing to the elephant's disposal, I heard another shout.

At the head of the column, Nikias and Aaye were having a heated argument about some whitish rocks someone had uncovered.

"All right," I said, "what's the matter now?"

"I say they are recent," said Aaye. "A matter of a few years at most."

"Centuries," Nikias mumbled, "dawn of time."

"Oh, what's the bloody matter, you two?" I said.

The two stopped their wrangling for a moment, and looked at me. Then they began again, picking up their convoluted thoughts in mid-ramble, leaving me as befogged as before.

"But then how do you explain the patina of age, the hardness of the rock in which they appear encased—"

"Hardness my foot! That vertebra was lying right out in the open!"

I knew I had not the learning to follow their argument, so I looked in the approximate direction of their wildly gesticulating hands. I saw bones. *Giant* bones.

When I say *giant* I do not use this word lightly. For these were bones of such creatures as I had heard described to me by my nursemaid as an infant, dwarfing by far the bones of elephants and rhinoceroi. We were standing on a ledge over a sheer drop of some hundred passŭs. Ahead, on the other side of the rift, which I judged to be relatively recent, were skeletons of serpentine creatures, half-sunken in the rock. "These are the Titans themselves," I whispered. "Yes, the very Titans who struggled for the possession of the world before the Olympian gods gained the ascendancy."

Nikias my boyhood tutor was beside me now; he smiled a kindly smile such as I had rarely seen since becoming a man, such a smile as when he used to read to me from the *Odyssey* until I fell asleep to the clash of swords or the gnashing of Polyphemus's teeth. "You were always such a romantic child. How I hated to tell you the truth sometimes!" he said. "But Aaye and I are completely in agreement on this one point, and you should draw encouragement from this agreement, vindicating as it does the whole purpose of our little odyssey ...that these bones are nothing less than the actual remains of silkworms!"

"Good heavens," I said, somewhat disappointed.

"But you see," he went on, "I think that these remains have probably been around since the beginning of our present age; that they predate the Roman Epoch by as much as a thousand years. This would make them contemporaneous with the Trojan War, during the transition from the Silver Age to the present Age of Imperfection. And again, quite possibly, they may even go back to the Golden Age itself. Therefore, while it is established in the writings of P. Josephus Agricola that the Chinish silk is indeed produced from the oral excretions of giant worms, the presence of silkworm fossils within these hills does not necessarily imply that the Chinish Empire—"

"You forget the important circumstantial evidence," Aaye said, "of the Chinook dictionary and the fact that silk is still traded daily in the marketplaces of the Empire—"

"Yes, but no one can tell us where it comes from, or how long was the journey that brought it into the boundaries of the Empire, or how many times it may have changed hands during that period to cause the merchants who deliver the silk to be completely unaware of its origins—"

"Wait a minute," I said. "Are you telling me that this *proves* the existence of China?"

"Well—" said Nikias. "At one time or another, I suppose China must have been somewhere near here—"

"Then not for nothing have we come all this way, and braved so much?" How exciting! For the first time since our odyssey had begun I was elated; I believed in our journey's purpose. I was a veritable Ulysses—a Jason—an Aeneas, leading an exploratory expedition of unprecedented importance! "Summon the legionaries!" I cried. "Summon the standard-bearer, summon even my wife! I want everyone to see this, to know that we don't have much farther to go!"

Our comrades had all caught up now, and stood gazing in awe across the gorge of bones.

"Don't look like no silkworms to me," one legionary said. "Them things is lizards, giant lizards."

"If I had a name for them," said a Greek, "I'd call 'em *dinosauria*. To coin a word, that is."

"How dare you lower the morale of the company?" I raged. "Fifty lashes apiece, on the double!"

"Begging your pardon, General," said the first legionary, "but we ain't been paid in three months."

"A hundred lashes! Two hundred!"

"Now let's not go overboard here," Nikias said. "They've a right to their opinion."

"True, O procurator!" said Aaye. "These simple soldiers cannot possibly comprehend the complexities of modern scientific inquiry and theory."

"Very well," I said grandly, "I suppose you fellows are not to blame for lacking a classical education. Commuted—but don't let me hear such rubbish again!"

"Thank you, General, sir," they both said, scurrying off.

"That's settled then." I gazed proudly on the bones of the Chinish silkworms. For the first time I felt truly in command of this mission. It was good, too, to have begun by commuting the soldiers' sentence, an act of clemency that could not but augur well for our success. In my excitement I had the late elephant, whose burial I had earlier commanded, exhumed, and had our traveling all-purpose priest examine its entrails, which were also remarkably favorable; and I ordered castra set up right there, in the Valley of Dead Silkworms.

Later I was to discover that my name for the gorge had not stuck, but that the soldiers had in fact named it the Valley of the Dinosauria, after that stupid Greek's incautious remark; thus it is that the ignorant rule the earth, and those who endeavor to enlighten them are invariably forgotten. But I did not know it then.

That night, we dined on broiled elephant's trunk and a choice mountain goat our sagitarii had brought down. We had no wine of decent vintage; but a keg of fermented barley-water, chilled with Saxosic snow, went far towards banishing our cares. We stayed up half the night, reciting Chinish phrases to one another; *nika ticky muckamuck*, which signifies *I wish to eat*, was a particular favorite. Even the burden of bedding the Lady Oenothea was not unpleasant to me. And in the morning we set off singing Greek drinking songs, as the mountains soared ever skyward and the flying saucers glittered golden in the dawnlight.

CHAPTER
XXII

THINGS WENT MORE SMOOTHLY FROM THEN ON—
for a while at least. The pass we had discovered
was, by Nikias's reckoning, southwest of the Montes
Negri. Northward lay some of the tallest peaks of the
Montes Saxosi; but to the south they were less steep,
and we were able to march along some reasonably un-
bumpy terrain. It was for the most part short, brown,
scrubby grassland, but adequate fodder for the remaining
half-dozen elephants.

A fortnight after entering this stretch of territory we
encountered the first of the backwards-flowing rivers,
proving once and for all the validity of Platonic Idealism.

"And if we follow this river long enough," Aaye exclaimed excitedly, "we'll reach the Persian Gulf—and
good old Roman Egypt! So it must be somewhere along
this river, this land of Chin...just beyond the eastern-
most borders of the Empire...truly, O procurator, we
Roman citizens have conquered all the world, if but this
small strip remains to be subdued...."

"Let's not count our chickens, and all that," I said, as I motioned our Chirochian mahouts to take the elephants down to bathe in the waters. "I know these Chinish are supposed to be philosopher folk, and are thus liable to be as namby-pamby as were the Greeks when our legions annexed their lands; and that there is no match for Roman strategy, cunning, and ingenuity anywhere in the world"—I thought for a moment of the Olmechii, but dismissed the uncomfortable notion of their possible superiority from my mind—"yet my father taught me always to be cautious in my dealings with barbarians of any type."

"An admirable sentiment, my lord," Nikias said.

"And Aaye, pray tell me," I said, "you seem to be the expert . . . precisely what river *is* this?"

"Without a doubt, General, it is the Ganges."

"I see." I gave out some more orders about the pitching of castra. "Oh, Aquila!"

"Yes, General?" For some reason he had chosen today to wear a bewilderingly gaudy robe, stitched with seashells of different kinds, and his head was adorned with a golden wreath, eagle feathers, and beads. Several scalps, one sporting a particularly long bone serial-number tag, hung from his waist and his painted shield.

"Good heavens," I said. "Is this a wedding?"

"No. I'm just preparing myself to meet this Chinish folk of yours on their own terms."

"So you've given up your notion that this Chinook is a savage trade language, and are forced to bow to superior wisdom?"

He began to laugh. "Sometimes I wonder how you people ever managed to conquer your own front porticoes, let alone the world."

"You'll eat your words, Aquila!"

As the days passed I discovered that ignorance had triumphed yet again: that the soldiers had decided to name the Ganges River the Flumen Serpentis, or Snake River, because of its many tortuous twists. As Aaye and

Nikias argued over whether the Montes Saxosi were in fact identical to the legendary *Himavantish* or *Himalayan* mountains where dwell the *homines abominabiles nivis* (abominable men of snow) frequently mentioned in those popular romances which so often attempt to pass themselves off as more rigorous *scientifictiones*, we descended onto a verdant plain that hugged the river for many miles on each side. It was lush, unspoiled land; there were a few native villages here and there, which we subjugated without difficulty, using the surprise value of our elephants to good effect.

Yet, as the mountain wall receded ever farther to the east, we still found no vast cities, no temples, no pathways such as might be made by the constant ambulations of silkworms. And the Lady Oenothea became subject to constant fits of weeping, which I was at a loss to alleviate.

"You don't love me!" she screamed, pummeling me with her fists as the elephant lumbered forward like a trireme in a storm.

"My dear woman," I said, "it seems hardly fair for you to expect me to do so, considering that the Emperor foisted you off on me purely for your symbolic value. Not to mention your spying."

"I'd rather be married to some savage who adores me than to you! Procurator of Lacotia indeed!"

"Given your perfidious nature, my dear, I'm not surprised. But you are hardly in a position to become shrewish at the moment—"

"General! General!" came a shout from the head of the column. "They're here! They're here!"

"Who? Who?" I kicked the elephant, hoping to hurry it on a bit; but no luck. The creature was in a most refractory mood. I waited patiently while all the pachyderms were led behind me to form what was supposed to be an impressive array, and for the little band to gather in some semblance of order.

"Canoes approaching, General, sir!" said a legionary. "Dozens of them, by Jupiter!"

"Very well! Infantry—set up scuta. Equites—here behind me. Heavens, try to look a little more menacing! We've lost a lot of discipline on this trip, I can see that! Standard-bearer beside me—bucinae, be ready to give them a blast upon my signal! At long last we're going to have a little spectacle around here!"

There was much clanking and bumping of heads as the soldiers, no longer used to proper formations and so on, ran around trying to find their places.

"Remember all the Chinish phrases you've been learning?" said Nikias from the neighboring elephant.

"Got them right here." I pulled out a scroll on which Aaye had copied a number of important phrases from the Chinook dictionary—in hieroglyphics and Nikias had glossed them with approximate pronunciations in Greek letters. "*Nika potlach muckamuck,*" I mumbled to myself. "*Nika wakeh kumtux. . . .*"

They were coming now, rounding a bend of this Ganges River. The canoes were manned by sleek--muscled oarsmen; their prows were carved into the images of frightful deities. The savages wore no silk at all—indeed, apart from a few decorative seashells, they were quite naked. I took the abundance of shells to be a good sign, suggesting that we were not too far from the Persian Gulf and from civilization; as for their lack of silk, it was not to be thought proper for mere galley slaves such as these to be wearing such costly materials.

"It is just as P. Josephus Agricola said in his treatise on the legend of China!" Aaye said from another elephant. "These canoes are nothing but the sloughed-off skins of silkworms, hardened with an unguent of naphtha and embalming fluids!"

"Look like wooden dugouts to me," said a voice from a more distant elephant.

"Silence!" I shouted, recognizing the voice of that

Greek skeptic who had dared rename my silkworms dinosaurs.

The canoes had reached our bank now, and I could see the Chinish men clambering ashore. They waved bone-tipped spears at us, but seeing our elephants came no nearer.

"Call a parley!" I cried, unfolding my phrasebook to its fullest. Aquila, garbed in his ludicrous finery, I, Aaye, Oenothea, and Nikias dismounted our elephantine palanquins and came forward, the aquilifer with his SPQR-blazoned eagle striding proudly ahead.

As we approached, the naked savages broke ranks; and some grand-looking chieftains of theirs emerged. They wore full bonnets of multicolored plumes, and impressive cloaks of animal hides crisscrossed with necklaces of seashells. At their head was a potbellied, hawk-nosed fellow who did not appear terribly pleased.

They made straight for Aquila and began to address him in strange, whining tones.

"What is the meaning of this?" I said, outraged.

"I can't help it," Aquila said, "if among those present it is I who have the most regal demeanor." With a superb gesture he stripped off his cloak and handed it to the Chinish chieftain.

There was a moment of suspense as the chief looked it over, examining its workmanship; then, with an equally majestic flick of the wrist, he took off his own and handed it to Aquila. Both went through the motions of surprise at having received so great a gift, and disdain for the small worth of his own offering. This ceremony being completed, spontaneous applause broke out on both sides.

"That's it, Aquila!" said Aaye. "We'll be trading silks in no time."

"Now wait a minute," I said, charging up to the two Terra Novan chieftains. *"I'm* in command here, don't you know! I'll do the parleying, if you don't mind!"

The Chinook chieftain turned his attention to me, and I got the distinct impression that he did not think very much of me. "You'll pay Caesar's tax," I whispered to Aquila, "on the trading of every one of those scalps hanging on that vulgar garment you just gave away!"

The Chinooks continued to stare at me. Aquila shrugged. It was not entirely up to me to negotiate some kind of treaty with these natives, with some provisions for the trading of silk, and perhaps for the use of a few silkworms in the arena—what a spectacle that would be! —and so I cleared my throat portentously and glanced over my scroll of Chinish expressions, trying to find one moderately appropriate.

Now, the left-hand side of the scroll, with its Chinook words transliterated in Egyptian and then reglossed with Greek, began something like this:

υικα τικι μουκαμουκ

υικα πωτλατς ιακα
κωπα μικα

There was no problem here; barbarous as the sounds were, it would not be too hard, by following the Greek subscription, to frame them to my tongue. It was when I started to look for the translation that I ran into trouble.

There wasn't one. Well, there was, but it was in Egyptian alone. Those blasted pedants!

What was I to do? I turned to the others of my party, but they were all awaiting my next move. The barbarians were waiting, too. The future of Chinish-Roman relations depended on what I was about to say.

I decided to start at the beginning and work my way through. *"Nika ticky muckamuck!"* I said sternly, hoping that my tone, if not the words themselves, would establish in their eyes the might and majesty of Rome.

The chiefs looked at each other for a moment. Was this a declaration of war? So much the better; I could send for reinforcements and annex the land in a matter of months. After all, with our Persian Gulf possessions on one side and our Lacotians on the other, we had them surrounded.

The head chieftain clapped his hands; a naked savage brought forth a magnificent platter piled high with salmon and other delicacies. Ah yes, I remembered in time, that was the sentence for asking for food. No harm done there. The Chinish continued to stare at me strangely; I decided that I had best look over the viands, take a bite or two here and there, to show a certain noblesse oblige. When I had eaten a small piece of fish they acted decidedly jollier. They strutted back and forth, looking over my men and our accoutrements; they seemed to take a special interest in the elephants. Their chief reached out a hand and prodded one of them gingerly. It drew back and trumpeted, causing all sorts of weapons to be leveled at us. It was time for me to say something else. I read out the next thing on the scroll: *"Nika potlatch yaka kopa mika!"*

The reaction was sensational. The chieftains turned on me, awe in their eyes. The naked oarsmen fell on their knees and gazed adoringly.

"Goodness!" I said. "Damn brilliant stroke of diplomacy, if I say so myself, eh?"

"You fool!" hissed Aquila. "You just gave away that elephant!"

"Oh."

"You've just given the fellow a present so valuable he can't possibly find anything of equal worth to give in return."

"So?" I said, trying desperately to act as if it were all part of some diplomatic ploy. "Now they'll be eternally in Rome's debt; won't they?"

"If he cannot repay you," said Aquila, "he will kill you. And if he *can* repay you and *you* fail to pay him back impressively enough, you will be shamed in their eyes, and they will doubtless kill you. The outlook is hardly promising. Not to mention the fact that these are *not* the Chinish, as I have been telling you for the past few months, but merely a race of western Terra Novans who—"

"Enough!" This was a little much to take in all at once. Now as I examined the chieftain's face, it was true that his expression was not exactly benign at the moment. It was, in fact, one of unmitigated animosity. In what was obviously a huff, he whirled round and began to confer in a huddle with his colleagues.

Nikias said, "My Lord, you were never one for languages. I'm afraid you've put us in quite a pickle by answering his gift of a plate of smoked salmon with something as huge and valuable as an elephant. You have, in effect, utterly ridiculed his largesse. Apparently this *potlatching* in which you have foolishly indulged is an important ritual activity which—"

"Well, I've no intention of insulting their religion," I said, "just of laying my hands on their silk."

The chieftain finished his discussion at that point and barked an order at his slaves. One of them ran back to the canoes.

He returned presently, leading by the hand the most beautiful woman I had ever seen. He motioned her towards me. *"Nika potlatch nika okustee!"* he said angrily.

The girl smiled: dazzling teeth, bright eyes, long dark braided hair, smooth fawn complexion.

"I do believe," said Aquila, "that our chief here has just *potlatched* you his daughter."

"The discus is in your palaestra now," said Nikias.

"Help me, Aquila!" I moaned.

CHAPTER
XXIII

"WELL," AQUILA SAID. "I BELIEVE IT'S NOW your turn to reciprocate, General Titus. Give him something clearly of greater value than a daughter ... then you'll be ahead of the *potlatching* game."

"I see," I said, although I didn't.

We had resumed our travel along the Ganges (or the Flumen Serpentis, as it was known by everyone except the members of my immediate entourage), the elephants and infantry marching along the river within sight of the vast convoy of gargoyle-prowed canoes. I and Oenothea and my little group had been reluctantly invited to share the canoe of the chieftain, whose barbarous name proved incapable of transcription into any civilized tongue, but appeared to mean something like He-Who-Hooteth-the-Names-of-his-Innumerable-Foes, the hooting referring to the owl, their bird of death. Nikias remarked that the Athenians had a not-dissimilar belief,

147

in that an owl hooting in the agora by day was deemed an omen of the direst import.

"Yes, even among us Lakotah a man who gives away all his belongings is accounted a great man, and so a pauper may be the most respected member of the tribe—"

"A strange philosophy indeed," I snorted, "which we Romans have endeavored to rectify wherever possible, teaching you the value of gold and silver, and—"

"Compound interest and corporate land-ownership—" Aaye added importantly.

"Be that as it may," said Aquila, "we Lakotah have never carried this custom to this excess. Why, it seems to be the whole basis of their culture!" He indicated a nearby canoe, in which two of the Chinish (as I still thought them to be) were engaged in a heated exchange of gifts.

"Good heavens," I said. "What a peculiar way to manage a civilization! Is it possible, then, that the silks for which our Roman matrons pay so dearly were actually *given* away by the Chinish, and that we could actually have silk for the asking, merely by proffering the right gifts in return?"

"Possible," said Aquila, "but you *will* persist in this delusion that this is China, when I tell you quite plainly that—"

"Silence, savage!" I said peremptorily.

"I can hardly wait," Aaye said, "to see their corrals full of silkworms, and to see their splendid worm-riders as they lasso the worm herds, taming their refractory spirits to the constant production of their precious sputum."

"Indeed," I said, "a magnificent spectacle."

We were passing through landscapes lush beyond belief now. Grass green as moss alternated with dense forests. Later we were treated to the sight of a canyon of titanic dimensions, and blazoned in rich hues of umber and maroon, which the Flumen Serpentis, surely a god of many talents, had carved from the living mountains; then there were more verdant plains rich with game, which my sagitarii hunted when we tired of smoked salmon, the savages' staple diet. The chieftain must have been, as savages went, a fairly important one; his "insignificant little escort," as he insisted on calling it, numbered some dozens of canoes, each painted in gaudy hues and manned by some twenty or thirty of naked oarsmen.

Soon, I thought, surely *soon* we will reach the Persian Gulf. Then it will be time to turn the tables; but until then, I had better dissemble, and I had better learn this game of *potlatching* well.

We were just circumambulating (to avoid dashing our boats and ourselves to pieces) an impressive waterfall, which I had decided to name after the Emperor Trajan (the name has not stuck), when I began casting about for a gift of sufficient value to match that of a chieftain's daughter.

My eye fell upon the Lady Oenothea.

"Dear wife," I said, "did you not once say to me that you would rather be married to some savage who valued you, rather than to Yours Truly, who does not?"

"Indeed, but—" she protested. But then she smiled grimly.

I was feeling better already. The chief's young daughter, whom I had necessarily bedded in order not to seem unimpressed by the gift, had proved not only companionable, but mercifully silent. I could present her to Trajan later on as a captive Chinish princess, and no doubt she could march in my train during my triumph as part of my spoils of war, decked with bolts of silk and the bones of silkworms . . . I was awakened from my reverie by the confluence of the river with one even mightier.

"Where are we?" I said, to no one in particular.

"My dear General!" said Aaye with tears in his eyes. "We have undoubtedly reached the great river Indus! We are not far from home at all!"

"Oh? I didn't know they were connected. I mean, the Indus and the Ganges."

"Nor did I. But it seemed the most scientific deduction I can make at the moment."

Chief Hooting-Owl grunted and addressed some commands to his paddlers. He had been ignoring us all through this journey, even as he plied us constantly with salmon, salmon roe, salmon pâté, fresh salmon eyes, salmon oil, and the like. It occurred to me that they must know nothing of the glorious decadence of our Roman banquets. I could not fail to notice, either, that the chief's language, when not addressing us, was quite different from the Chinook we had been using. A little doubt nagged at me; perhaps Aquila had been right all along, and these were mere savages such as the Lacotii themselves had been? But no; Aquila was surely merely jealous. After all, no one could possibly *like* the idea of a more civilized culture coexisting upon the same continent as one's own, could they? It was thus that I rationalized away Aquila's scornful remarks for the time being.

Perhaps, I thought, I should try a little conversation.

"Um . . . how's the silk this year?"

The question was translated through Nikias and Aaye, who had to use some tremendous circumlocution to describe silk.

"Silk?" said Hooter in a surly tone. "What silk?"

I concluded that its manufacture must be some sort of religious secret; after all, I, who was a general and a procurator, knew nothing about the workings of motorcars or bicycles. We traveled on.

"Have you met, O Hooter-of-et cetera, my good wife, the Lady Oenothea, Princess of Cilicia?" (I shall henceforth omit the complex ritual of translation and its concomitant ballet of elucidatory gesticulatons.)

"She is wondrous strange."

"She's yours."

The chief looked at me long and hard, as if trying to

ascertain whether or not I had made him the butt of
some cruel joke...and at long last he laughed aloud.
"Thank you, O stranger," he said. "A brilliant move in
the game of *potlatch*. But you won't get out of this
lightly." He beckoned Oenothea to his side; she went
quite willingly, it seemed. "I have a most tremendous
potlatch planned for our arrival in my home city, such as
the Kwakiutl have not seen in a thousand moons of
moons. No foreign chieftain with mysterious two-tailed
beasts-of-burden is going to beat *me* at the ritual of *potlatch*! Here, *ticky muckamuck*?" He threw me a piece of
raw salmon liver.

"Delicious, I'm sure," I said, wondering why he had
referred to his people as the Kwakiutl, and not the Chinish race. I must also mention that all of these people, the
beautiful daughter not excluded, stank most abominably
of raw fish, and had I not been obliged by the exigencies
of diplomacy to deal with them, I would probably have
had them long since executed or at least sentenced them
to the nearest arena. But I needed the silk as evidence
for the Emperor Trajan. I tried asking again about the
silk, and about the giant silkworm bones I had seen earlier.

"Oh, they're giant lizards," said the chieftain.

I diplomatically swallowed my disbelief. I had heard
from Aaye, who frequently quoted the works of P. Josephus Agricola to me, that the Chinish are an inscrutable
race; it was not impossible that this whole production
was an elaborate ruse.

"Oh, they are, eh? Jolly good."

"Titus, the sea!" Nikias exclaimed.

And sure enough—

A salt smell assailed out nostrils. We could as yet see
very little of the ocean; it peeped out through distant
crags. My heart leapt with excitement. The Persian Gulf!
Or the Arabian Sea, perhaps...at any rate, proof posi-
tive that the world was round!

And now we saw dozens of huts lining the river; the

canoes were being towed to the bank, and women and children, quite as starkers as our oarsmen had been, began rushing into the waves to greet us. Huge wooden lodges stood out from the houses; and each was guarded by a solemn pillar of wood, sculpted into a pile of those hideous demon faces which had decked the prow of each canoe.

Meanwhile, our elephants had come charging behind us, spraying the mob with their trunks and making a fearful racket, mostly to the delight rather than the terror of the mob, however; from this I gathered that an advance canoe had been sent with news of our impending arrival.

As our chieftain stepped off our canoe, he began to bellow forth an announcement in his own Quaquiutish speech, which was rapidly translated into Chinook for our benefit, and thence into Greek by Nikias. It was to the effect that we were chieftains from a distant land, and had presented him with an elephant and a princess; and that there would shortly be a grand *potlatch* of unprecedented proportions.

During the entirety of his speech, Lady Oenothea clung to him, practically devouring him alive. The chieftain did not seem at all bothered by this, however; it seemed to be the way he expected all women to behave.

"This is it," I said. "We shall either return to Rome laden with silks and carrying a treaty (which Trajan can proceed to break at his leisure) or we shall end up as spectacle-fodder. It might be the most brilliant deplomatic coup of my life."

"And then again," said Aquila, "it might not."

CHAPTER
XXIV

IN THE MORNING MY SMALL COMPANY AND I WENT OUT
to the seashore and looked out. It was a clear, warm
day; gulls cried, and many of the local peasantry were to
be seen in their canoes, spearing fish and what have you,
by the ruddy dawnlight.

"You know," I said, "considering the evidence *in toto*,
somehow I don't think we're in China any more."

"What nonsense!" Aaye said. "How can you go
against every shred of scientific evidence?"

Nikias said, "I am not as loath to give up an implausi-
ble theory as you are, Aaye. I suspect that China is still
... farther off."

Aquila gave an I-told-you-so sort of shrug.

"So what shall I do?" I said to him. "You always seem
to know what to do."

"Well, you'll have to figure out some way of subju-
gating them; Trajan will perhaps be mollified at the news
of a new province."

"Indeed. But what of the dictionary? It worked,

didn't it? They *do* speak this Chinish speech here, after a fashion. And the silkworms' bones . . . surely incontrovertible proof—" said Aaye.

"Will you be quiet, you . . . you . . . *Egyptian!*" I said. "Now, the question remains: how shall we put a good face on all this?"

"We could leave," said Nikias, "before we come even more embroiled in this *potlatching* business."

"*I'm* happy to be left here," said Oenothea, who had emerged positively radiant from the marital bed of Hooting-Owl.

"A true Roman wouldn't run away," I said.

"I suppose not," said Nikias.

"In the meantime, there are all these new places to be named. What, for instance, of this great ocean we have discovered? Trajan would like it named, I'm sure; he thinks that naming things gives one power over them."

"Well, it looks awfully peaceful," said Nikias. "How about the *Oceanus Pacificus*?"

Everyone nodded, except me. "It's too much of a cliché. We should name it *after* someone; one of the gods, perhaps, or some Emperor."

"How about the *Oceanus Papinianus*?" Aaye said slyly, trying to inveigle himself back into my good graces.

"That sounds . . . that does have a certain ring to it," I said, hardly able to contain myself. "And after all, I *am* the first *civilized* person to set eyes upon it, the first trueborn Roman . . . you fellows being, of course, merely foreigners who have been granted the citizenship."

"The Oceanus Papinianus it is," said Aquila, "you conceited man."

Ah, perfidious fate! The name did not stick, and instead the new ocean is invariably referred to by that nondescript, absurd name, quite unsuited to its grandeur and magnificence, the Oceanus Pacificus.

"Look!" Nikias cried.

"By the mons veneris of Isis!" Aaye said. "Another of those infernal saucers!"

Sure enough, there it was, skimming the sea-surface in the middle distance.

"Curse you!" I shouted at it, more in sadness than anger. "You lead us on to the very edge of the world, taunting us, never answering our questions. If you are gods, you are the most recalcitrant of them all. By what mysteries should we propitiate you? By what rites ensure your goodwill? What have I done to so incur your wrath, to make me into a veritable Ulysses of the modern age?" It was a passable piece of rhetoric in a style then fashionable in certain Athenian schools of sophistry; and the others applauded me as I finished.

"But perhaps," said Aquila, "they are nothing more than what they have told us; creatures from the distance future in pursuit of a criminal guilty of altering the very fabric of the universe."

"Bah!" said Aaye. "If even our Greek and our sage Egyptian philosophers cannot understand the nature of reality, how can you, a savage, presume to expound on this subject with such simplistic remarks, not even bothering to dignify them with the barest modicum of rhetorical figures and classical paradoxes?"

"Nevertheless," Nikias said, "when it comes to the nature of the One, Aquila may have touched upon a point—"

"Will you shut up with your damned ontology?" I said, exasperated. "The fact is, the were-jaguars are behind all this, somehow, Jove knows how. And I think we should keep them happy. What about those jade werejaguar amulets that they gave us in Olmechia? I for one have always worn one ever since then, as a lucky charm."

"And I," said Nikias.

"And I," said Aaye.

"And . . . even I," said Aquila. "Well, there are times

when dancing doesn't quite do the trick, and it's best to be prepared."

Suddenly—

"What was that?" A deep thundering noise boomed from the village.

"The drums! The *potlatch* is beginning!" my comrades shouted all at once. We made haste towards the village of these people, whom we now knew to be the race of Quaquiutii.

As we approached the main lodge of the village, the drums grew ever more deafening. Quaquiutish minstrels chanted and dancers capered. The door was guarded by some twenty of those pillars-of-gruesome-faces, which we had named *totem poles*. As we entered we saw more of the totem poles, and at the far end of the lodge, a sight to chill our very marrow.

There was a totem pole, larger than the others, and on it was sculpted several times—

The face of the godlike were-jaguar, rider of the flying saucer, sustainer of the Olmechian super-science!

And then I noticed the other face, with which it alternated.

It was neither bear, nor ape, nor man, but a hairy combination. Its fangs were bared. I could not tell what it was, but I knew instinctively that, unlike the rest of the totem poles with their stylized representation, and like the image of the were-jaguar, which I had seen in the flesh . . . that this monster had been carved from life!

"What is it?" I said.

"It is nothing less," said Aaye, "than an exact reproduction of one of the *homines abominabiles nivis*, or abominable men of snow, said to be found in the Himalayas. Aha! My theory has been vindicated after all! This *is* China!"

"Well, we know the were-jaguars really exist," I said. "It strongly suggests that these creatures, too, exist. I think we're in for quite an adventure."

The chieftain and his people began filing in, decked in all their finery.

"By Jove!" I said. "Imagine all this barbaric splendor as a side show in the arena."

For the Quaquiutii had covered their naked bodies with woven-sea-shell garments of brilliant hues; and drums pounded, chilling the blood. Hundreds of men and women filled the wooden lodge, chattering and giggling, and bevies of children ran chirping without any proper Roman discipline at all. It was this appalling lack of the sense of *order*—for a firm sense of order is inculcated into the minds even of civilizations inferior to our own—that convinced me, in the final analysis, that this was not China at all, but some enclave of hideous savages who might at any moment execute me horribly for some unknowing breach of their inscrutable barbarous customs.

The music welled up. I stood immutable, every inch the Roman procurator, I thought; my new wife, my tutor, and the rest of my entourage seemed rather to be enjoying the vulgar rhythms of the savage bards, and rocking to and fro to the music. Presently the barbarians performed a number of dances, most of which seemed to consist of marching ungracefully around in a circle to the accompaniment of deafening poundings and wolflike howlings. Then followed dances of bacchanalian wildness, performed by dozens of men in wooden masks, decked in feathers and robes of beaten cedar-bark. The dimness of the cavernous lodge was now illumined only by the flickering of wood fires; the flames seemed to lap at the grotesque wooden faces of man and totem pole, to accentuate their crevasses of darkness. And among the dancers too, I noticed, were sculpted masks of the were-jaguar and the abominable snowman; here as with the totem poles, these particular faces seemed to breathe with verisimilitude by contrast with the stylized stiffness of the other gods' visages.

"And now," Chief Hooting-Owl declared, after the seemingly interminable proceedings had become a little less noisy, "I shall present the Bulbous-nosed Chieftain from the East such presents as he has never seen before! Never let it be said I am niggardly in my *potlatches*! Never let it be said that I, greatest and most generous of the Quaquiutii, can give less generously than a mere foreigner!"

I could not suppress a laugh. "Why," I said to my companions, "the man is actually besotted enough to believe that *he* is the civilized one, and *we* are the barbarians!"

"Truly it is enough to awaken any man's compassion," Aquila said, and though the sentiments were natural enough I couldn't help but detect a note of sarcasm in his utterance.

"But, Nikias and Aaye . . . *our* gifts!" I went on. "Are they prepared? We've not come unequipped to deal with this savage on his own terms, have we?"

"Heavens, no!" Aaye said. "I intend to make a good showing of the Egyptian art of diplomatic razzle-dazzle."

"It had better be good," I said, remembering our debacle with the Olmechii.

The chieftain turned to me. First he lifted off his amazing headdress; it was made of wood and human hair, and chiseled into the shape of a whale—an astonishingly fine work of art to have come from savage hands. With an air of utter disdain, he laid it in front of me. "This royal headdress," he said, "is a thousand years old. It came to me in a grand *potlatch* last year, when we roundly routed the Northern Tlingit by superior show of generosity. Take that, barbarian!" More things were laid at our feet by slaves: delicate sculptures of wood and whale ivory, bark blankets curiously hand-dyed into the shapes of mythological scenes. Young slave girls and boys bound with leather ropes, naked to reveal their physical perfections, their skin sleek with fresh salmon oil. They were quite beautiful as long as one held one's nose; after I'd cleaned them up a bit they'd fetch me a fortune on the auction block in Rome. I remained impassive, however; I realized that to be impressed was to take a resounding loss in this bizarre diplomacy.

I smiled. I no longer made the mistake of essaying the Chinookish tongue; I left it to the scholars in my party. At a gesture from me, centurions tramped into the room with gifts of my own. In order to lend the show an air of mystery, our resident expert on hokum, Aaye, had ordered that the offerings be hidden behind three huge arrases cut from the fabric of one of our tents. We hadn't brought much, so I had perforce to rely on the alienness of our presents and Aaye's brilliant propensity for mendacity. Oh, it galled me to have to trust to an Egyptian's wits; but the Empire must use what resources it can to further its great mission, the civilizing of the world. And better, of course, to have a foreigner be dishonest, than to sully the purity of a Roman's tongue.

"In the first place," Aaye said, "we'd like to give you our remaining three elephants. These are magical beasts that when properly trained render one invincible in war."

The chief snorted. "You have already given me one of the beasts-with-two-tails," he said. "And of the remaining three of yours, one is a mere infant, the other aged, the third suffering from a continual flux of the bowels. Indeed, your generosity overwhelms me!" The assembly of Quaquiutii laughed uproariously; we were obliged to follow suit, but our own laughter sounded pitiful by comparison.

We had on hand, behind the first of the tapestries, a finely worked Persian carpet, which we laid on the ground. Upon it we had placed the most valuable objects from my tent; two flagons of greenish-blue glass, which Aaye had filled with a foul poultice of elephant dung and wine.

"Behold!" Aaye cried impressively, as the cloth was drawn back.

"This is all you can produce? Beware! I am not easily mocked," said the chieftain.

"Lo, the wonders of Roman technology!" Aaye continued, unfazed. "Look at the quality of this glass, this rare substance manufactured from the tears of the gods themselves . . . and within, a potion that renders the most impotent man a towering edifice of passion! That restores full hair growth to the bald! That—"

"Indeed," said the chieftain, rubbing his head thoughtfully. He was not terribly impressed. When he picked up the glass flagon, it shattered, befouling his costly robe.

"Perhaps—you would prefer to peek behind curtain number two?" said Aaye.

"You mock our sacred rituals!" the chieftain said.

"Go through the whole script," I whispered urgently. "At least we can buy time." For we were heavily outnumbered, of course.

"Behind curtain number two—"

"This is foolery!" the chieftain shouted, striding forward to rip down the makeshift canopies. Behind the second were some jars of unguents and a few out-of-date newspapyri, which Aaye had planned to pass of as ritual formulae and incantations ("For," he had told me, "our own priests habitually practice such deceptions on the common populace"), and a rusty steampipe from a defunct motor-car which one of our Greek soldiers had kept as a souvenir, and which Aaye intended to pass off as a device for detecting fine shifts in the motions of the stars.

Aaye began his explanations, but the chief raged on. "Fools! And to think that I greeted you as messengers from a distant civilization as advanced as our own, when all you offer me are meaningless scribbles on thin sheets, breakable jugs, and an old shit-pipe! And what's behind curtain number three? More rubbish, I suppose!" He marched towards it and pulled it down. I gulped. For

behind it was one of our catapults, and it was intended
that, at the signal of the curtain being torn down, it
would shower the chieftain with gold. Instead it clouted
Hooting-Owl firmly in the jaw and sent him sprawling
across the lodge.

A less mighty-thewed man would have been knocked
cold, but not this one. He rose up again, furious, shouting for his masked dancers to surround us.

"Hold!" I screamed. "I was but testing you, foolish
ones. One gift have I yet!" I tore my jade were-jaguar
from my neck and threw it onto the floor. The others of
my company swiftly did the same.

All the Quaquiutii recoiled in horror; then they fell
prostrate at our feet.

"That's more like it," I said, feeling better already.

"My lord. . . ." The chieftain cringed visibly at my
baleful glare. "We will give you everything! Our homes!
Our villages! Our lands! Our salmon! Only have mercy!"

"I'm sure Caesar, your White and Greatest Father,
can be prevailed on to show compassion," I said at
length. "Very well, we accept your offer of eternal servi-
tude."

When this was duly translated, a change came over
the chieftain, and he began openly to weep. "What is the
matter?" I said, trying to show the proper admixture of
severity and mercy, yet inwardly gloating over our victory and reflecting on the fact that the flying saucer-
creatures had saved our lives yet a third time.

"Alas, our lands are not ours to give you, O Bulbous-
nosed Chieftain," Hooting-Owl sobbed. "We are thralls
to a terrible and evil power. But you . . . wear the symbol
of the little green masters. Surely you can aid us."

"What power?" I said. "Tell us. Caesar is omnipotent!
I myself shall lead an expeditionary force against who-
ever dares molest you." I was in my element now, acting
out the role of the great general.

"You will truly save us from our overlords, our oppressors?" said Hooting-Owl.

"My word as Caesar's mouthpiece on it!"

Slowly a smile formed on the savage chieftain's face. I did not like the smile. The crowd parted; looking straight ahead, I saw the largest of the totem poles, in its place of honor, lit by the flickering firelight. I saw the master whom they feared most.

The face of *homo abominabilis nivis*.

"Sasquatch," the chieftain murmured.

"You expect me to go against . . . *that*?" I shuddered at the fierce features, animated by the flames, at the huge hollow eyes, the glistening fangs so chillingly rendered in whalebone.

"You have given your word, haven't you? As the mouthpiece of the High One."

Slowly it dawned on me.

"By Jupiter!" I stammered. "I've been tricked!"

I stared from Aquila to Aaye, back and forth, unable to believe that I had bungled so badly as to get myself conned into going against a possibly supernatural foe. For if I balked now, the honor of Rome itself would suffer, and I would almost certainly end up as an unwilling celebrant in one of Trajan's miserly spectacles. And this time I wouldn't be laughing about Trajan's tawdry taste, either.

"I should never have attempted this ludicrous alien diplomacy!" I shouted.

My two old comrades nodded sagely, for once agreeing with me completely. I knew who had won the game of *potlatch* that day. I'd never had a chance.

Chief Hooting-Owl started to screech with laughter, a hideous racket. So that's how he'd come by that name!

We stared at the image of the abominable snowman for a long time, awed, hushed. At last the silence was interrupted by the voice of old Aaye. "I knew it!" he was saying. "These barbarians could never have been the mighty Chinish civilization. It is *this* that is the final link in the puzzle! Legends of abominable snowmen in the mountains beyond India—and now these Sasquatii: a race of giants, masters of super-science! It all makes sense now! Gentlemen . . . we have the honor of being the first civilized creatures to gaze knowingly on the likeness of . . . a Chinaman!"

Chapter
XXV

T HUS IT WAS THAT I FOUND MYSELF, MY SMALL CO-
terie of querulous old men, and Aquila, stalking off
into the lush thick pine forests of this land that was not
China, at the head of a decidedly ragtag band of centurions. The ground was disagreeably wet; ferns snagged
continually at our caligae. We had no idea what we were
up against—man, magic, or divinity. All we knew was
that our feet were muddy, our noses stuffy from the constant damp, and that each of our experts had a pet theory
to which I was forced to listen at length. One consolation
was that we had been permitted to retain our Olmechian
jade were-jaguars; it was possible that these talismans
might save our souls again, after all, unlikely as it
seemed.

Our path was clear enough. Every now and then a
little abominable-snowman-shaped totem pole peered
from the ferns. Following these signposts, we trudged
ever deeper into the forest.

Needless to say, I was not pleased at this turn of

events. Far from cleverly fooling some simpleminded peasants, we had actually been tricked by them into seeking out and attacking some legendary beast!

"And they can't lose!" I moaned. "If we are killed, the better for them; if we dispatch the Sasquatii, we vanquish their oppressors for them! These Quaquiutii are *masters* of this *potlatching*."

Yes. Over a banquet of whole smoked salmon, mountains of salmon roe on dishes of curiously carved whalebone drenched with salmon oil, which had impressed us Romans by its quantity if not its variety, Hooting-Owl had told us the whole story. For generations, the Sasquatii had been settlers in the area, exacting a tribute of salmon and slaves. Occasionally a were-jaguar would be seen too, but no one knew what their place was in the scheme of things, and so it was thought wisest to propitiate both. And the flying saucers? There had been more than usual in the past few days, but they were not considered particularly unusual.

"How many days have we been traveling?" I said.

"About five hours, General," said Nikias.

"It seems like an eternity. Let's eat."

"We only have a few days' supply, General, and it's all dried salmon."

We trudged onward.

Presently we came to a clearing in the forest, where there was a sort of circle of the miniature totem poles.

"This must be the place Hooting-Owl told us of," said Aquila, "where they leave their offerings to the abominable snowmen, and run quickly away before they're caught."

"Look!" cried Aaye. "Monstrous footprints!" He had tripped and half-fallen into one.

"What an enormous footprint!" I said.

"You know," Aaye was saying, "it would be nice to give the creature some proper name, rather than this barbarous *sasquatius*. It doesn't sit well on the tongue."

"You're right," my tutor said. "How about *megapus*? Look at the size of that footprint."

"*Megapus*. Yes. *Bigfoot*. A good Greek word. Has a certain majesty to it. I think that the scientists back at the Academy will be very pleased—"

"In the name of Jupiter Vacantancae!" I said. "What does it matter what it's called, when it's going to kill us any moment?" Dread gnawed my innards as I scrutinized the gargantuan footprint. "What now?" I said.

"Wait," said Aquila. "Build a campfire. Smoke."

"But—they could be hiding behind these very trees!"

"We do not know that. Best to make our minds still. It is a good day to die, eh, what?"

"It's never a good day to die," I grumbled.

"Come, young Titus!" Aquila said. "When I first met you, you were ready to commit suicide at a moment's notice. You are older and wiser now, no? Be of good cheer. Listen, I'll sing you a song! *Eya-ha-ha*—"

"Lovely, Aquila, but—"

Just then, we heard a deafening roar. And a ponderous, pounding footfall. And a hideous, earsplitting laughter that seemed to rock the very forest. "Good heavens!" I cried. "The Sasquatii are approaching already!"

They were all around us, suddenly, a couple dozen of the creatures, well over five cubits tall, their toothy jaws slavering, their arms waving wildly.

"What are we to do?" I screeched. "Quick, form a phalanx!" We huddled together. One of the *megapodes* lumbered forward and shoved some centurions aside, guffawing horribly.

"Pila! Scuta!" I shouted. But our weapons had been knocked out of our hands. There was only one thing left to do. I yanked my were-jaguar talisman off my neck, and bade the others do the same. Then we advanced, holding them up like the insignia of exorcizers.

"Begone," Aaye was intoning, "in the name of the sacred Olmechian were-jaguar—"

It was a ludicrous spectacle, and should not have

stopped them for a moment. But to our surprise they halted and looked at us long and hard; and then they ceased their attack. The tallest of them, his fur a mottled yellow-white, ambled forward and saluted us.

"*Shalom*," he said distinctly, and then muttered some words which were in a tongue I half-recognized—

"Good heavens!" Nikias said. "The Judaean speech! These Sasquatii are Jews!"

The head *megapus* bowed gravely to us and said (his speech was translated for us by Nikias, who had, in his boyhood in Alexandria, known many speakers of Aramaic, and had also a nodding acquaintance with the Hebrew tongue), "Greetings, O children of the little green masters! Forgive us our peculiar and unprepossessing appearance, which is alas, not our doing; all will be explained to you shortly. My name is Abraham bar-David, and I am the patriarch of this merry band here."

"But—but—" I said.

"Not a word more! You shall be our honored guests. I shall be most happy to lead you to our humble city, and to introduce you to the little green masters themselves. They are, I am sure, dying to meet you."

With that he turned around, gestured expansively with his furry arm, and led us further onward into the forest.

Chapter
XXVI

WELL, DEATH HAD BEEN STAVED OFF FOR AN HOUR or two at least. We followed the tall Sasquatii deeper and deeper into the woods; presently the rough path broadened into a paved road with a gleaming surface. The trees thinned, and suddenly, gasping, I could see what lay behind them, in the vale beneath.

"A city!" I shouted.

"A vast and splendid city!" cried Nikias, as we saw strange metal columns and curious spires, and flying saucers soaring back and forth among them.

"At last," Aaye said smugly. "We have been vindicated. There is indeed a splendid civilization here. The Sasquatii and the Chinish folk . . . are one!"

"You are terminally stupid, Egyptian," said Aquila. "You should stop bending the facts to your theories, and accept truths as they come."

For once I had to applaud the old Lakotah chieftain. Barbarian he might have been, but the Emperor *had* made him a senator, and when you were used to his funny ways, he wasn't a bad sort.

The road wound downward toward the city, a splendid agglomeration of metal spires and curiously shaped columns. There stood expansive platforms perched on gilded towers, where fleets of the flying-saucer things waited, ready to swarm skyward at a second's notice. What an outlandish city it was! The buildings were in pure geometrical shapes of the kind I had learnt about from my tutor, as a young boy struggling with Euclid: they were icosahedrons, octohedrons, domes, and glittering spheres that swam of their own accord in the very air, emitting an otherworldy music.

"The resonances are positively Pythagorean in their primal purity!" Aaye babbled happily.

There were little green men everywhere. Some resembled the were-jaguars of our previous acquaintance; others looked like nothing so much as those mannikins of dough that old women love to bake. Others still were like enormous lobsters or fibrillating octopodes.

As some of the more monstrous miscreants approached, our Greek and Romans made signs to ward off the evil eye; our Lacotian centurions, however, seemed to accept it all with equanimity, and the Sasquatii, human though they claimed themselves to be, were utterly unmoved by the sight of these prodigies.

"What city is this?" I asked of our host, the self-proclaimed Jewish patriarch.

"It is a city," he said impressively, "neither here nor there; neither within your time nor out of it; it is the Time Citadel of the Dimensional Patrol Corps."

"Foolish man!" said Aaye scornfully. "Still trying to hide the fact that we have stumbled at last upon China itself." At which the Sasquatii burst into raucous and abundant laughter.

"At least," I said, "if this is truly the land of our old friends the were-jaguars, we should be safe here. They have never meant us any harm, which is more than can be said for, say, Caesar himself."

"True, O procurator," said Nikias, as we ascended by an elevating device up one of the saucer parapets, "but it would be nice to know what this all means; and if our friends here are indeed Judaeans, what god has metamorphosed them into such terrifying shapes."

"Oh, I expect the little green masters will want to tell you himself," said Abraham bar-David. "It's a long story."

We entered now—this is the truth, I swear it upon the maidenhead of Artemis—into a transparent bubblelike vehicle, which carried us through the air into the heart of one of the golden flying spheres. Soon we stepped out into a chamber of dimensions huger even than the Flavian Amphitheater or Colosseum of Rome itself; and there, before our very eyes, enthroned in splendor, sat—

"Jupiter help us!" I said. "It's V'Denni-Kenni, himself; I'd know him anywhere!" Actually I wasn't a bit sure; but as we neared the seat of power I became convinced that this was truly the very were-jaguar whose flying saucer had plucked us off the sacrificial altar so long ago, that day of the solar eclipse in the land of the Olmechii. I could hardly contain my joy. "Do I dare to hope? Ah, V'Denni-Kenni, our old friend—may I call you friend, O sublime one?—once more you have appeared at the moment of our direst need!" In my enthusiasm I no longer spoke any of the barbarous languages I had half-mastered. I broke out into the Emperor's Latin, and jolly proud of it, too. I knew that the walls would be implanted with translating devices, and that they would shortly reverberate with the Green One's reply.

And reply there was.

"Those infernal Romans again! For god's sake, K'Tooni-Mooni, can't you *ever* steer a straight course through those transdimensional disjunctive nodes? Sometimes I despair of you!" One of the giant lobsters emerged, then a large green octopus; they began conversing in their language, ignoring us completely.

It was Aquila who finally got through to them.

"Now look here," he said. "You may be gods or men of the future; I care not. For all I know, I may be at this moment relaxing in the comfort of a sweat-lodge back in Lacotia, smoking dreamweed, and am here only as a wraith, a traveler on a spirit journey. You may all be phantasms. But my aching bones certainly don't think so. I'm an old man and a chief of the Lacotii, so perhaps you might begin by telling me if I'm still in this world or not. And after, I think the General has a story to tell."

"We apologize," said V'Denni-Kenni. "You *are*, in a manner of speaking, in this world. And as for your tale —proceed."

And so it was that I blurted out the entire story of our mission. Of Trajan's parsimoniousness. Of the Lady Oenothea's unpleasant embraces and the subsequent charms of Hooting-Owl's daughter. Of the attack of Siannii. Of *potlatchings* and the skeletons of silkworms.

"And all I want now," I said, "is for you to send us back. I don't know what vast conflict you may be involved in, whether there's war in heaven as there was during the time of the Trojan War—but I don't want any part of it! I don't see why you should send your flying saucers after us, following us up and down the River Miserabilis, bobbing up at every crisis, and not even telling us what's happening or where we're supposed to be going—"

I was weeping now, in full view of my men. It was a shameful, disgusting sight, but I was beyond caring about the old Roman virtues and dignities. I didn't want any part of anything at all.

"Blasphemy!" Aaye was saying to me. "You make demands of the very gods?" And even Abraham, who only believed, of course, in that rather nebulous, invisible Judaean god, looked a little sheepish.

The green lobster, were-jaguar, and octopus conferred among themselves for a few short moments.

"O men of the distant past," said V'Denni-Kenni at last. "You saw flying saucers all along the way here?"

"Yes," I said.

"You have details of all the sightings? Dates, directions, numbers of saucers spotted?"

"I think Nikias and Aaye together can supply you with them." And the three green creatures listened as the old sages told all they could remember about our sightings.

The were-jaguar nodded gravely. "It is just as I thought! Ah, I deplore the directive that prevents us from manifesting ourselves throughout the continua we must police! Otherwise *we* could have spotted the criminal long before this. The final confrontation is about to happen! The moment of ultimate truth! Yes, some of your sightings we can account for, you know, regular traffic between Olmechia and here, but others . . . yes, it is clear! The Time Criminal is near, and analysis of your data indicates that he has moved westward, towards the island at the nexus of the universes! We must ready ourselves for the coming battle." And he made as if to leave the room.

"Wait! What about *us*?" I said.

They stopped for a moment and looked us over.

"Oh, you tiresome Romans again," said the lobster. "Well, you've helped us, and I suppose we owe you some sort of explanation. An oath of secrecy, though, first."

Aquila laughed. "You think anyone would believe us even if we told?"

"I suppose not," said the octopus. "Well, here we go. . . ."

Thus it was that V'Denni-Kenni told us the following incredible tale:

"There are," he began, "billions upon billions of universes; they lie side by side within a transdimensional continuum, and each is but a hair's breadth different from its neighbor. You might think that billions and billions would be enough for anyone; but there are always others who want more. And thus it was that the Time Criminal came to be.

"No one knows his identity. But we, the Dimensional Patrol, have detected his presence through a series of shattering paradoxes that threaten the very fabric of the universe. For some years ago (in our own time, unimaginable to you) it was noticed, during routine policing of the time-lines, that neighboring universes were no longer just slightly askew from each other. Someone had been traveling through the time-lines, changing here and changing there, wreaking havoc with the flow of causality, you see. It's as if we had caught a child throwing stones into the rippleless Lake of Being. I hope this isn't too heavy for you?"

It was, but we, stunned by the offhand way in which the godlike were-jaguar spoke of the fate of universes, were actually speechless.

V'Denni-Kenni continued:

"The Time Criminal invaded your universe, you see, centuries ago. He found himself in what is now Judaea; and he abducted hundreds of Hebrew tribesmen from the desert for his genetic experiments, creating chimaeras and monstrosities and finally...the abominable snowman himself! Yes, your Sasquatius is a member of the lost tribes of Israel. Becoming bored of these pursuits, the Master of Chaos jumped around in your continuum, causing you Romans to discover steamships a thousand years earlier than in our history books. The abominable snowmen he deposited all through dozens of the known worlds, as evidence of his having come and gone. They have been here, in the land of the Quaquiutii and Tlingit, for a century now, gentle tyrants who demand nothing more than an annual tribute of salmon."

"Indeed," said Abraham bar-David, "we stayed here so long only because we have an irresistible appetite for this smoked salmon, which we devour constantly with a kind of round, holed bread loaf smeared with creamed cheese."

"Why," said the were-jaguar, ignoring this, "does the Time Criminal leave these Sasquatii scattered throughout the universe? Assuredly as clues for us...for the man wants war, you see. He wants to bring about the Final Spectacle, a battle of the universes whose magnitude you puny creatures of the past cannot possibly imagine. Even if it means the destruction of a million universes. He is a madman, a megalomaniac such as we thought had been eliminated centuries before our time.

"Your evidence—insignificant as it may seem to you —has been a great help to us in tracking down our enemy. I wish there was some way to reward you—"

"There is, Divine Ones," I said, prostrating myself in my awe at his mystic, incomprehensible words. "We are far from home, and perhaps if Your Augustnesses would care to drop us off a little nearer home, as you were kind enough to do last time—"

"That is, alas, impossible!" said V'Denni-Kenni. "All our Dimensional Patrol vehicles will be needed now for the coming fray. Unfortunately, in the grand scheme of things, you see, a few humans from the distant past, from an anomalous universe that should not even have existed in the first place, have little significance. I wish I could help you...but you are as dream figments, you folk; and the man who dreamed you up is on the loose, and very dangerous indeed. We must go to him."

"Well!" I said. "I like that. Here we are, we've trudged goodness knows how many mille passūs, we've told you everything we know to help you on your quest for something we can't even understand—and you have the temerity to tell us that we're just figments of some evil god's imagination!"

"Surely," said Aaye, "a sophist's argument only, and not intended to have any connection with reality."

"Be still, little one," said the lobster. "We will help

you in any way we can, given the haste with which we must now uproot the Time Citadel and vanish in pursuit of the Evil One."

"Well," said Aquila, "we do have a more pressing problem than returning home."

"Yes," Nikias said. "We must return and face the Quaquiutii. We can't claim to have subjugated their oppressors, so we'll lose this *potlatching* competition and they might even kill us."

Abraham the *megapus* laughed. "Is *that* all you need! I think I can probably help you here. How would you like to take me back to Rome with you?"

I turned to see the Sasquatius beaming jovially, his fangs glistening in the light from the gold-covered walls of the vast rotunda. One could hardly say no to such a creature.

"I'd be proud, most proud," I temporized.

"Ah! It will be wonderful, too, to return to Israel, of which I have heard only in old songs and legends. Tell me is the Temple in Jerusalem built yet?"

"Actually, the Emperor Titus burned it down thirty years ago," I said.

"Ah. Well, I do seem to be a little out of date. Well, are we ready to go back and scare the living daylights out of your Quaquiutii?"

"I suppose so."

And so saying, he led us out of the huge hall. The creatures of the future had long ceased to notice us; and no one stopped us as we wandered out of the strange city.

One spectacle yet remained, however, and it was the most impressive of all.

As we strode up the hill road that led back into the forest of pines, we heard a low rumbling. Our very bones quaked. "What is it?" I said in alarm, remembering tales of the eruption in Pompeii.

"Oh, it's nothing," said Abraham. "Just the city taking off, that's all."

I turned around to look, as the roaring began, pounding my ears. Nothing I'd ever heard before had been so loud—not the screamings of ten thousand Parthians as their army advanced upon us! And then I saw whence the deafening din came: it was the Time Citadel.

It was glowing now, the tops of the towers blindingly incandescent; and the flying saucers were hovering like hummingbirds over the parapets. The city shook. An involuntary shriek escaped our collective throats as the whole megalopolis tore loose from the ground and shot skyward like brimstone from a catapult. Flames enveloped the field. In a few seconds the city had become as a comet, so bright as to dim the very summer sun; and its only remnant was a charred and blasted plain that spewed forth little fountains of fire.

"What a spectacle," I said. "Imagine reproducing *that* in the arena. . . ."

"No time for such thoughts now," Aquila said. "We must return to Hooting-Owl."

And we trudged onward into the darkness, our minds hardly able to believe what our very eyes beheld but moments before.

CHAPTER
XXVII

I T WAS A SIMPLE MATTER TO DESCEND BY STORM INTO
the Quaquiutish village, with some dozens of Sasquatii
—or *megapodes*, to use the proper Greek appellation—at
our head. The natives ran screaming from their houses as
we took possession of the wooden lodge where but a day
before we had been made to look like blithering idiots.
Afterabout ten minutes of lumbering and shambling, we
reduced the Quaquiutish chieftains to gibbering helpless-
ness, and they prostrated themselves before us, pleading
for mercy. Mean-while, in an attempt to propitiate these
furry gods, the village dancers masked themselves and
were working themselves into a frenzy of leaping and
caterwauling.

"Well, well, Hooting-Owl, old chap! Quite a reversal,
isn't it?"

"Have mercy! Have mercy!"

"Very well, I shall be compassionate. I claim this entire village and its environs in the name of his August
Majesty, the Emperor Marcus Ulpius Trajanus, White

and Greatest Father of All Terra Nova! You, Hooting-Owl, I will set up as regent in the Emperor's name; for it is not our way to annihilate the local customs of underling nations, but to preserve the good and gradually introduce the better. And I command that you never again have the hubris to play *potlatch* against *me*, who am, after all, the mouthpiece of Caesar Himself."

"Your Omnipotence is . . . more generous than I deserve. . . ."

Hooting-Owl prostrated himself firmly in the mud as Aquila, Abraham, Nikias, and Aaye came up behind me. "Well, it's all settled then."

"Except for one thing," Aquila said. "What about—China?" And he began to laugh.

"Oh, there's no such place," I said. "Trajan will just have to be told, firmly and finally, that this land does not exist. Not *here*, at least." I shuddered, thinking about ending up as arena fodder. "I suppose I must now resign myself to some painful death. Perhaps I should stay here, go native, wear a breechclout and feathers—"

"No need for that, General Titus!" Aquila said. "Have you forgotten, dear General, that you have carved out two whole new provinces for Caesar? East of here lies Siannia, with its capital city of Tachyopolis . . . and here Quaquiutia, at the shores of this Oceanus Papinianus, a land rich in salmon. You have single-handedly *doubled* Rome's might in the new world!"

"But . . . but Tachyopolis is just a fort with a couple of wooden lodges!" I said. "And Quaquiutia's capital city is just—" I waved my arms about the village, where natives still cowered behind totem poles and Sasquatii still ambled about, their arms swinging.

"Ha! Not by the time *I'm* through with it!" said Aaye. "I am, as you know, an Egyptian, and by my very nature a master of all that is dark and mysterious. I'll paint a word-picture of the frights we've faced, of the hordes of savages we've overcome . . . let them say, O procurator, that you came, you saw, you conquered!"

"Well . . ." I said. "I've seen ample proof of your verbal skills before, but—"

"Oh, he'll do it, General," said Aquila. "It is, after all, *his* hide we're talking about."

I was beginning to feel better already. We would winter here, in this village of now properly subservient savages; we would have ample time to prepare a whale of a story for the August Caesar. In our wild-goose chase after a legend, a dream, we had come up with some very real Roman provinces; well, almost. By the time Trajan heard about things in Rome, I'd have long since dispatched troops to mop up my operation.

For a moment a thought nagged me: what was it the were-jaguars had referred to? *The Final Spectacle.* Oh, to see such a thing! The fate of million universes! I felt a sliver of curiosity insinuating itself into my little noggin.

The final spectacle!

But I dismissed the thought from my head. Right now I was Papinian the Conqueror who had stormed through the Montes Saxosi in a blaze of glory, and carved great provinces out of this untamed continent. I practiced a languorous wave of the hand; the Quaquiutii quickly scuttled about, fearful of my every gesture. I permitted myself a gracious smile.

"And now," I said majestically, "I think I'm ready for a piece of smoked salmon liberally covered with creamed cheese and served upon an annular loaf!"

"Yes, your Lordship, at once!" the Quaquiutish chieftain crooned, as the Sasquatii began to lick their chops menacingly.

"That's the spirit, my good man," I said.

CHAPTER
XXVIII

AND SO, LADEN WITH MANY TALENTS' WEIGHT OF smoked salmon, and accompanied by an honor guard of a hundred Quaquiutish braves decked in their finest robes of beaten bark, whom I would later elevate to my personal guard, we set off on the long trail home. Our elephants we managed to palm off on the unfortunate Quaquiutii, who immediately began the process of worshipping them and of sculpting totem poles in their image. As a result of using elephants in thier woodcarving, the always pragmatic Quaquiutii were also able to invent a new use for their totem poles; for their elaborate cloaks could be hung on the extended wooden trunks, and thus the totem poles served both as deities and as coatracks.

Well! It had been more than a year since we had set off from Caesarea-on-Miserabilis; for we had wintered in Quaquiutia, and set forth in the spring, arriving in my capital city in high summer. Our journey home was uneventful enough; once entered into the great plains, we found aurochs aplenty to eat, and the Siannii did not venture to attack us too often, for the tales of our ability to summon the Olmechian flying saucers had had a year in which to grow in the telling.

To my delight, I saw as we approached the Siannian-Lacotian border that the fort I had set up in the vicinity of the Montes Negri, which we had somewhat hubristically named Tachyopolis, was still fully operational.

More than operational! Tipis were clustered all around it. A ramshackle sort of arena had been built, and we were able to experience some small-scale spectacles: legionaries riding bareback on wild horses while attempting to lasso aurochs; men dodging wild bulls; and other sports. Not as bloody as most of the spectacles one is used to, perhaps, but it *was* different, and seemed to require skill. I gave the word that such new arts were to be encouraged.

A courier from Trajan awaited me; this I did *not* like. A message stated that His Magnificence now wished to repeat his vast successes in Alexandria-in-Iracuavia in this, the most remote Roman Province of Lacotia; that he had heard of my most admirable exploits, was deeply moved by them, and wished to honor me by journeying all the way from Rome to Caesarea to preside over my official Triumph!

I shuddered.

Well, I thought: at least I'll have some months to prepare yet. How long ago had it been since I'd sent that self-aggrandizing missive to the Emperor, telling him of the annexation of Siannia? Could it have been a year ago?

That would have given Caesar plenty of time.

I gathered my forces together in some semblance of grandeur, and we set out for Caesarea at forced-march speed. As I reached the outskirts of my governmental seat, I realized that all my worst fears had come to pass.

For hundreds of grand-looking tents were clustered at the West Portal of the city, many of them blazoned with the imperial colors. From a distance, an imposing sight: close up, one saw the frayed fabrics, the unsewn holes in the tent walls. Clearly His Parsimonious Majesty had not changed in the slightest.

And in the sky, hovering over the city, anchored to the ground by huge boulders, were vehicles that I had thought never to see again—that hot-air balloons that we had first seen in the land of the Olmechii!

"What has happened?" I cried out to my friends, dismayed. "Have the Olmechii left their southern lands, and sought out new conquests in the Roman Empire?" For I knew that they had the might to do it, impious though such a notion might seem to a true Roman.

As I looked about me in consternation, a familiar-looking palanquin borne aloft by familiar-looking burly Nubians came plodding towards our group. Quickly I dismounted and began the complex prostrations that had been taught me by the Emperor's eunuch before. "Anyone but Trajan!" I whispered, hoping against hope. "If only I'd had time to prepare a decent report—"

The palanquin's curtains were drawn, and I gazed once more upon the face of my earthly master.

"*Ave*, Caesar!" I said, saluting smartly.

"Ah, Papinian. You see how good We are to you! Having received the good news in Rome, We immediately set forth hither, to do you honor by granting you a triumph into your own capital city! Not to mention, of course, that by having your official triumph here, rather than in Rome as is the custom, We save the fearsome expense of bringing you, your troops, your spoils, and your captives home by ship."

"Your Majesty's . . . ah . . . financial wizardry is astonishing."

"Of course, of course. What's more, I have no wish to see another man almost deified before the Roman throng, as I was in the days before my elevation to divinity, when I was granted a triumph after each fresh conquest. Another's triumph in Rome, you see, might make the populace suspect that We are not their god. As for triumphs in front of remote peasants, well. . . ."

"I am overwhelmed, Caesar!" I started to salute again, but his eunuchs ran forward and I was instructed in some ritual forms of greeting even more elaborate than those of the last time I'd greeted my Emperor. By the time I had prostrated and genuflected in the correct directions, some ten minutes had elapsed, and Trajan showed no sign of allowing me to skip any part of the ceremonial.

I took it that he was not altogether pleased.

"Ah, done, are you? Bores me stiff, meself, General, all this bowing and scraping, but you know, We *are* the Emperor."

"Beyond a doubt, Your Magnitude. But let me tell you of our new conquest in the west, Caesar! Since my last missive to you, we have annexed yet another province, wherein dwell the Quaquiutii, a race of fishermen, and the Sasquatii, a race of Jewish monsters—"

He waved his hand for silence. "Later, Papinian, later. Meanwhile, what do you think of Our new hot-air balloons?"

"Your Majesty, I hardly think that the conquest of a new territory one thousand mille passūs wide can be brushed off—"

"Silence! You did not think to tell Us about them, did you, when our late predecessor the God Domitian sent you to the southern lands. Nor about the jaguar-gods, or the military threat posed by the Olmechii—"

"Sire, I doubted you'd believe me," I said, cringing before my earthly master just as, not many moons before, Hooting-Owl had cringed to me.

"Well, a lot has happened in the past year and a half, General! In the first place, the gods of the Olmechii, in their flying chamber pots or whatever it is they travel around in, departed Olmechia completely, leaving the natives somewhat in the lurch; they sent an embassy to Gaius Pomponius Piso the Younger, Procurator of Iracuavia, begging for a mutual defense treaty of some kind. It proved not difficult to negotiate a treaty, even though conquest seemed out of the question in view of their still superior technological achievements. As a result, we obtained those ... vehicles you see above our heads and many other delightful gifts."

What could I say? No longer was I Papinian the Conqueror, come back to see his Emperor in a blaze of glory. While I'd been slogging through the mountains, history had calmly passed me by; for I knew that contact between the Imperium Romanum and the Imperium Olmechiorum was an event infinitely more momentous than the winning of a game of *potlatch* or the building of one miserable little wooden fort. I looked around desperately for Aaye, who had promised to give an impressive account of our mission; unaccountably he had vanished. I stared at my Emperor, quailing in terror, while his face grew redder and redder. "You have failed, you nincompoop! China was what I sent you to find, not fishing villages and tent-huts of savages! So tell me then, is China under control?"

"Sire, before we reached the fabled silkland, we ran into an enormous ocean and were forced to turn back. I have taken the liberty of naming it the Oceanus Papinianus—"

"Oh, really, General! Such overweening hubris! And the Lady Oenothea?" he said sharply.

"Your Majesty ... I have made a properly dynastic match for her with the regent of Quaquiutia, a native."

"Excellent, excellent!" The Emperor beckoned for some eunuchs to come cool his brow with a poultice of snow and sweet orange juice. "Have a complete report sent to Our accounting office, will you? Expenditure and outgo, and what have you. I don't want it said that Our campaigns lose money."

"Lose money! Lose money!" I was so furious that I forgot myself for a moment. "Your Majesty, I've been on the trail for the better part of two years! I'm tired, I've

widened your realm with two new provinces"—I'd practiced saying this so often that I now believed it—"and I
hope you'll take the value of the two provinces into con-
sideration when you have the accounts done! I'll not
stand here while your eunuchs hand me a bill for the loss
of a dozen elephants!"

For a moment we stared at each other, both appalled
at my outrageous lack of propriety.

Then he slowly clapped his hands. "Bravo, Papinianus! Never thought you'd show any gumption, old boy.
That's more like it! A good general should stand up for
what he believes in. And now: remember that you
haven't found China. And *that*, Titus Papinianus Lacoticus, was your mission! You should be begging for
mercy, not bargaining over money matters like a pimp in
the agora! I've half a mind to order your execution this
very minute! To have you crucified like a common criminal, in fact!"

I thought back to that day, so many years ago, when
Father had taken me in the old motor-car to see a man
being nailed to a cross along the Via Appia. Suddenly I
saw him again in my mind's eye: an imposing figure of a
man, his toga praetexta and his white hair billowing behind him as the slaves stoked the boiler of the old motor-
car, lecturing me and the young curly-haired Nikias on
the sober Roman values. I was heartily ashamed of myself now: for I had not only turned my back on these
values, I had actually disported myself in the manner of
a savage, eating raw aurochs and speaking the vile Lacotian tongue and Jove knows *what* other dreadful pursuits!

"Your dread Majesty," I said humbly, switching to the
Latin tongue of awesome and sober utterances instead of
the Greek of frivolous conversations, "at least give me
leave to dispose of myself in the customary Roman manner"

My entourage had gathered around me now. Nikias
was twiddling his thumbs, despairing of me, looking the

other way. Aaye was striking a superciliously cada-
verous pose, as if by endeavoring to resemble an Egyptian mummy he could avoid the impending fate of
becoming one in fact. Aquila alone seemed tranquil
enough, though he was shedding his toga and seemed
about to embark upon another crazed dance.

"And what's *that* thing?" said the Emperor, pointing
to our friend the *megapus*. "Something for the arena, I
trust?"

"Heavens, no!" I almost shouted in his face, since all
was lost and I might as well be hanged for a sheep as a
lamb. I'd show His Miserlihood some general-like gumption before those eunuchs dragged me off! "That's Abraham bar-David, our friend, *if you please*; he's not to
blame for looking funny, he was mutated in a genetic
experiment, he's a Judaean I tell you—"

"Bah! I knew we should never have conquered Judaea!"

Abraham made one of his horrid forward-lumbering
moves.

"Oh, very well, very well," Caesar said, trying hard to
regain his composure, "I shan't execute any of you. I
suppose it's not exactly your fault there was a bloody
ocean in your way. But you have failed me, and I cannot
brook that! You'll go again! This time I'll give you ships.
I'll give you these Olmechian hot-air balloons if you like.
After all, this ocean of yours can't possibly be much
wider than the Mediterranean, if that. In the name of
Jupiter Optimus Maximus, find bloody China before it
bloody finds *me*!"

The gods know I have never asked for adventures.
"Yes, Caesar, of course," I said, wondering the while
whether crucifixion would not be the less painful alter-
native. So the odyssey was not yet over! I was non-
plussed beyond all measure.

"It's not so bad," Nikias said, laying a comforting arm
on my shoulder. "After all, we may get to see the were-
jaguars again. We may even participate in . . . what was it

they called it? *The Final Spectacle*. Don't be upset, Titus."

The Final Spectacle!

"I never want to see anything green again!" I growled. But the thought nagged at me for a few moments.

Then I looked at the walls of my capital city. I could see the marble temples, the graceful columns of the Forum Papinianum; on the slope of the central hill, the citadel itself and the walls of my palace. The trumpeting of distant bucinae lanced the summer air.

"General!" Trajan said. "Your triumph awaits you!"

Then a page-boy came up to me, carrying aloft a flagon of the finest Lesbian wine; and I knew that the fate of a million universes could wait a day or two at least.

PART FOUR

AQUILA:
THE FINAL
CONFLICT

CHAPTER
XXIX

I T IS ALL VERY WELL TO BOW AND SCRAPE AND AGREE with everything that is told one, when one is in the august Presence of Marcus Ulpius Trajanus, White and Greatest Father, Caesar Augustus, Pater Patriae, and so on so forth, and he has taken the trouble to cross the Oceanus Atlanticus and brave the wilderness to address the procurator of a remote province in Terra Nova, most distant, most intractable and most eccentrically barbaric segment of the Imperium Romanum; quite another thing, I'm afraid, to go ahead and obey his commands once he has departed for Rome and is almost a year's journey away.

Trajan had told me to take the hot-air balloons he had obtained by trade from the southern land of Olmechia, and to cross the Oceanus Papinianus (as I still insist on calling it, despite its vulgar appellation of the Oceanus Pacificus) in search, once again, of the land of Chin and a direct route to the silklands across Roman territory. This was an Imperial command, and as such issued from the mouth of deity (or prospective deity at the very least); but it was still a ludicrous impossibility. Nothing would induce me to go up in the air in one of those things. It wasn't natural, simple as that. Even as prosaic a conveyance as a paddleboat made me sick; I had traveled by motor-car in my childhood, by ship and by horse in my young manhood, by elephant across the Montes Saxosi in my middle age... and I wasn't about to try anything new now! Now with the Emperor safely tucked away across the sea, at least....

For I had returned in relative triumph to my governmental seat of Caesarea-on-Miserabilis. We had no gold or silk, true, but we did have a considerable booty of smoked salmon obtained from the Quaquiutish natives of the northwestern country, and we *did* have Abraham bar-David, the Judaean sasquatch, to exhibit as proof of our prowess; not to mention the two hot-air balloons which I ordered permanently anchored to a little Temple of Mars just outside the town walls, in our little equivalent of the Campus Martius. But after a day or two of the usual ballyhoo, and after I'd celebrated with the usual games, gladiatorial combats, and so on, and done the usual sacrifices, I was all ready for a few years of quiet. Nikias and Aaye went back to running their Academy of Sophistry and Casuistry, built with money from my own pocket; the Emperor Trajan, who had stayed in Caesarea for a month, with considerable drain to the city coffers, had finally left me with nothing to show for it but the title of *Sasquaticus—conqueror of the Sasquatch*, and an enormous bill for some triumphal arches that he had had built at all the major crossroads of the town. These latter were truly absurd: those who knew about art had a field day criticizing their monumental gaudiness, and our miserable peasants and merchants cursed them roundly for congesting traffic.

Well... there it was.

Trajan was gone, much to everyone's relief; Abraham bar-David had been adopted by Aaye and Nikias, and

was professor of Hebrew studies at the Academy, which
lay on a prime piece of land beside the Via Augusta, on
the left bank of the Miserabilis. The Lady Oenothea was
happily ensconced as Queen of the Quaquiutii and wife
to Chief Hooting-Owl; now and then she'd send me a
chatty letter, to which I would occasionally respond. The
chieftain's lovely daughter I renamed the Lady Cervilla,
for she reminded me always of a little hart; she was my
pride and joy, and after a year or so she was chirping
away happily in Greek and even Latin. What an idyllic
life it was!

If only Aquila hadn't. . . .

Yes. I was partaking of my Iracuavian wine (the vine-
yards in the vicinity of Eburacum Novum, especially
near the Algonquian border, had begun to yield their
grapes, and with time had come a dulling of the palate,
so that I could hardly tell the Iracuavian from a decent
Lesbian or Chian vintage, especially after it had been
thoroughly resinated in the Greek manner) in the main
atrium of my palace in Caesarea when a message came
from Aquila. It was brought to me by a young boy, one
of the octogenarian's innumerable offspring—the old
codger was, by all accounts, randy as a stallion, and indefatigable in his pursuit of the *ars amatoria*, not to
mention the amatory arse—who burst in quite rudely
bearing a message-tray on which was a scroll sealed with
Aquila's personal seal, an eagle astride a laurel wreath.

"Hey, procurator!" aid the boy rudely. "My father
wants you to have this." He thrust it at me and started to
leave.

"Ha! *Toki ya la hwo*?" I said in my now fluent Lacotian: that is to say, *quo vadis*?

"Aquila is dying. He wants you."

"Didn't he teach you any manners?"

"Oh, sure, your Lordship. But he says I don't have to
bow and scrape to a bumbling bubble-nosed general like
you."

"Succinctly put," I said, trying not to be bothered by

this diminutive monstrosity. "And he wants me to see him before he dies, I suppose, eh, what? He sends me this twit of a messenger to call me to his deathbed? Well, I never! Glad to see him go, in a way; always full of himself, never did see the innate superiority of the Roman way. Still, I'll miss him. Is he ill?"

"No, of course not, you dimwit!" the child piped. "He's hale and hearty as ever."

"Then what's all this about?"

"Good day to die, that's what he says. Made us children spend the whole day gathering all his pipes and paraphernalia, getting all his buffalo robes ready and what have you. What a nuisance! I'm surprised he even had time to think of *you*. Well, General, I have to be off, now. I've to go to the Academy and tell Nikki and Fuzzyface and the Old Fart about it. Ta-ta!"

"Wait!" The boy turned beneath the statue of Aquila which still adorned the atrium, though I seldom had time to anoint it with rotten fruits anymore. I didn't quite know why I'd called after him. Perhaps it was just to make sure I hadn't lost my touch, you know. Voice of authority and all that. If I couldn't order a mere stripling around, how was I to command armies? I hadn't been in the field itself for years, actually; didn't care to much now. I'd developed a considerable paunch from the high-aurochs diet of the great plains. I looked at the boy for a moment.

"Well, you little hemiobol, you might show a little proper grief at the man's death, you know!"

"He told us to rejoice!" said the boy defiantly. Suddenly I noticed that he was holding back tears. I looked at him for a while longer; then I tossed him a bronze *as*.

"Golly! Thanks a lot, General!" he said, and then squirmed off down the corridor.

"I'm getting soft," I said to the empty atrium. Sitting down at my table, I signed half a dozen crucifixion warrants and a score or two of floggings; all in a day's work. "Soft, soft, soft!" I doubled some poor wretch's poena to fifty years' enslavement on a paddleboat treadmill. I went back and tripled the number of lashes on all the flogging warrants. But I still wasn't satisfied. "What's the damn matter?" I shouted to no one in particular.

Then I sat back, quaffing away at my wine, thinking of the past. Of Aquila and me facing the Olmechian high priestess. Of the flying-saucer people. Of the ridiculous elephant odyssey and the mad *potlatching* ceremony in which we'd participated. And finally I remembered the flying city of the saucer people; the green were-jaguars muttering about the Final Spectacle, the Final Spectacle—

And suddenly I understood the true cause of my unease.

The Final Spectacle!

For a year it had haunted my thoughts, a recurring daydream. I wanted to see this thing, to participate in whatever it was...the conflict of the million universes, whatever it was called. We needed something to enliven our existences; governing this remote province was a dreadful bore really, and the arcane sophistry of Nikias, Aaye, and Abraham was often quite unintelligible to the Lacotians to whom it was expounded, so there probably wasn't too much meaning in *their* lives either. It was time to do something! But we couldn't do it without Aquila. I made up my mind.

"Slaves!" I cried out. Several scurried in, bearing my mantle of office, my wreath, my sword, and so on. "Have my chariot ready. I shall go outside the city gates. Oh, and summon a couple of homines medicinae, will you? I'll be needing advice on native customs and so on. Especially funeral rites."

"*Toki ya la hwo*, domine?"

"To the sacred burial grounds!" I said grandly, as they started to deck me in my most impressive robes.

CHAPTER
XXX

I RACED THROUGH THE CROWDED LANES OF MY HOME city, pausing now and then to urge my yoked horses out of a rut. With tempestuous celerity I hurtled through the agora, as vendors scurried to cower behind wine vats and food bales. I did not stop as I usually did to examine the gorgeous main street with its statues of Vacantanca, Minerva, Caesar, and me, but hurtled madly towards the city gates, ignoring everything. Soon a dozen young boys and girls, each dressed in his finest toga praetexta or gown, eagle-feather wreaths, and leggings, each with that excruciatingly memorable aquiline nose and supercilious smirk, were following after me, hollering madly: "Aquila's funeral! Aquila's funeral!" and I heard the shout taken up everywhere. Soon we were joined by a horde of young women, all blessed with those same familiar facial features, ululating madly as is the funerary custom among the Lacotians, bawling and caterwauling as if to wake the very dead. In a trice we were at the city gates and the guards hastened to crank the portals open.

"This is quite the merriest funeral I've ever encountered!" I screamed at the charioteer, as we went through the gates onto the Via Augusta, lined with oak trees and with the odd crucified criminal. Now and then I reached over to touch the driver a bit with my quirt, you know, remind him who's boss; more often than not I missed, for the road was bumpy. Soon it seemed that half the population of Caesarea-on-Miserabilis was jogging behind me.

"Don't forget," I shouted, "to stop off at the Academy!"

We lurched down a side lane, and presently were at the Academy's decorative iron gates, over which stood the superscription "No entrance without mathematics." This was a tribute to the ancient Academy of Plato, of course. "Well," I said, as we halted, "I've never been much good at figures, so I suppose I ought to wait here." Behind me the women came to a lull in their wails of mourning.

A new chorus of ululations issued forth from within the Academy, however, as the three academics, followed closely by their wives (for each of them had taken a native spouse), emerged; and they were a comic spectacle indeed, for each had decked himself in the mourning style most appropriate to his country of origin: Nikias had shorn off a lock of his gray hair and rent his chiton; Aaye the Egyptian was in a long white robe and one of those metal pointed beard-things and was lugubriously waving various scepters of power, as though he were about to officiate over a mummification; and the sasquatch, his head covered with a veil, was rocking from side to side and weeping copiously. At this astounding sight, those behind me resumed their chorus of consummate grief.

"Jove help us!" I said. "I'll be deaf by the time we reach the sacred burial grounds."

I called for an oxcart to transport the gray academicians and their wives and lackeys, and the procession continued apace along the Via Augusta. Our destination, a hillock some three or four mille passūs from the city, could already be seen. Soon we had left the main road and were bumping up and down as we negotiated a pathway composed in equal parts of mud and boulders.

"Don't they ever fix these roads?" I said. "Considering how much I tax these natives, we ought to be able to afford to pave the way to their sacred places, at least!"

We stopped again. The children were mobbing my chariot; I noticed among them that smug and smarmy urchin who had first given me Aquila's summons.

"Why are we stopping?" I said.

Two impressive braves on horseback rode down the hill to greet us. "You are trespassing, O procurator!" they said in almost perfect unison. "This is sacred land."

"But I'm the bloody governor!"

"General, you will recall the treaty signed by General Pomponius Piso the Elder more than fifty years ago," said the first brave, "when, at the Battle of the Flumen Pulveris, or Powder River, your general was roundly defeated by Chief Aquila. It was agreed upon that no Roman would ever molest our sacred burial grounds again, was it not? This is Lakotah land."

"What do your native superstitions mean to me, who am the mouthpiece of Caesar Himself, your supreme god? Let me pass, I say!"

"Let him through, Taurus Sedentarius!" the child piped up. "Aquila invited him to the funeral."

The two conferred among themselves for a moment. Then the second spoke up. "You may pass," he said. "But give this earth due respect."

"I'll be happy to officiate at whatever sacrifices seem necessary, as representative of the Pontifex Maximus—"

"Be silent!" the brave said. "Come." We followed him. Soon what passed for a road evaporated into a mass of rocks and shrubbery. Here and there stood a pole topped by a sacred aurochs skull painted in red, black, and white, the three colors betokening the three sacred attributes of Earth, Night, and Day. The wailing began once more. Now there were platforms raised up on poles, decorated with feathers and scalps and skulls, on which lay skeletons, all dressed in the finest of buffalo robes; they were covered with things precious to these Lacotii: with rattles, favorite weapons, and strings of beads dotted here and there with Roman coins. Yet these were old skeletons; I saw none recently dead, and no coin newer than from the reign of Nero; so I knew that these were braves and chieftains who had died as long ago as that famous Battle of the Flumen Pulveris.

"This must be the wrong place," I said. "I don't see Aquila anywhere. Besides, there's no rotting smell such as you'd find, say, in the Roman catacombs."

At this the hideous little brat began to cackle uproariously. "Why, you silly old general," he said, "this is just the *old* part of the burial grounds. My father wouldn't lie among *these* old fogies. Besides, if you can't smell, I 'spect you do have eyes, don't you?" He pointed upwards. I saw vultures circling. I shuddered.

"This way," said the dour braves who had come out to meet us. We rounded a bend of the hillock; and there I beheld the most astonishing sight.

In a clearing shaded by oak trees stood more of the death-platforms; but these were not mounted on poles, but on miniature Ionian, Dorian, and Corinthian columns of fine marble, and the aurochs skulls rested in niches carved with cupids. "Good heavens!" I said. "Roman culture comes to the barbarians even here, then!"

And I saw one platform up ahead. A sign over it, engraved on a plate of marble, read

AQVILA

followed by a lengthy inscription in the Greek-alphabet transcript of the Lacotian tongue. I couldn't really tell much about what it said, though it did mention the number of times he had counted coup and had a brief account of his adventures that seemed none too flattering to me!

Beneath it, the old man was dancing madly, waving a rattle from time to time and wheezing strangely. Around him watched a curious crowd, many of them in tears.

"Ah, there you are, General Papinian. You're just in time to witness my final dispensement of deathless wisdom," Aquila said, coughing a little. He seemed frail; his skeletal frame hardly filled the senatorial toga that he wore, and the eagle-feather wreath came halfway down his face.

"You don't look too well, old friend," I said, and went to embrace him. All the while he pranced feebly up and down and sang.

"You're very lucky to be able to hear my death-song," Aquila said. "An eagle taught it to me once, long before you were even born; it was on a spirit journey that I took when I was a stripling no bigger than this nipper here." He looked fondly at that selfsame obnoxious brat. I glowered. "This is my youngest child," he said. "As regards my death song, General Papinianus ... I give it to you, if you can remember it. It is my parting gift to you, a man of whom, despite your cultural chauvinism and impenetrable denseness, I have become a little fond. *Hechitu welo!* Those were fine adventures we had, eh? The Parthians. The Olmecs. The Quaquiutii. The Were-Jaguars. The *Megapodes. Hechitu welo!* I wish I had it to relive all over again."

"Can't *I* have your deathsong, pop?" said The Brat.

His father patted him fondly. "No, *michinkshi*. I have already given you many songs."

"But they're not real ones! You just make them up as you go along!"

"Eya! Just like life itself, eh, General? Now listen carefully to these words—" He began to wheeze again, and despite my grasp of Lacotian I could hardly understand him.

"Stop!" I said. "You can't die yet!"

"But it is a good day to die! The sun is shining, the weather is warm, so I won't freeze to death as I lie there thinking about the Great Mystery."

"But I'm planning another expedition!"

"Bah! Take The Brat with you."

"Don't you want to see China? To ride the hot-air balloons across the sky? To take ship over the Oceanus Papinianus, and see the Final Spectacle promised us by the flying-saucer people?"

"I'm old, I tell you!" he said a little doubtfully.

I pressed my advantage. "Just think of it! To fly like the eagle itself, the *aquila*—to be king of the wind—"

"But I *will* be, my dear General, and soon! My grandfathers are calling me."

He began to caper ever more energetically, and it looked as if he would drop dead at that very moment. Some Lacotian braves were preparing a stretcher on which to lay his body, lining it with buffalo robes and silken cushions and were-jaguar jade amulets and a Roman war helmet and a fascis medicinae full of fragrant herbs.

The ululating of the women reached fever pitch.

Suddenly, from nowhere it seemed, stormclouds began to gather overhead. Lightning flashed dramatically. There was a deafening peal of thunder. I nearly jumped out of my skin. Then it started to rain.

Abruptly, Aquila stopped dancing. "Bah! Wrong dance again! I really *am* getting old," he said.

"There you are! It's not such a good day to die after all, Aquila. You'll be drenched! Now, how about a nice long soak in the caldarium of the Caesarean baths, followed by a nice massage from some nice voluptuous handmaidens, a goblet of wine chilled with Saxosic snow . . . and a nice long discussion of the logistics of our next adventure?"

Aquila looked a little dubious.

"Well?" I said. "Tell me there's some life in your aged bones yet!"

Aquila looked at me for a long time. "You only want me with you," he said, "so I can save your life again!"

"Well, you've already saved it half a dozen times, old chap. I need the insurance, you know."

"Eh! Well, I suppose I can always die some other time," he said, shrugging.

"There's an oxcart waiting at the foot of the hill to take you back to the city."

"No thanks. If I'm to go adventuring again, I'd better run. Keep in shape, you know. Hey, little Brat! Race you to Papinian's palace!"

When I turned around they were gone. And so were the vultures. Now by what magic had he conjured up the storm and forced me into this blasted adventure? Now I couldn't turn back.

"Confound this accursed savage!" I screamed. "He planned this whole thing to force my hand! I've no wish for any more of these bloody adventures!"

I walked back and forth among the throng, remonstrating, pleading. "I'm just an average sort of governor of a remote quiet province, and all I wanted was to be invisible to the baleful eye of the Emperor . . . I've just been sitting at home, minding my own business, and—"

Why was no one listening to me? I forced myself to stop making a spectacle of myself—this was, after all, not even my own funeral—and to conduct myself in a more sober manner as befitted my station. I drew myself tall, fiddled with the clasp of my cloak, which had loosened in the sudden downpour, and resolved my face into a veritable grimace of authority.

But everyone just laughed at me, and I knew that once more, despite all my good intentions, despite my total commitment to the glorious old Roman ideals, I had succeeded only in playing the role of buffoon.

CHAPTER
XXXI

WELL! WESTWARD AGAIN IT WAS, AND THIS TIME with the largest strangest force ever assembled within the confines of the Roman Empire; for I had decided that if we were indeed to find the fabled land of Chin, or to encounter that Final Spectacle of which the were-jaguars had said so much, it would be best to meet spectacle with spectacle, to try to do Mother Rome proud. Moreover, since we would, theoretically at least, be traveling within the confines of the Empire, we could afford to move slowly and with pomp, and without fear of attack from the savage hordes, at least till we reached the shores of the Oceanus Papinianus; thenceforth, of course, we would be on our own.

There were to be no elephants this time: I had learnt my lesson among the Quaquiutii. Apart from that—for I have no particular desire to describe the same scenery twice—our progress from Caesarea-on-Miserabilis to Tachyopolis, now a bustling market town, and thence onward through the Montes Saxosi into Quaquiutia, was much as I had related in a previous chapter.

There were, however, a number of differences. I was Titus Papinianus Lacoticus Sasquaticus Dux et Imperator now, not one of your carping nobodies who had risen to power by bribery or by bedding the Emperor or his appropriate concubine; and this time I traveled in style. Behind me marched an entire legion—six thousand men—not the old Thirty-fourth of which I had such fond memories, but a new Thirty-fourth made up mainly of Lacotii, Siannii, and the odd Iracuavius or Seminolius, with only a few Europeans. We carried scorpiones, ballistae, and catapultae aplenty; and soon we were to need them all.

For my...ah...conquests to the west of the known Empire had not proved quite as thorough as I had led Caesar to believe, of course. Every now and then, a pack of Siosionii or Siannii, or even the far-ranging and brutish Apaxae, would come charging up to us, and we would be forced to dispatch them in true Roman fashion, staying put in the testudo formation while the savages dashed themselves to bits against our unassailable war engines.

Thus we spent a pleasant summer; I and Aquila would ride on ahead, whilst my gaggle of academics, serving wenches, and other human paraphernalia proper to a traveling procurator's court followed behind in a new kind of conveyance recently become popular in Terra Nova, the covered wagon.

If only that bloody child, Aquila's youngest, hadn't bawled his way into our company! Equus Insanus, for that was the Latin translation of *Shunkawinkte*, his barbarous name, was constantly underfoot, and the legion had made him their mascot besides. What a nuisance!

But let me not carry on in this vein too long. The idyllic trek through Roman and almost-Roman territory led us all too soon to Quaquiutia and to Hooting-Owl's village. We'd set him up, you recall, as an interim gover-

nor, and he was now married to Oenothea the Vast. Our
rather impressive company trooped into the village, and
soon the legionaries were everywhere: gawking at the
totem poles, making cow eyes at the women, and *potlatching* away their helmets and daggers for plates of
smoked salmon. Trade with the Empire having enriched
Hooting-Owl considerably, I noted with pride the begin-
nings of culture. The old wooden *potlatch*-lodge was
now dwarfed by a huge structure of marble: a circus, by
Jove, ready for the performance of a full-blown spectacle! Ahead of me was a forum in the classic style, although the fact that the columns were neither Dorian,
Ionian, nor Corinthian, but were instead merely marble
totem poles, did upset me a little. Still, they *were* only
savages, and at least they were trying.

And just then Hooting-Owl and Oenothea came out to
me on twin palanquins borne by some stubby-looking
slaves who were, despite the sweltering weather, covered from neck to toe in furs.

"Oh, I say, old chap!" came Hooting-Owl's voice. My
goodness, he'd changed. More Roman than the bloody
Romans, if you ask me. He jumped down rather ungracefully from his litter and trotted up to embrace me; I
took care to turn my nose upwind, for the stench of raw
and rotting fish had come wafting towards me even at
fifty paces. Even with my nose held stiffly erect, I could
not miss the odor, unpleasantly blended as it was with
attar of roses.

"I see you've taken to using perfume," I remarked. At
an aureus a vial, attar of roses (even laced with rancid
fish) was not to be sneezed at.

"Oh, heavens, yes. Got it by *potlatch* from some
Roman traders, you know, in exchange for the marvelous elixir that you yourself, O procurator, once vouch-
safed to me! A cure for baldness, eh, what? Renders the
male member indefatigable in its ministrations to the
fairer sex? Am I quoting your Egyptian friend aright?"

"My dear fellow—"

"Pshaw! No hard feelings, Titus old bean. Capital idea of yours, this 'behind curtain number three' business and all that, you know. Did it to all the neighboring tribes. The Tlingit don't know *what* hit them! That's how I got these pudgy furry slaves, you know. They're Aleutii from the roof of the world—*very* scarce, let me tell you! Yes, all this Roman savvy and *potlatching* expertise has certainly taught me a thing or two, old thing!"

"How shameful!" Aquila snorted. "That you should so far forget the ways of your ancestors—"

"Well, I say, you're hardly in a position to complain, old chap. Senator, eh? Toga praetexta, eh, what? Gilded laurel wreath? Ancient ways my arse! Let's face it, Rome is the wave of the future, and I'm happy to throw in my lot with her. Oh, and procurator . . . you like my new arena?"

"I can hardly wait," I said, "to see my first spectacle there!"

"Not for some time, I'm afraid. We've no funny animals out here; and no one seems interested in getting killed, either. Ah well. These savages still have a lot to learn."

"You can say that again . . . oh, Aquila, don't get upset, the man's at least having a go at being civilized, and . . . Equus Insanus, come back at once!"

"Shut up, pumpkin-nose!" said the child, as he darted among the Quaquiutian women, pausing now and then to tweak the odd steatopygial cheek.

"I shall have you flogged, you little *faex avis*!"

"Can't catch me, can't catch me. . . ."

"Perhaps," Oenothea said sweetly—it was the first time I'd heard her voice in a year—"the General and his friends would care to join us for a light supper?"

We were ushered into Hooting-owl's garish, lavish imitation of a Roman-style manse, where a rude repast awaited us in a triclinium; couches had been set out, one table for me, Oenothea, Aquila, and my host, a second table for the intellectual trinity of Greek, Egyptian, and sasquatch. The latter group was constantly interrupting our conversation, both to ridicule my use of rhetorical figures and to correct Hooting-Owl's Greek grammar, for our host had acquired some smattering of the language of Homer and Sophocles, which became him as felicitously as a silken gown might a Barbary ape.

"Looking for China again, eh, General?" he said, pouring me a vinegary red liquor of dubious vintage into a goblet as capacious as it was tasteless.

"Indeed," I said. "But the main question now is whether our primary goal should be the search for the silkland per se, or whether it should be the pursuit of that Final Spectacle of which the were-jaguars spoke."

"Bah!" said Aquila. "Already I begin to miss my platform in the sacred burial grounds, and to regret that you prevented me from singing my deathsong! For each of your quests is as crazy as the other. Can't you see that there is a huge body of water in between you and your goal? And we know only that the were-jaguars went west, not how far."

"Can't be more than a week's journey," I said. "Why, I'll wager the Oceanus Papinianus is no wider than the Mediterranean! It's simply unthinkable that the world should be any bigger than this, Aquila; otherwise how could it be said that Rome rules the world?"

"You read many books, O procurator, but have you ever actually looked at the world about you? Surely you must realize that the world will not transform itself merely to conform to your notion of who must be destined to rule it! Why, how do you even surmise that China is to be found on the other shore of your ocean? Perhaps we'll find some mythic kingdom; perhaps some unearthly domain such as the Land of Many Tipis, to which I was bound before you so rudely dragged me from my deathbed."

"Bull's pizzle, Aquila! Of course China's there. Where else could it be?" An affirming chorus came from the next table, with Aaye quoting the Book of the Dead,

Nikias quoting Herodotus, and the Sasquatius intoning choice passages from the Talmud in a lugubrious baritone to corroborate their various cosmologies.

"Here, Titus dear," said Oenothea, "have some salmon!"

I glanced at the plate in front of me. "I had my cooks copy it from a Roman recipe," Hooting-Owl said proudly. "First you take some salmon eggs and you sew them up inside some lightly braised baby salmon. Inserting this carefully into the bellies of medium-sized salmon, you grill the whole lightly in a marinade of salmon oil; then you carefully stuff the fish into larger fish and bake them, basting constantly with salmon oil of course; then, after leaving the entire operation to hang for seven days, you insert it into the largest available salmons and fry them with plenty of salmon oil and—"

"Good heavens!" I said. As I remember it, that recipe called for olives stuffed inside hummingbirds stuffed inside rabbits inside mallards inside peacocks inside boars inside venison. . . ."

"Ah yes, General, that is how the recipe came down to us when I obtained it in a *potlatch* from some Greek trappers, but you know how it is. We don't have any of those funny animals around here. Have to improvise, you know. Bloody shame, but we do our small part here, you know. Long live the Emperor, eh, what?"

"You'd not say that," I said, "if you'd ever met him."

"But General . . . not to take your mind off this banquet . . . how *do* you plan to cross the Pacificus?"

"A week's travel time to China, eh?" I said, politely stuffing my face with the salmons-within-salmons, which tasted, by the way, nothing like the dish it mimicked. "Well, I'd say that these hot-air balloons of ours could take care of it very nicely."

For it was known that the balloons could stay aloft as much as a fortnight, and we had a good dozen of them, copied from the Olmechian model and, I must say, somewhat improved. Each balloon was made of some fabric

—linen, I think—which sprouted from a platform some two or three passūs square. These platforms were light-weight wooden things; on each of them four or five could squat uncomfortably with room for provender and fuel in sacks dangling from the corners; in the center was a charcoal brazier tended by two slaves. This was, at least, the principle of the thing, though I, being no scientist, am at a loss to explain the more technical aspects. Suffice it to say that we Romans had been able to improve considerably on the Olmechian model, which had been used mainly to haul their enormous stone heads from quarry to temple, and which had been presented to them, out of as-it-were whole cloth, by the godlike were-jaguars. For the Olmechii, despite their apparent techno-logical edge over the Romans, were at heart barbarians; they could accept gifts from these superhuman beings, but they had none of our Roman ingenuity. We Romans, on the other hand, with our great expertise in the matter of applying heat to large volumes of air, as witness the caldaria of our baths, had applied true scientific thinking to the Olmechian gift; our scientists, inspired no doubt by the memory of Epaminondas of Alexandria, had added a monstrous equippage of cogs, valves, and slave-operated fans to the hot-air balloon, enabling the heat to be more thoroughly concentrated and controlled, and with far greater economy of fuel...lest this sound like one of those expository lumps so beloved of the writers of scientifictiones, let me retreat forthwith from this di-gression and continue apace with the scintillant dinner repartee of Hooting-Owl, Aquila, Oenothea, and the three pedants.

Hooting-Owl was smiling expansively at me. "It's set-tled then," he said.

"What? What's settled?" I said.

"I'm coming too."

I sighed. "What do you mean? The Empire needs you to govern Quaquiutia!"

"My dear fellow...how lucky you are not to have

remained wedded to the Lady Oenothea! I have learnt, the hard way, who won the final victory in *that* game of *potlatch*. Eh, what?" He winked at me. "Moreover," he added, "why shouldn't I promise to come with you? It's the one safe promise I can make, you know, since I know you'll not last five minutes up there—"

"What nonsense!" I said. "Our hot-air balloons are capable of—"

"I know what they're capable of, General. But have you considered the wind?"

"What do you mean, the wind?"

"In all my years here, O procurator, I have yet to encounter a single westerly wind. Oh, I mean a brief storm, perhaps, lasting no more than an hour or so... but a wind that'll actually carry you fellows westward for an entire week? You ask too much!"

"Foolish savage," I crowed, confident now that despite his newfound veneer of Romanness he was still at heart as much of an ignorant sod as ever. "Have you forgotten the Manifest Destiny of the Roman Imperium? Have you forgotten whose side the gods are on... not to mention that Trajan Himself happens to be a god? If the wind will not blow in our direction, surely the right sacrifice will change its mind. We are not, after all, mud-eating savages who pray at random to capricious forces of nature. We Romans have reduced the control of the universe to an exact science. Though your wind may be recalcitrant, it will surely heed the bidding of Jupiter! Not to mention Vacantanca, and the various other local deities recently adopted into the Roman pantheon."

I took a deep slug of this Quaquiutian wine. "Jolly good stuff," I said. "After you've downed a few gallons, you can hardly tell it isn't Lesbian."

Indeed, it was quite some time before a westerly wind sprang up; several creatures were duly sacrificed, including a young elephant left over from my previous sojourn in the land of the Quaquiutii. I despaired of the gods paying any heed at all, until. . . .

It was morning. We staggered to the beach. I'd been drunk, very drunk. I remember bedding the Lady Oenothea, with Hooting-Owl and Aquila on either side of me, urging me on and taking bets. Through the fog of my hangover I saw that half a dozen balloons had already been inflated. Each bore the legend SPQR in gilt letters on fabric dipped in the finest purple. Equus Insanus, who never left his father's side, was throwing our cloaks over us and chattering furiously.

"And the wind came this morning," he was saying, "and we all saw it and the bucinae started, and I ran to get you and—"

"Quam spectaculum est!" I cried; my heart stirred at the sight of our proud hot-air balloons, still roped to the tops of totem poles, straining hard against the wind. Pennants hung from their sides, and an aquilifer stood proudly on board the largest of the platforms, eagle raised high and glittering in the bronze light of dawn.

The legion, which I was quartering in the village to await the return of my small band of adventurers, was out in force; as I raised my hand they let out a cry of *Huka hey! Ave, O Papiniane, Dux et Imperator!*

I ran for the flat-hot-air-balloon like a little child. I was to share it with Aquila and some centurions; the others were to follow in their lesser balloons. I gave the signal; the moorings were loosened. I lost my balance as the thing swerved upwards, tripped over the slave who stoked the brazier, and singed off half my hair.

Aquila was laughing at me. "I have just the thing," he was saying, "this magical poultice—"

But I couldn't listen. We had been airborne for but five minutes, and already I was leaning over the side, raucously anointing the Oceanus Papinianus with a purée of half-digested salmon.

CHAPTER
XXXII

FOR AN HOUR OR TWO ALL SEEMED WELL. THE BRA-
ziers that heated the air to keep our vehicles aloft
served also to cook our food. Each hot-air balloon had
strings of salmon trailing from the corners, gifts from
Hooting-Owl's people; when we hungered we simply
reeled the line in a bit, skewered a fish, and threw it on
the fire, which slaves continually stoked and fanned.

The skies were blue and sunny, though cold; a high
wind blew us steadily westward; and the sea below
looked wondrously peaceful, almost meriting the absurd
appellation of Oceanus Pacificus with which the vulgar
had chosen to baptize it. The child Equus Insanus prat-
tled endlessly; he seemed utterly devoid of Roman discipline, and his father only laughed when he addressed me
rudely or stole a fish from the coals. A proper Roman
paterfamilias would long since have thrashed the bugger
to a pulp, but Aquila merely humored him. It was the
Lacotian way, he told me, to correct their children's ill
behavior by laughing at them.

"How absurd!" I said scornfully. "Surely only severe beatings can make a man of one. We Romans, who have conquered the world, thrive on the lash."

"*Hechitu welo!* But can you creep up *this* close to an aurochs without making a noise, and reach up to slit its belly open?"

"Bah! What matter of man could do that?" Suddenly I felt stubby little hands around my neck. "Get off me, imbecile!" I shouted, yanking forth the minuscule monster by the hair.

"You see?" Aquila said triumphantly. "Caught you quite by surprise. Believe me we Lacotii can go cloaked in the wind."

"Idle boasts, Aquila; hyperboles are natural to a conquered race, after all. Look at the Greeks."

"Look indeed." Aquila shrugged I turned to see the denizens of the next balloon ensconced in a vehement argument.

"Daddy, why are they screaming at each other?" Equus piped up, fiddling with the deerskin leggings beneath his toga praetexta.

The odd phrase drifted towards us on the wind: "Essential nature of the One . . . the quincunx being the perfect figure, the quintessence the natural consequence of . . . false syllogism, if you examine it from the point of view of prior and posterior analytics . . . Aristotle . . . Euclid. . . ." Considering the esoteric nature of their conversation, the Greek and the Egyptian seemed remarkably crimson in the face, even at this distance; but Abraham bar-David, the Jewish Sasquatius, seemed perfectly placid, and was, in fact, scribbling on a scrap of parchment.

"Who's he, the referee?" said Equus Insanus.

"No," said Aquila. "Actually our Judaean friend has turned writer."

"Oh?" I said. "It's not a piece of scientifictiones, by any chance?"

"No," Aquila responded, "our Abraham's work is by

no means scientifictive, but rooted firmly in reality; it is entitled *Peregrinus Perplexus*, a travel guide for the bewildered tourist."

"Heavens," I said.

"Just the book *you* need, General!" said the little boy. "You're always bewildered."

"Leave His Bulbosity alone, *michinkshi*." And they both began to cackle offensively at me.

It was in such frivolity that we passed the first few hours of our voyage.

"It's wonderful, isn't it, what a little Roman knowhow can do?" I was saying to Aquila. "All we need now is for the weather to hold out for a day or two, and then... China! The mythical, magical silkland! Oh, how exciting it is, Aquila, to be alive at this moment; to be the vanguard of the greatest discovery in the history of the Roman Empire!"

"*Hechitu welo*," said Aquila. Then... the weather changed....

"What's the matter?" I shouted.

"I do believe we're running into a storm," Aquila said. "Clearly, the westerly wind of an hour ago was merely part of a spinning wind, and will now carry us back to Quaquiutia!"

"Well," I said, shrugging. "We've nothing to worry about then. We'll simply rest a few more days in the village, sacrifice another creature or two, and be all set for a more opportune moment for departure...."

"Oh, I say," I said, pointing ahead. "What's that?"

I could not believe my eyes. In the distance, hovering over the ocean, was a huge and impossibly perfect triangle of mist.

"A strange phenomenon indeed," said Aquila. "Only in spirit journeys had I seen such a thing. It only goes to support the thesis that we are no longer traveling in earthly planes."

"Superstitious twaddle!" I said uneasily. I looked above; the clouds were getting quite dark. "You haven't been doing one of your rain dances, have you? I mean, not that I set much store by your savage mumbo-jumbo, but—"

"No, I believe that they are perfectly natural thunder-clouds, General."

"Well, don't just sit there, old man! Caper! Hop to it! Dance us up an antidote, old chap!"

"My dear General Papinianus," Aquila said. "The homo medicinae who taught me to dance gave me this vital maxim: *Never perform*, he said, *when you know it's not going to work*! You're on your own. O procurator. How about some good old Roman ingenuity?"

"For this I saved your life?"

"Saved my life! For this I left a comfortable deathbed, surrounded by dozens of weeping relatives?"

"Fire's gone out, master!" cried the slave-stoker. Unthinkingly I lashed out with my quirt.

"Sirrah! Fan the flames!" I cried, as hail the size of crab apples began to battle the sides of the balloons. One hit the slave on the head, and he passed out.

"But—but—" I shouted. Looking eastward, I suddenly saw another of our balloons plummeting, I saw legionaries grasping at the sides, I heard their screaming through the pelting of the hail.

"Bloody adventures!" I cursed; my voice was drowned out by thunder. "I should never have left Caesarea! Curse you, Aquila, for giving me this insatiable taste for risking life and limb. . . ."

But I could speak no more. The wind sprang up; we were tossed up and down, my stomach churned and relieved itself of another salmon dinner, and the next thing I knew we were all on top of each other, falling, falling, and the triangle of mist was careening towards us, growing and growing. . . .

"Wake up, General!" It was the child again, tugging me from my lethargy. I felt dry vomit in my throat. Where was I? Was I dead? Surely—

"The others . . . safe?" I groaned.

"Come, General! They're all waiting for you." I rubbed my eyes. The child's visage swam hazily before them for a moment.

I saw palm trees and lush verdure such as grow in the vicinity of Carthage. Here and there lay gigantic ribcages oddly familiar-looking.

Aaye was running up now, hardly able to contain himself. "Procurator, it's true, your predictions were completely accurate! Behold, it is even as you said . . . the living proof; bones of silkworms such as we found in that gorge en route to Quaquiutia, but these not petrified at all; the worms cannot have been dead a month or two!"

"Good heavens," I said, thanking the gods that we had been let off so lightly. I rubbed my eyes and my arse and stood up. "This is a veritable paradise!" I said. "I don't suppose these Chinish will be any threat to us at all; for we all know that the inhabitants of warmer climes are by nature sluggish and indolent, and given only to hedonistic pursuits. Let us explore more."

My group fell in behind me. We had lost several balloonsfull of legionaries and spear carriers; but all the major figures were still in one piece: Nikias and Aaye in mid-epistemological argument, Abraham writing on a scrap of papyrus, and Chief Hooting-Owl maintaining his composure by a muttering recital of his past achievements in battles of *potlatch*.

"Well, Aquila, what do you think?" I said. "We've really stumbled upon it for sure, this time, haven't we?"

"Of course we have!" Aaye interposed. "This time there can be no doubt that the very next creature we meet will be, in absolute verity, a Chinaman!"

"I will hold my peace," Aquila said, "since I am

wholly ignorant of this land of Chin; yet might these not be bones of giant lizards or other animals?"

"Silence, savage!" I said. "The scholars have spoken!"

"*I* have not spoken yet," Abraham bar-David said mildly.

"Then speak, so that all will have had a turn and we can continue on our mission."

"I have nothing to say," said the furry creature. "I was merely observing that I had not yet spoken, thus proving your statement a false syllogism—"

"Precisely what I mean!" Nikias interjected. "When the *all* is alluded to, as it must be in the statement *All the scholars have spoken*, it follows that, ontologically speaking—"

We had walked right into a sort of earthy mud-embankment. Giant ferns grew everywhere. And, resting atop the crest, its tail lost behind the tall vegetation, was a creature. It was long and smoothly serpentine, but about a man's width, and perhaps as much as ten cubits long; it was tapered towards the tiny head, which dozed contentedly in the mud.

"By Jove! A silkworm at last!" I could hardly contain myself, for I knew that this must be the creature which, according to the writings of P. Josephus Agricola, produced a sputum that quickly solidified into strands of sheerest silk, and which the Chinish folk used as a pack-animal, driving it sluggishly forward by means of lead-tipped goads.

Aquila looked at it. "By the Great Spirit!" he said. "The Egyptian's predictions *do* occasionally make sense."

"Well, what are we waiting for?" I said. "Let us gird up our loins and mount the creature. I assume it will need breaking in, before it is ready to be ridden in triumph back to Caesarea-on-Miserabilis." Of course, I didn't even know how we were going to get back across the Oceanus Pacificus at that point: but the Chinish folk could not be far away, and if they did not help us, we could always conquer and enslave them, as we had done with every other nation.

"You want us to ride this thing?" Aquila said dubiously.

"Of course!" Aaye said. "It must learn to know its master."

"And who, pray, will be the first?" Aquila said.

We all looked at each other.

"Let me, Daddy, let me!" It was The Brat. He was already running up to leap onto the great worm's flanks.

"Well!" I said. "Let it not be said that Romans are outdone by children—and savage children at that!" I hastened to clamber up the mudbank, pulling myself up by means of the ferns.

"Our noble general has spoken!" said Aquila, laughing.

"Giddyup! Giddyup!" Equus Insanus squealed gleefully, digging his feet into the creature's side. In a moment I was at the top, and about to jump on behind The Brat, when I chanced to turn around and look over the other side of the embankment.

I screamed! "Look—it's a monster—" I shrieked, as more and more of the beast came into view: the body, huge as a good-size temple, the hillock haunches, the prodigious legs. "Run for your lives!" I started to get off what I now knew to be merely the neck of a creature of stupendous magnitude.

Down below, my scholars and savages were all hooting with laughter. "You don't see what I see!" I yelled down at them, but they laughed all the more. Suddenly the neck began to move.

"Hold on, Equus Insanus," I said, trying myself to grasp the slippery, slime-crusted skin of the animal. The beast reared up its neck now; its eyes opened, its tongue darted out to uproot a clump of ferns.

I heard the shouts of the others. "Help! Help!" I
cried, but all I heard were remarks like ". . . definitely
reptilian, eh, Aaye? . . . jolly big it is. What would you
call such a thing? . . . well, being a lizardlike being, and
being so ponderous that its very footfall must sound like
thunder, I would suggest the appellative *brontosaurus*
myself; what about you, Abraham, eh?" . . . endless de-
batings in this vein.

"Dance, Aquila!" I shouted. "Maybe the flying
saucers will come and rescue us!"

"I'm too old to dance. My joints are weak. Besides,
all I know is a rain dance."

"Do that one then! You always get them wrong anyway, maybe you'll accidentally summon the saucers—"

Just then the brontosaurus rose impressively to its full
height. Its neck craned up and down with frightening
agility, and I was holding on with both arms and both
legs, yelping in terror. Equus Insanus wasn't having such
a good time either; indeed, he had burst into tears.

Dutifully, Aquila began to dance and wheeze, a tiny
figure below me. Hooting-Owl began declaiming in his
native tongue, offering to trade our lives for his freedom,
for *potlatch* is a game of perpetual back-stabbing. The
reptile we were on began stomping slowly away, each
step it took shaking my very marrow and blasting my
eardrums.

All at once, I heard a familiar whirring sound. "The
flying saucers! Hold on, Brat, and we'll be rescued in no
time!"

And indeed, the shiny disks were beginning to descend upon us out of the sky; and the earth began to
rumble mightily, and burst asunder in the middle distance, much in the manner of a volcano's first eruption,
spewing forth fountains of fire at the center of which
emerged—Jove strike me down if I lie—an enormous
palace, resembling in every particular the celebrated
Golden House which the Emperor Nero had had built

when I was but a little boy—rising phoenixlike from the blazing infernum that surrounded it.

A shriek of terror escaped Equus Insanus's lips; he lost his grip and tumbled down towards the exploding earth. The academics were running in circles, and only the two savages seemed unconcerned; indeed; Aquila was still dancing.

"Save us! Save us!" I cried out to the descending saucers. But as I screamed I heard the heavens resound with raucous mocking laughter, a laughter that had EVIL stamped all over it . . . and I realized that they were the wrong flying saucers. . . .

"Stop dancing, Aquila!" I shouted down at the prancing old man. But it was too late. Gigantic nets were being spun out from the bellies of the nearby flying saucers; and before I knew it, our whole gang, including the brontosaurus, were being borne skyward. The beast did not, as can be imagined, take too kindly to its sudden change of habitat; it thrashed about, emitting a high-pitched honking from its throat, and had I not let go of the neck, and climbed up to the top of the net, forgetting in my distress that I was hundreds of passūs in the air and that I have a terrible head for heights, I would have been flattened into a papyrus.

My comrades, caught in the same net, all followed my lead, scrambling for the less dangerous positions near the top. We were moving slowly towards the Neronian palace. Nervously, I began counting heads.

"The Brat's gone!" said a voice. I started; it was Aquila, hanging on for dear life beside me.

"Surely not—" I looked around wildly. Then I remembered: the last I'd seen him he was plummeting headlong towards the golden palace. "Oh, what's to become of us?" I said. "China indeed! When I get home I'll take every single work of that self-styled expert P. Josephus Agricola, put them all in a heap, and personally set them to the torch. Silkworms my arse! Yellow-skinned folk who paint their faces with a poultice of gold, and ride around on giant caterpillars! Scientific-tiones rot the mind...I'll have them banned from the Alexandria Library, I'll have them—"

And then, to my surprise and no doubt to Aquila's great relief, I fainted.

Chapter
XXXIII

WHEN I CAME TO, I COULDN'T MOVE. NOT EVEN an eyeball, that is; I was staring straight ahead, and unable even to blink. I thought I would be in a dungeon, but far from it; the room I was in was airy and pleasant, and I could see that it opened onto an atrium where a marble fountain played. Once, as a boy, when my father still enjoyed the favor of the Divine Nero, I had been in this very room in the Golden House; it was, I recall, a room that held several Asiatic eunuchs, which Caesar employed to search his guests for daggers, poison, and suchlike, the advantage of eunuchs being that it was unnecessary to have sexually segregated searching-rooms, since neither man nor woman could claim to have had his or her virtue impugned (of course, His Divinity Himself had a tendency to take care of that later). Since I seemed to have been frozen solid, there was little to do save entertain these memories of the distant past....

Before me, resembling absurd caryatids, were Aquila, Hooting-Owl, Nikias, Abraham, and Aaye, as frozen as I myself was; their expressions ranged from equanimity (Aquila's) to hysteria (Aaye's). The spectacle was quite amusing, though I was unable to laugh.

After a very long while, I heard another outburst of that chilling laughter which had accompanied our capture, and I regained the use of my body. The others, too, were gradually coming to life, and Aquila, I saw, had seized a knife and was about to cut off one of his own fingers.

"Good heavens," I said.

"I mourn for my son," Aquila said. "Besides, what does one finger more or less matter? It is clear that the Land of Many Tipis cannot be far in the future for us all."

"Come, come, Aquila, don't talk like that! Lower the morale of the cohorts and all that, you know, what."

"What cohorts?" said Aquila, and everyone else moaned.

"I hear the owl call my name," Chief Hooting-Owl added in a lugubrious tone.

"'Call no man happy,'" Nikias was quoting from Euripides or one of that crowd, "'until he is dead.'"

"Dust thou art," the sasquatch droned dismally, "and unto dust—"

And Aaye was mumbling some Egyptian gibberish, lines from the Book of the Dead I had no doubt.

"Now wait a minute," I said incensed suddenly. "Where is your love of honor? Your pride in your Roman citizenship? How can you say that all is lost? We are, after all, in a room of the Golden Palace of Nero; perhaps we have by some supernatural means actually been returned to the bosom of Mother Rome herself!"

"My dear General," said Aquila, "if you wish to stop entertaining such a silly notion, I suggest that you look behind you." I turned round; there was a portico that led to a balcony, from which there was a view of the city beneath. I saw a few temples and things, and in the distance the Flavian Amphitheater (or Colosseum, as it is sometimes known); and at first I heaved a sigh of relief. But after a while I started to notice that nothing was quite what it seemed. For one thing, the city came abruptly to an end, and beyond were fields, swamps, and lush vegetation such as we had encountered on first landing within this Mysterious Triangle. For another, the streets were devoid of people, which would have been a most singular occurrence in Rome. For yet another, the Flavian Amphitheater contained—I could recognize it clearly even from this distance, since it filled fully a quarter of the arena—an old friend of ours: that brontosaurus whose neck we had thought to be a silkworm.

"Indeed," I said, "this isn't Rome; and it bloody well isn't China, either. In fact, I've a feeling it's no earthly place at all!"

More raucous laughter filled the room. Where was it coming from? "In fact, I'll wager that we have fallen into the very lair of the Time Criminal of whom V'Denni-Kenni spoke, that Mastermind of Evil with whom the were-jaguars plan to perform their Final Spectacle!" I turned my back on the view of pseudo-Rome only to find that my companions had once more been transformed into statues. "Now look here," I railed at the empty air, "I don't care who you are; I'm the Representative of Caesar here, and my person is inviolate—"

More hideous cackling. And then, in a puff of smoke, someone materialized in front of me.

"By Jupiter Optimus Maximus!" I said, agape at this latest apparition. For it resembled nothing so much as a sort of enormous green pig, with curiously delicate antennae and bug eyes. Once more, it screeched with that laughter that one instinctively knows must belong to a creature of consummate Evil.

"Ah, General Titus Papinianus Lacoticus Sasquaticus," the creature purred menacingly. "How frightfully clever of you to have guessed who I am! Well, don't just stand there, say something! Cat got your tongue, eh, what? Or are you surprised that I speak your language?"

"I—I—"

"Bah! What do V'Denni-Kenni and K'Tooni-Mooni mean, anyway, by sending such creatures as *you* against me? Have they lost all respect for me? Aren't I Evil enough to merit better than this?"

"If you please, Your Evilship, the were-jaguars didn't send us . . . looking for China . . . hot-air balloons. . . ."

"A likely story!" His breath was fouler than a legionary shitpit. "You came for the Final Spectacle, did you not? Well, spectacle you shall have, and in abundance. Indeed, you will have more than your fill of it. Ho, ho, ho! But first . . . since you are, after a fashion, a leader among your inferior race, I shall give you the grand tour of the palace. I'm rather proud of it, actually; Roman history's my specialty, you know. I've already made over a hundred continua branch off at the Roman nexus, you know. Though I doubt if such futuristic remarks will make much sense to you. Well, before you . . . ah . . . pass on to the Elysian Fields, let's show you what we have here."

I was not terribly pleased at this turn of events. I reached for the little dagger I always carry in a fold of my tunica for moments such as these, and rushed towards him; but I had not even reached him when I was repelled by some invisible force.

"That," said the Green Pig, "is future technology for you: a force-shield, if you please."

"Wonderful," I said.

"Now, if you'd care to follow me?"

He led me down aisles, through corridors, across atria. "As you may have guessed," he said, "this Mystic Triangle into which you have fallen is actually what might be called a Spatiotemporal Anomaly. It is created by my own diabolical invention, the Spatiotemporal Bewilderizer, which I have set up within the actual confines of the Flavian Amphitheater there."

"You snatched the Amphitheater out of Rome itself?"

"Ha, ha! Not *your* Rome, you ignorant insect, but another Rome, in another universe, where things happened a little differently from yours . . . because *I* willed it so through the use of the Spatiotemporal Bewilderizer! Same with this palace, I may add. It's a jolly nice one, isn't it? And don't mind the brontosaurus; it wandered in one day when I accidentally toggled a switch I shouldn't have, and set it to a hundred million years ago instead of a hundred. Even we Time Criminals make mistakes sometimes, sad to say. Ah, here we are."

We had entered a vast hall of the palace; if boyhood memory serves me right, it had been one of Nero's throne rooms. But makeshift stages had been set up everywhere, and upon them were tableaux of people, some in outlandish costumes, and yet so verisimilitudinous that I knew them immediately to be people frozen out of time, in precisely the way I and my companions had all been frozen.

"Behold my collection of Great Historical Moments!" said the Time Criminal, his viridian jowls quivering with excitement. "I snatched them all from various time-lines, you know, and have preserved them here so that I can replay them whenever I want. Here's one you have heard of—"

He clapped his hands. On one platform there stood a bald, middle-aged man in a senatorial toga and laurel wreath; another man, brandishing a dagger, was frozen over him in mid-stab. As the Time Criminal clapped again, they came to life, the knife came ripping through cloth, and I heard the bald man distinctly say *"Et tu, Brute!"* before the scene abruptly ceased in mid-gesture. I simply gaped—for the assassination of Julius Caesar was something that had happened more than a hundred years before!

We went by other scenes: some seemed familiar, others impossibly alien, as one in which a man in metallic garments that covered him from head to toe, wearing over his head a kind of transparent jug, was walking about on a desertlike landscape waving a pennant of stripes and stars. "Oh, that's the first man on the moon," said the Time Criminal nonchalantly, "I've got half a dozen of them."

It was in the next room that I began to get very frightened indeed. For I saw the Emperor Domitian himself—the first to have sent me on the fruitless quest for China—seated upon a throne. Though I knew him to be but another souvenir in this Time Criminal's picture book of the universes, yet I quailed, especially when the Criminal awakened him for a second, long enough for him to see me and cry out, "You too, Papinian, you too...." before returning to his spatiotemporal stasis.

And then I saw Trajan too. I saw, indeed, about a dozen Trajans, and all seemed to glare at me. "Look, old chap," said the Time Criminal, "none of these Trajans is *your* Trajan, you know. That one, for instance... wonderful ruler. Enlarged the Empire all the way to Parthia. Pity he vanished mysteriously on the eve of the final battle."

"But...how irresponsible! What happens, then, to those worlds from whom key historical figures have been so casually excised?"

"Oh, they muddle through," said the Criminal. "Besides, after a while the Elastic Effect comes in and time bounces back onto the right track; and of course, the actual people of the continuum have no idea that I've tinkered with them! This is such fun, you know; it certainly beats creating hairy monsters and dropping them in the Himalayas."

"Indeed," I said.

"Yes, your period is something of a special love with me; that's why I engineered this fantastical alternate history, with its steamships and motor-cars a thousand years before their time. I'm a visionary genius, you know! I suppose you'll tell me I'm mad, though. They all do."

"You are positively bonkers!"

"How terribly banal. How can you possibly comprehend the grandeur of my conception? Thousands of histories twisted beyond all recognition. But, as I say, this period is my favorite. Look, I've prepared an exhibit just for you, which I'm sure you'd like to gaze upon before I sentence you to your regrettable demise—regrettable for you, that is, though I shall enjoy it well enough. When you do die, by the way, which will be tomorrow, if all goes well, I trust you'll have no hard feelings? Stiff upper lip and all that? After all, it isn't much fun sitting around being Evil for centuries on end, you know. Any diversion is welcome. I've a lot on my mind, what with the Final Spectacle coming up and K'Tooni-Mooni's cohorts heading here at top speed; thanks to you and your blabbermouth friends, who gave them all the details of my movements in your continuum! Where was I? Ah yes. Lo! Gaze upon my prize specimen, which I obtained for your edification as soon as I knew you were coming!" At another handclap a curtain was drawn, and I was gazing into an alcove.

"I captured this figure from the nexus right next to this one; indeed, it would be a virtually identical world, had I not . . . ah . . . fiddled with it. This specimen is, as I'm sure you'll recognize, a certain Roman general. I snatched him up for my collection at the precise moment when his Emperor had condemned him to death for the crime of not discovering China."

Terror seized me. For, standing in that recess in the wall, his face pale with fright, his eyes wide, his every feature distorted in some ultimate horror . . . was me!"

For the second time since I had been elevated by Caesar to the august position of Dux of the Thirty-fourth, I did something which every red-blooded Roman male would be heartily ashamed of.

I fainted.

CHAPTER
XXXIV

I WAS NOT TERRIBLY AMUSED, UPON REGAINING CON-
sciousness, to discover that I had been crucified.
That I was face to face with a brontosaurus only com-
pounded by discomfiture. Nor was it much of a relief to
me that my tormentor had not used nails on me, but had
merely strung me up with rope; I knew very well from
experience that the latter form of execution, working as
it does by a slow asphyxiation induced by the continual
abrasure of the shoulder blades upon the lungs, was in
fact by far the more protracted, the more undignified.
My first impulse was to call out: "How dare you do this
to me, a citizen of Rome and representative of the Prin-
ceps Himself?" But I realized that such talk would have
little effect upon my pitiless captor, whose mentality was
as porcine as his appearance.

I saw him now, sitting in the Imperial Box of the Flavian Amphitheater (for, as my gaze circumnavigated the
surrounding area, I saw that this was where I was at) to
my left (I had been strung up unceremoniously just

above the gates of death), dressed in the Imperial purple. The purple dye contrasted most vulgarly with his viridity of visage. Shambling back and forth across the sand was the brontosaur; however, he could not reach me, for one of those force-shields such as had prevented me from touching the Green Pig stood in its way. In fact, this force-shield seemed to begin at the corner of the Imperial Box, so that His Evilship was seated to my side of it, and as protected from the creature as was I.

I struggled to hold myself up, knowing that if I were to let go, the asphyxiative process would not be slow in following.

Beneath the Imperial Box was a machine of some kind. I had read of many marvelous devices in the scrolls of scientifictiones to which I was addicted; none came up to the reality. For this apparatus had cogs, wheels, levers, flashing lights, antennae from which issued jagged blue lightning bolts, dials, and ranks of buttons of every color. The entire device glowed as if lit from within. This must indeed be the fabled Spatiotemporal Bewilderizer! I strained hard against the post, desperately trying to stay upright.

Chained to the machine, and completely frozen, were Aquila, Hooting-Owl, Aaye, Abraham, and Nikias. Only I was conscious, then. I was fated to watch the entire spectacle through to the end, and no doubt to be served up as dessert to whatever ravening monster the Green Pig would summon up next.

Soon I heard the familiar laughter.

"Ha, ha, ha!" the Time Criminal said, his voice amplified a thousandfold by the excellent acoustics of the Flavian Amphitheater. "Little did you know, Titus Papinianus, that you would end up as spectacle fodder on an island in the midst of a mystic, misty Triangle that doesn't even exist in your universe...did you, old chap?"

"I would spit on you if I could," I said. "Only my proper Roman breeding restrains me."

"Not to mention thirty cubits of stout rope! Hee hee! Ah well. First, my dear fellow, you will watch your compatriots die; then you shall perish in some fiendish manner that I shall extemporize. But first, a little hors d'oeuvre, don't you think? More monsters, perhaps. Oh, ancient history is my passion; I've always loved dinosaurs, Romans, and Indians. Now that I am master of the Spatiotemporal Bewilderizer, I actually get to play with them all—in the same arena!"

"They're not Indians," I said irritably. "They are Terra Novans. I don't know of any Romans who have even set foot in India." I started to sag again, and strained harder.

"I'll call them whatever I please," said the Time Criminal. He clambered down some steps to his machine, elbowing the living statues of my friends out of the way, and began to push buttons.

Suddenly I heard a tiny voice in my ear. "Watch! He'll push the red one next. I've been watching him. That's the Time Portal."

"What the—"

A tiny hand flew over my mouth. "Shush, you silly general! You'll give us all away!"

"By the maidenhead of Venus!" I was struck speechless.

"Aren't you going to ask me how I got here?" said Equus Insanus, who was perched behind me on the crosspiece, his slight form completely hidden by mine. "Look, I'm going to rescue you now, so just take it easy."

"Wonderful! You incomparable child, I shall promote you to tribune as soon as we get home—"

"Will you shut up! Act dead or something. I'll wait for an opportune moment, and then untie you slowly, starting with the feet. When I give the signal, you'll slither slowly to the bottom. Now's as good a time as any to start work; I'm not as strong as Daddy, so it'll take a while."

No sooner had he begun that a most hideous sight assailed my senses. For beneath the brontosaurus, a huge portal of blackness, taller than the amphitheater itself, materalized. I shrieked; the boy ducked behind me.

I heard him whisper. "That dial on the far left; I'm pretty sure that's a time-zone selector or something. Picks the period from which he's going to collect his next souvenir."

"How do you know, you little toad?"

"I've been watching him all day."

"And how did you get here anyway?"

"What a dumb old general you are! I'm saving your life, and all you can do is ask dumb old questions. I walked, of course. You think I'd just lie there in the mud and wait for the Roman cavalry to come over the hill?"

"But—"

"No buts! Watch! It's pretty fun to try and guess what's going to pop out next."

And to my dismay, a horrible creature came charging out of the doorway of darkness. It was as tall as the brontosaur, but elongated; it had huge fangs and a thrashing tail, and it stood on its hind legs. Its forepaws were incongruously petite. It immediately made for the brontosaurus, and, as our porcine host giggled and guffawed, began attacking the unfortunate creature, who in attempting to flee merely bumped against the invisible force-shield. Not an intelligent being, it continued to run in place, bashing its neck again and again on the barrier.

The Time Criminal hooted with glee as the battle proceeded. "I'll have to awaken the other frozen ones," he said, "so that I can laugh over their expressions of terror." He clapped his hands, and the chained figures on our side of the barrier came to life. As the three academics caught sight of the two raging titans, they began to wail and to pull against their chains, to no avail. Aquila relaxed against his restrains and surveyed the scene with a bemused expression; and Hooting-Owl turned to the Green Pig and was attempting to strike a bargain with him.

Presently the academics noticed that the barrier was preventing them from getting hurt; so they settled down to a discussion of nomenclature.

"Clearly a nobler beast than the brontosaurus. I suggest calling it the *tyrannosaurus rex*," said Aaye.

"What? And mix the Greek *tyrannos* with the Latin *rex* within the same name? Surely that is tautologous," said Nikias. "One or the other, my Egyptian friend, but not both!"

As they spoke (the more taciturn Sasquatius interrupting now and then with a learned word) the two beasts began to go at it with a vengeance, the tyrannosaur lashing away with his tail, the brontosaur's neck darting with surprising agility. Tireless, the tyrannosaur worried away at the brontosaur's flanks, honking eerily the while; indefatigably the brontosaur battered against the indestructible force barrier, until its head was cut open and its neck raw in a dozen places.

"In a less confined space," Equus Insanus whispered in my ear, "I'd give them more or less equal odds; as it is, the one with the big teeth is bound to win. For one thing, it's hungry, and the brontosaurus only eats vegetation."

"How do you know all this?"

"I told you, I've been watching this dump for a day and a half!"

"I'm sure Aristotle says nothing about the feeding habits of these silkworms-cum-giant lizards."

"Who's Aristotle?"

"That," I said, finally showing myself to be in some small measure superior to this midget of a savage, "is for you to find out when you learn to read and write, like decent Roman citizens do."

"Oh, I can read all right. But I only like reading scientifictiones," he said, pulling away at a recalcitrant knot in my crucifixion-ropes.

I heard the voice of the Evil One. "Oh, I say, Papinian! Having a good time, eh, what?"

"Marvelous, Your Evilship!" I temporized, as Equus Insanus slithered into hiding behind me.

At that moment, the brontosaur, harried beyond endurance by that monstrous predator, tumbled to the ground and expired, bringing down several tiers of marble seats. The tyrannosaur, its appetite whetted, stalked about screeching.

"What next, my friends?" the Time Criminal said, and with another handclap he had dissolved the force-shield, for the dinosaur was making its way towards *me*! "What next? Shall I put the two Indians" (I don't know for what perverse reason he insisted on referring to my Terra Novans as *Indians*; surely such a supreme master of super-science would not confuse such an obvious detail) "—shall I put them against the dinosaur, and force them to protect all the others?" He made a gesture, at which Roman catapults came rolling out of the Time Portal, and a bin full of exotic weaponry. At another gesture the chains fell from Hooting-Owl and Aquila; they both rushed to the weapon bin while the academics screamed continuously.

"The catapult!" I heard Aquila cry; Hooting-Owl helped him load with a pitch-ball, which they set alight; it hit the tyrannosaur on the head, but it continued to advance towards me.

"Dance!" I cried to Aquila. "Dance as you have never danced before! Perhaps this time the right flying saucers *will* appear!"

Aquila yelled back, "You're out of your mind!" And he seized a lance and began to lunge at the creature (he came up to its calf or thereabouts) while Hooting-Owl worried it with fireballs. The creature was as stupid as the other one, though; for when struck it would not react for several moments, almost as though its brain had to assimilate the extent of the damage before determining an appropriate screech or maddened lunge. Aquila danced to and fro, stabbing the thing now and then in the legs; suddenly it snapped up the lance in its jaws, and all I saw was a pair of withered legs, wriggling madly; but then the lance broke and Aquila landed safely on the carcass of the brontosaurus; the tyrannosaur, distracted by the sight of the dead beast, began to rip ravenously at its innards, while gore streamed from its fangs and down its neck.

Just at that moment, Equus Insanus finished untying my bonds, and I half-slithered, half-lurched groundwards.

"What the—" The Time Criminal stormed from his booth, ignoring the tyrannosaurus as it continued to feed, and staggered towards me, his hands threateningly outstretched.

"Keep him at bay," cried Equus Insanus, "while I sabotage the machine!"

Unthinkingly I obeyed the savage child—for I had lost all dignity now, and sought only to save my own hide—and began to run hither and thither as the Green Pig gained on me. Meanwhile, Equus Insanus ran to the Spatiotemporal Bewilderizer and began to fiddle with the controls.

"That's my son!" Aquila shouted gleefully, returning with Hooting-Owl to the operation of the catapult, and bombarding the tyrannosaurus with rocks. The huge predator scarcely noticed, though, as he gorged; would a man notice a few gnats, if a plate of delicate bear's hams or unborn dormice dipped in honey, or some other such costly dish, were placed before him?

"Curses," the Time Criminal cried, and ran to protect his invention. "Keep your filthy hands away from that thing...if you turn the time knob, you've no way of guessing what thing will come crashing through the portal, and—"

"I'm turning it to the present," the little boy said, and then he banged repeatedly on the red button.

"Not the red button! Not in the present! No! The spatial coordinates have been centered on *me*!" the Green Pig shouted; but it was too late. We heard a whistling sound, as of a projectile being loosed from a scorpion or catapulta—

It was another Green Pig!

"What are you doing in my time-line?" the first Green Pig said angrily, flapping his Imperial robe.

"And what do you mean by summoning me from mine?"

Another pig popped up beside the first two. More whooshing sounds. We all turned round and stared at the Time Portal, whence more Green Pigs were being ejected at the rate of one every second or so. Equus Insanus continued to bang unmercifully upon the red button.

The sandy arena of the Flavian Amphitheater was now completely full of Green Pigs, with more arriving every second. One by one they came to blows and presently the whole arena was one writhing sea of pugilistic Green Pigs.

It was at this point that the tyrannosaurus decided that he was hungry again. Rising from his bloody feast, he began to stomp around wildly, here and there crushing a Green Pig. We had by then lost sight of the original Evil One, but all present seemed equally nauseating, so we felt few regrets as the tyrannosaur scooped one or two of them into his jaws. But then he seemed to catch sight of us.

"Help! What'll we do?" I said.

"Search me," Aquila said, shrugging. "Want me to dance up an invisibility medicine?"

"Quick!" little Equus Insanus shrieked. "Up the cross!"

It was each man for himself as we shinnied up the cross upon which I had so lately been strung up. I managed to make it to the cross-piece, and squatted uneasily on the end; the sasquatch had hooked his legs securely round the X of the cross, and was balancing Aaye around his neck, Equus Insanus under one armpit, and Nikias, who was clutching onto his legs; Hooting-Owl was squashed in between me and Abraham bar-David's other armpit, and as for Aquila—

He was actually balancing upright on the opposite arm of the cross, hopping from one foot to another, and singing some Lacotian song!

"What *are* you doing?" I said, as the tyrannosaur gazed longingly at us, much as one might stare with hunger at a tree full of ripe figs.

"I think," said Aquila in between wheezing utterances, "that I'd better teach you my death song now. I suspect you're going to have to be using it in a moment."

He danced unsteadily, croaking out the incomprehensible words of his death song.

Suddenly I felt the cross giving way.

"We're falling! We're falling!" several of us were screaming (as if that were not obvious) as the cross began to creak and sway. In that split second I knew at last that I was going to die. A superstitious dread overcame me, for I had no wish to enter Hades and have to answer to the judges of the afterlife . . . what could I do? I didn't even have a coin to shove in my mouth to pay the ferryman. Would I be condemned to walk the nether shores of darkness forever, then? Above the tumult I heard Aquila singing still. Almost without thinking I began to repeat his words; mumbo jumbo or not, they were better than *nothing*. Presently, as we began to tumble down towards the throng of angry Green Pigs, I raised one arm and began shaking an imaginary rattle. "O Jupiter Vacantancae," I prayed, "help me . . . help me. . . ." In that final second of life, I raised my eyes imploringly to the heavens—

Hundreds of flying saucers were materializing in the sky! They were streaming downwards towards us!

"We're saved!" I shouted, as the ocean of pig-heads buffered my fall.

Chapter
XXXV

Blinding light filled the sky. Terrified, I closed my eyes tight. When I opened them, the tables had turned: the tyrannosaur was completely immobilized (its gaping maw but a cubit or two from my neck) and the several hundred Green Pigs were all transformed into statues.

In the distance, the fabulous Time Citadel, which I had once glimpsed taking off from a valley in Quaquiutia, was slowly coming to rest on what would have been the Capitoline Hill if the Time Criminal had bothered with a complete reconstruction of Rome; it was a tangled mass of glittering spires and mosaic domes that flashed with a thousand colors.

Flying saucers were swooping down from overhead; they were gathering up the thousands of frozen Green Pigs in nets, much as we ourselves had been gathered up by the Time Criminal a day or two before.

I gathered my motley group together; and we staggered towards the whorl of brilliance that was the Time Citadel, for we knew whom we would find there.

And sure enough, in that selfsame resplendent hall in which we had last met him, we found V'Denni-Kenni, the green were-jaguar who had first told us of the Final Spectacle.

He was standing at one end of the hall, conversing with the equally green giant lobster and octopus who seemed to be his under-officers. He looked up and saw us; immediately he dropped his business and came towards us, beaming, his arms wide open in a gesture of welcome.

"Was that it?" I said excitedly. "Was that the Final Spectacle you spoke of?"

V'Denni-Kenni laughed, a kindly laugh that resounded all around us, for the translating-devices, implanted in the edifice's walls, were operating as usual. "Alas, you poor little primitives; you had a little spectacle of your own, but you did not see the great battle we fought, the decisive battle between our saucers and his saucers. That took place far from here, out in the emptiness of space; for were it to have taken place near the earth, who knows what continents might have been sliced in half by accident, what earthquakes, tempests, floods might have ensued? That is why we were late in rescuing you. Nevertheless, old chaps, you did in fact save us a great deal of trouble . . . I am astonished to say that you moronic savages of the remote past have actually saved the entire universe! More than one universe, in fact, for you assembled in a single spot all the Time Criminals from all the alternate universes in which the fellow is known to have operated."

I noticed them then; dozens of the enormous nets were hanging from the ceiling, and each contained a hundred or more exact duplicates of the Time Criminals; they were no longer statues, but wrigglingly, kickingly, and bickeringly animate.

"What will be done with them?" I asked wonderingly.

"Surely for creatures of such consummate Evil, even crucifixion would seem far too lenient a punishment."

V'Denni-Kenni laughed again. "Good heavens, you ancients are a bloodthirsty lot. We don't do that sort of thing anymore, you know. Perhaps we'll have their brains erased or something."

"Sounds like execution to me," Aquila said. "I wonder what their scalps would look like hanging on my death scaffold."

"Surely, Aquila, you are not thinking of that again!" Nikias said. "We've saved the universe, haven't we? We should sit back and enjoy the kudos for a while at least!"

"Indeed! It was Equus Insanus who saved you all by memorizing the operation of the Spatiotemporal Bewilderizer while you lot were busy with your philosophical arguments."

"You are right," Nikias said. "Bless you, child!" And Equus Insanus ran giggling forward, to be hugged and petted and made much of by us all.

"To be saved by a child . . . and a savage one at that!" Aaye groaned, as he gave the child a diffident pat on the head.

"Perhaps you understand now," said the were-jaguar, "how I feel. You are a little embarrassed, perhaps, that a young one has saved your lives; what must we feel, to have had our universes rescued by creatures whom we barely recognize to be our remote ancestors? If the child has taught you humility, you fellows have taught it to us in equal measure. But now we must think of the future."

"What future?" I moaned. "I have seen my future! It is to be sentenced to death by the Emperor Trajan for not discovering China."

"What you saw, Titus, was only a ghost of the truth; it was what has already happened in a universe to which you do not belong. In your own universe, who is to say?"

"But you are from the future! You *know* what will become of me."

"And if it should so happen that you *find* China?" said the were-jaguar. And it seemed to me that his eyes sparkled strangely.

"China...."

"Ah. To you we must seem like gods; yet we owe to you the very integrity of the lives we will lead, millions of years in the future though they be. We're not supposed to grant wishes, you know... that would be interference. But in the case of *your* universe... well, things have been so mucked about already, I don't suppose another dose of futuristic technology is going to make any difference. So... how about it, my good men? Requests will be heard and granted."

"China!" the three academics shouted in unison, and then they explained severally how the sight of the land of Chin would serve to settle their many disputes over its nature, and to corroborate or discredit once and for all the writings of that genius-or-charlatan P. Josephus Agricola.

"And you, Hooting-Owl?" said V'Denni-Kenni, turning to the Quaquiutius.

"To hold the greatest *potlatch* in the world," the savage said humbly.

"And you, General Titus Papinianus Lacoticus Sasquaticus, Procurator of Lacotia and Overseer of Siannia and Quaquiutia?"

"I want to go home."

"And you, little one who has saved so much?"

Equus Insanus said, "I want to be just like Daddy when I grow up."

The were-jaguar nodded gravely and said, "Child, you are already as like him as you could possibly be. Strange that you, who have done the most, should ask for the least." He looked pointedly at us. "And you, Aquila?"

"It is a good day to die," Aquila said.

"And what to you *is* death?"

"I do not know, O wise ones. Perhaps it is to be like you; free to visit all lands and times, yet always outside them. Perhaps *you* are the grandfathers who have been calling me these past few years."

"Well, we could certainly use you in the Dimensional Patrol. But we will grant all your wishes before we leave your universe forever."

I looked up at the thousand wriggling Green Pigs. A thought nagged at me; I had to ask them. "What will happen to us? Will we ever be cast back on the track that was originally intended for us, and live the history that we were intended to live?"

"No," said V'Denni-Kenni. "Your world has gone so radically askew that it might be considered a rogue universe. You wouldn't want your old universe back anyway. It was very boring. The Roman Empire fell, you know."

"You're pulling my leg, I take it."

"Heavens, no! What's more, Terra Nova was never discovered by the Romans, but by a fleet of Indians under the Maharaja of Jain, after the invention of sailing-ships by a scientific genius named Ashoka, using principles developed by Aristotle after Alexander the Great made him a satrap of Western India."

"Good heavens," I said.

"A vast Indian Empire of Sanskrit-speaking Lacotii arose in Terra Nova, known by the Indians as Greater Bharata. It was they who conquered Rome shortly after the reign of ... of. ..."

"Yes?"

"... ah yes ... the Emperor Papinian ... the less said about him the better. ..."

"What are you talking about?"

"One Titus Papinianus, having bribed his way into Imperial favor, next usurped the throne from Trajan and was subsequently ignominiously ousted by one *Shunka-winkte*, Maharaja of the Lacota."

"What! That's Equus Insanus's name in Lacotian."

"I do believe you're starting to see the picture, old chap," said V'Denni-Kenni. "Perhaps you'd care to transfer to the universe I just described? You could change places with the other General Titus, and none need ever be the wiser."

"I'll pass," I said, glaring at The Brat, Aquila's hideously precocious offspring. To be deposed by that! Unthinkable. A fate worse than death. Perhaps I should have the child executed as soon as we got home. Uppity little monster. Why could *I* never have a son like that? My little Cervilla appeared barren, and the thought of siring a child off the vast and sweaty Lady Oenothea, my first wife, was frankly less than appetizing. I resolved to name this Shunkawinkte my adopted son and heir as soon as we returned to Caesarea-on-Miserabilis. Nip it in the bud, you know. Wouldn't want the little bastard getting any ideas from listening to were-jaguars and other itinerant gods.

Aquila spoke up, then. "How do you know you've caught every single copy of the Time Criminal?" he asked our host.

"We believe we have."

"But if a single one has got away?"

"Then, alas, the whole bloody spectacle starts all over again!" the were-jaguar said, sighing.

Of our flight over China I shall say little; suffice it to say that we flew over a vast and verdant land in V'Denni-Kenni's flying saucer. We saw the cities with their teeming thousands; we saw the young men riding silkworms and the women gathering up the strands of dried sputum and entrapping coagulated moonbeams to weave into silk. The countenances of all these folk were gold; indeed I saw the powdered-gold paste that they use, which bubbles up into little brooks of gold from subterranean sources.

Indeed, what little we saw of China agreed with the writings of P. Josephus Agricola in every particular, much to the delight of our sophists. *So* similar was it, indeed, that I had my suspicions. We never talked to them much, you see, except to hold the enormous *potlatch* in fulfillment of Hooting-Owl's wish, as a result of which we obtained a hundred bolts of silk as proof for the Emperor. We were simply whisked up and down in V'Denni-Kenni's machine, shown a view here and there, and then off we'd go for another five-minute tour of some other part of the country.

I have formed my own theory of this, which I have confided to no one, for I am no scientist, and have no wish to be laughed at out of hand by a gaggle of verbose pedants.

The creatures from the future told us often enough that the number of possible worlds is infinite; if so there must exist every possible variant, even those conceived in the febrile and fertile minds of the writers of scienti-fictiones.

If this be true, then were it not simple enough for the were-jaguars to dig out some alternate universe that resembled writings of P. Josephus Agricola...and then transport us there? Out of, perhaps, a desire not to have our future go too far out of alignment by means of yet another unforeseen meeting of cultures?

For it is true that, after we were shown the land of China briefly, we were then told that no vessel or vehicle in our possession would ever be able to take us there again. It was to have been a private glimpse, nothing more. Did they not trust us? I suppose they saw no reason to. We were to them as apes are, man-mimics only, lacking the gift of intelligence.

Was it, perhaps an illusion?

As a result of all these adventurous peregrinations, it was clear that I had finally acquired the gift of skepticism...I was no longer the dupe, the gullible one, the buffoon. I had even acquired some measure of humility.

If China exists, perhaps I *will* go there one day.

We were escorted to a hillside just outside Caesarea-on-Miserabilis. I was almost sick with joy to see in the distance the city I now called home.

And then V'Denni-Kenni and his Dimensional Patrol departed our continuum forever.

Except for one *final* Final Spectacle.

I had known it was coming for some weeks now, but dreaded it. As my chariot careened up the hill slope of the sacred burial grounds for the second time, I knew that I could wring no reprieve out of Aquila—that he was absolutely determined to take that final journey to the Land of Many Tipis.

It was nightfall by the time I reached Aquila's scaffold. He was dancing and shaking his rattle just as the last time; the women had gathered around him, ululating, and the men were chanting and banging away on drums.

When he saw me, old Aquila stopped for a moment. "Ah, Papinian!" he said, very softly. "Have you come to learn my death song?"

"My dear fellow—I'm quite overcome—" I said.

Equus Insanus led him towards me, for it was dark and his eagle senses were rapidly failing him.

"You've come," he said, "I suppose, with some new harebrained scheme in mind, eh, Papinian? Perhaps you suspect that it wasn't really China—"

"Arrant nonsense!" came Aaye's voice from the crowd. "Dying, he still denies the evidence of his own senses!"

Aquila chuckled; only I could hear him. Suddenly I was reminded of the first time I had ever seen him; that day on the field of battle in Cappadocia—or was it Parthia?—when he had seemed to condense out of the very shadows of my tent.

"I will be with you always," he said.

"Of course, old chap, of course," I said, swabbing at the sweat on his brow with a fold of my toga.

"No, General, I don't mean in a figurative sense. I mean literally." He pulled an eagle feather from his laurel wreath and handed it to me. "This for remembrance." I stared at it curiously.

"Yes! I shall always be watching over you!"

I nodded; the Lakotah have many superstitions, and the omnipresence of the dead is one of these; I wasn't about to contradict him on his dying day.

"Let me go now. I will sing you the song, and then I will depart."

He slipped out of my hands like a ghost. The drums pounded again.

He shook his rattle, croaked a few words, and jumped up and down a couple of times, and then he vanished.

Vanished!

A whistling noise in the night sky. The whole crowd looked up at once—

And there it was, a single saucer, gleaming silver in the moonlight, arcing high, high, high into a bank of cloud.

For a moment, a collective hush, a catch of breath ... and then at once a cry of joy burst forth from all sides, and they started to beat the drums once more, resounding with the pounding of my heart. For I knew now what he had meant when he told me that he would be with me always.

Later there would be those who would say that the gods had honored him with *katasterisme*, that is to say that they placed him among the stars. This makes little sense, when you reflect that no new constellation has joined the signs in the night sky. I knew better.

I knew that Aquila had joined the Dimensional Patrol; that he had become one of the company of those that travel between the infinite universes. His Land of Many Tipis was all of time and space. And though there was a part of me that envied him, I knew that I could never be like him. I had to be content with the rather mundane task of ruling over several hundred thousand people, a chore enlivened only occasionally by the odd execution; for having once been crucified myself, I seldom had the stomach to mete out such punishment to others anymore.

Enough. Drums were banging and throngs cheering. I saw Nikias smiling; I saw the Sasquatius and the Egyptian agape with wonder for once, and Equus Insanus weeping for joy. I saw the Lady Oenothea and the Lady Cervilla, who had become good friends, laughing in each other's arms; and I saw Hooting-Owl, splendid in his toga, cloak, and Quaquiutish mask, nod sagely and clap his hands. Elation surged in me. "Bloody good show!" I shouted at the darkness, for only a streak of light remained to remind us of the passage of the flying saucer. And then, remembering my grave Roman sobriety just in time, I added, "For a mere barbarian, that is."

Something tickled the palm of my hand. Ah yes. The eaglefeather. Without thinking, I stuck it in the wreath that I had lately begun to wear to conceal my incipient baldness.

It has remained there to this day.

> —*Alexandria, Rome, Paris, 1981–82*
> *Los Angeles, 1987*

About the Author

Somtow Papinian Sucharitkul (S. P. Somtow) was born in Bangkok in 1952 and grew up in Europe. He was educated at Eton and Cambridge. His first career was as a composer, and his musical works have been performed, televised and broadcast in more than a dozen countries on four continents. He was artistic director of the Asian Composers EXPO 78 in Bangkok and was chosen Thai representative to the International Music Council of UNESCO. In the late 1970s he took up writing speculative fiction and won the 1981 John W. Campbell Award for best new writer, as well as the Locus Award for his first novel, *Starship & Haiku*. His short fiction has twice been nominated for the Hugo Award.

Somtow now lives in Los Angeles. He is working on more satirical novels, a serious, ambitious horror novel, and has recently written the script for a forthcoming motion picture. *The Aquiliad: Aquila in the New World* is the first book of a trilogy. The second two books will be published by Del Rey Books in 1988.